DEATH, DICE & SOUTHERN SPICE

SIGRID VANSANDT

Death, Dice

&

Southern Spice
Helen and Martha Cozy Mystery

by
Sigrid Vansandt

❀ Created with Vellum

For Stace and Amy.
Truest friends, loved beyond time, now Heaven's angels. Thank you with all my heart for being the sweetest of souls and sharing your lives with me. Until we are together again...

Chapter One

Present Day
Monday

"LADIES AND GENTLEMEN, OVER THREE THOUSAND MEN DIED ON the field in front of you during The Briar Ridge Battle, in the first days of March 1862."

The volunteer docent, Deb, her name tag teetering precipitously upon the left side of her well-endowed bosom, was a stout woman in her forties, sporting a bleach-blonde hairdo and a Kewpie Doll-type face. With a turn and a sweeping Vanna-like arm gesture, Deb pointed to the far-reaching, grass-covered fields stretching out behind her.

"Arkansas was less than a year into its secession from the Union, and a skirmish between US and Confederate cavalrymen on the banks of The Missouri Creek not far from here was the first combat the state experienced. Militarily, politically, and philosophically, the line between North and South would be hard-won, especially here, in the mountain regions along Arkansas' Missouri border."

The view Deb indicated through the museum's massive

windows appeared exquisitely peaceful in its picture-postcard way. Bound on one side by heavily treed hills aglow with their first autumn colors, the gentle, rural vista was more reminiscent of an iconic, American landscape painting by Edward Hopper or Andrew Wyeth than a place bloodied by violence, death, and brutal human misery.

The tour group stayed mute. Each adult, aware of the deceptiveness of the field's bucolic splendor, focused their attention through the panoramic viewing room's swath of ten-foot-tall windows.

"Briar Ridge National Military Park is one of only a handful of national Civil War battlefields where the modern-day visitor may visibly experience a landscape quite similar to the one a soldier, farmer, or traveler would have in the 1860s."

Collectively the group made utterances of awe and surprise at this novel visual experience, bringing a smile to Deb's bubble gum-colored lips.

"Shall we move on?"

The crowd followed like baby ducks behind their stately, full-bodied mother to the next display. Two mannequins dressed in Union blue uniforms, one with a dirty bandage wrapped about its head and the other stuffing an iron ball into the mouth of a cannon, were the catalysts for the docent's next chapter in her polished script.

"Over twenty-three thousand Union and Confederate soldiers engaged in a two-day battle, which when it was over, secured Missouri for the Union and lost two well-seasoned generals for the Confederacy, plus approximately two thousand soldiers their lives."

A five-year-old boy near the front tugged on his father's shirtsleeve but was instantly hushed with a stern look and a parental finger-to-the-lips. Deb continued with her account of the Confederate's retreat and their eventual reassignment to support Tennessee's army, thereby leaving Arkansas utterly defenseless to the marauding bands of murderous bushwhackers, mauling over the area like a dark ravenous plague of hungry locusts.

Standing at the back of the group was an elegantly dressed man of Caribbean descent. His attire and regal aloofness set him apart from the park's typical middle-aged tourist, military enthusiasts, or retired RV ramblers.

With a bespoke dark suit and a silk salmon-colored shirt, the gentleman's stylish dress made him stand out from the crowd, the way a Malay Lacewing butterfly would among a group of brown moths.

"In this exhibit, we see two Union soldiers attempting to man the cannon on their own. Typically, this was a job for at least eight well-trained artillerymen, but as the battle progressed and lives were lost, two men working steadfastly together could fire the canons."

Again, the boy pulled on his father's sleeve.

"Daddy," he whispered, "did soldiers wear the same sneakers as basketball players?"

With a short, terse head shake, the father maintained his attention upon Deb, who'd moved on to relating staggering figures regarding casualty facts.

"During the American Civil War, of the approximately six-hundred and twenty-thousand men who were killed, more died from infectious diseases, primitive medical procedures, and appalling conditions in camps and internment prisons."

The young boy raised his arm, wiggling his five fingers and waving his hand. With an imperious gaze, Deb lowered a wintery look upon him, pursing her pink lips into a tight bow at what she most likely deemed to be an impertinent and trivial interruption.

Flicking a searing look in the direction of the boy's father, she asked, "Yes? Do you have a question, young man?"

It was clear from her tone she wished more parents prescribed to the nineteenth century notion of children being seen and not heard.

"What killed that dead soldier? The one wearing the sneakers?"

All heads turned to look where the child pointed. Sure enough, curled up within the exhibit but behind a pile of ammunition barrels and a row of spindly, artificial display grasses was a man, a dead man, stabbed in the back with a heavy pointed dagger.

True to their duckling nature, the entire group began squawking in unison. As if the knife might whirl free from the expired body and fling itself into the next indiscriminate, unsuspecting human, they bounced about like ping-pong balls in a lottery machine, knocking into one another, until finally stampeding from the room, leaving Deb, the man dressed in the suit and the body alone.

To her credit, a cool Deb stepped behind the display's split-rail fence barrier, slipped around the stacked fake ammunition barrels, knelt over the dead man, and moved away his dark, curly hair to see a handsome face.

"What type of knife is buried in his back?" the gentleman asked, his accent indicating he hailed most likely from Jamaica.

"It's a knife called an Arkansas Toothpick."

"A what?"

"A dagger first made by a man named James Black in the early 1830s. He may have also made the Bowie knife for Jim Bowie."

"Do you recognize the dead man?"

Deb shook her head.

"No, but he's got something pinned to his shirt. Give me a minute..."

Bending closer to see, she let out a gasp.

"What is it?" he asked.

Quickly getting to her feet, Deb flashed her only companion a terrified expression as she scanned the room for anyone left standing around or watching from down the hallway.

Looking from her to the body, he saw there was a piece of paper penned to the dead man's shirt, displaying a triangle with numbers at each corner. He asked, "What does this symbol mean?"

"I don't know—how they—," she said, her voice sounding raspy with fear, as she crawled free from the display.

"They? Who are they?" the man asked, his tone indicating his interest may be more than someone who was inadvertently a witness to a murder.

Clearing the split-rail fence around the display, Deb didn't look at him. "Trust me; you're better off not knowing."

The man reached over and put a steadying hand on Deb's arm, arresting her movements. Turning her face upward to meet his eyes, he could easily see the complete deterioration of her once confident manner.

"Did you see anyone strange in here today?" he asked in a low, urgent voice. "Do you recognize something? Please tell me."

Her gaze locked onto his. Minuscule vibrations from fear, agitated her eyes almost imperceptibly within their sockets.

"Leave it alone," she whispered. "For your safety and those you love, leave *it* and him alone. Nothing good ever came from sticking your nose into *their* business."

"Please," he said, his voice low. "*Whose* business?"

Deb's mouth twitched at the left corner, as her eyes canvassed the empty museum room for possible witnesses to their conversation. Wrenching her arm free from his grasp, she headed for the reception area, saying over her shoulder: "It's their business and best not interfered with, if you know what's good for you."

Chapter Two

Atlantic Ocean
The Fortunata
1672

A BREEZE SO SOFT, IT FELT LIKE A KISS UPON IAN'S SUNBURNT
skin, flirted and capered about the *Fortunata's* massive wooden
deck. Staring up into the limp topsail, he clenched his jaws
together in frustration as the canvass flapped pathetically in the
windless air. For more than a week, the *Fortunata's* sails had rested
flat, leaving the sloop marooned in a seaman's worst nightmare, the
Atlantic's becalmed horse latitudes.

"What wouldn't I give for a strong wind?" he asked himself, as
he studied his sloop's rigging. "Even a typhoon would be welcomed
or a ride on the back of a great whale. Anything is better than
this."

Like a teasing coquette, who whispers sweet, empty nothings,
Ian watched as the wind continued to flippantly toy with his
topsail causing it to flutter with listless impotence. From his lowly
vantage point, he bitterly considered her fickle nature as the

zephyr flitted away once again, most likely to fill the sails of more steadfast, loyal seamen.

To him, the wind was always like a woman. One day she was full of gentle caresses and encouragement, while on others, she battered him with ferocious howls and torrents of angry tears at some known or even unknown transgression. A mercurial temper was her privilege, her nature, and he'd come to honor and even enjoy it until now.

In the last week, she'd abandoned all real interest in his endeavors and treated him with a growing indifference bordering on the cruel. Ian knew the fault of her cooling ardor lay at his own faithless, adulterous doorstep. He'd brought a woman on board, a beautiful woman; and this act, he believed, had lost him his first mistress's grace and ultimately her patronage.

A creeping truth had settled upon him like a foul-weathered fog bank he'd known once off the coast of New England. If a good, strong breeze didn't come soon to free his ship, Mother Nature would extract her payment. All aboard would die a blistering, thirst-crazed death, and the *Fortunata* would be left to drift like a ghost ship upon the ocean.

Drinking water had been rationed to two cups a day and no gin or rum whatsoever. Larkin, his quartermaster and confidant, said the talk among the crew was ramping up against him. They accused Ian of angering fate by bringing the woman, always a harbinger of bad luck, on a privateer's ship.

"Five more days, and we'll make Bermuda. Get me there and I'll hock mother's necklace and lay ten pieces of eight in the plate of St. Peter's," he murmured upwards to the cloudless blue sky. "Captain's honor, I will do it, if you'll but fill the sails with an easterly wind."

Internally, he chided himself. He'd long since given up any pretense of paying homage to whatever Supreme Being orchestrated the lives of men. Besides, when it came to knowing the cut of a man's jib, God was no fool. For the last twenty-seven years, Ian proved time and again to be an extremely untrustworthy, faithless fellow.

By the age of seventeen, he was fully aware of his dark good looks and had mastered the ways of charming women to get what he wanted. Though he wasn't his mother's first son, he was her favorite; and when she found out he'd been dallying around with one or two of her housemaids, she found him a position in the Navy to keep him out of harm's and arm's way.

Before he left, he gave her a loving kiss, tenderly wiped the tears from her eyes, and with excellent deftness lifted one of her diamond necklaces from her jewelry box. He considered it his inheritance and a bit of insurance for the new life to come. Ten days later, as he shipped out of Plymouth for New York, Ian Edward Harrington Warwick, the third son of the Duke of Warwick, became a Midshipman on the HM Prudence, and he never looked back.

Within six years, he'd risen to Captain of his ship. He'd learned how to be a man, how to answer for his mistakes, and had determined that bartering with God was a fool's game; but he'd never been in this situation before, and he was getting desperate.

Quickly, he scanned the deck to see if anyone may have witnessed his foolhardy mumblings. Seeing no one but Larkin heading down into the hull, Ian found cover from the sun under the shade of a sail and relaxed, leaning against the ship's railings. His mind drifted back to a fortnight ago when he'd first seen the woman, standing like an apparition upon the deck of an adrift, Dutch ship, the *Spiegel*.

At the time, it seemed Fate had chosen to favor *Fortunata's* return journey from Lisbon to Bermuda that day by letting Ian cross paths with the Dutch merchant ship dead in the water, but still flying the Republic's red, white, and blue flag. With the renewed war between England and the Dutch for the primacy of the Atlantic sea trade, Ian, as a privateer who carried a letter of marque from King Charles II, could attack with impunity any enemies of England and carry off their cargo to Bermuda where he and his men would be well rewarded financially for this legal and profitable act of piracy.

When they'd come upon the *Spiegel*, a gale was stirring up from the East, and the ship was sitting low in the water, meaning her hull was full of cargo. Ian hoped this meant she carried sugar, tobacco, and with any luck, silver, but a ticklish problem presented itself as soon as he leveled his spyglass upon her rigging. Flying limply from the main mast was a white flag. There was disease onboard.

Reports of plague in Europe, especially Amsterdam, had come to Ian when they docked in Bermuda three months ago. There was a chance the captain was flying the white flag as a way to sail unmolested by the many privateers, pirates, and even French buccaneers who prowled these waters like sharks hunting for their next meal. Though merchant ships were modestly armed with canons, they were slow beasts and easily outmaneuvered by a sloop like Ian's.

After a quick discussion with Larkin, he'd decided to risk the plague for profit. It had been over three months since they'd hit on a good revenue opportunity. His men had agreed, and the *Fortunata* fired two shots to announce themselves and plowed ahead with intent to board the merchant ship.

As they came within five hundred feet, Ian scanned the *Spiegel's* deck with his spyglass. No living soul walked upon her boards. She appeared to be utterly unmanned. An eerie quietness settled upon his ship as he and his crew studied the *Spiegel's* torn, untied sails flapping freely in the growing gale's gusts.

He remembered wondering if it was a ruse by the captain to deceive possible enemies or, if not, how long the *Spiegel* had been adrift with her dead. In the end, the bait was too tasty, and he'd hoped Death's hunger had been satiated and the plague had run its course.

Looking back, he knew Fate hadn't dealt him a good hand by finding a fat pigeon of a merchant ship, but instead, she'd played him for a fool. If he'd only listened to his gut and not suppressed the feelings of unease whispering through his mind at the time, he'd be happily drinking rum at Old Henry's near the wharf in Bermuda at this moment.

Instead, he'd handed the glass to Larkin and said, "What are your thoughts?"

Taking hold of the proffered instrument and applying it to his left eye to scan the Dutch ship, Larkin had been quiet for a moment.

"The plague's taken them all," he'd said, but an instant later, he cried, "Wait! Look, Captain!"

Ian had taken the glass and pressed it to his eye. His brain had momentarily stalled against its normal tide of thoughts as it tried to make sense of what his eyes were seeing.

A white-clad thing, a specter of sorts, floated across the *Spiegel's* deck toward the starboard gunwales. Its flowing, loose garments were being pulled and grabbed at by the wind's invisible fingers.

Raising its hand to hail them, it became clear to the men what appeared to be a wraith was a woman—a beautiful, living woman.

Ian's heart, stung by such beauty, stopped, floundered in his chest like a fish pulled from the ocean, and screamed for the signal to beat once more. The girl's gaze fell on him, their eyes met, and Ian's heart lurched into a new cadence, a new rhythm, and it had begun to beat only at the command of a new mistress.

Chapter Three

New York City
Present Day
Tuesday

MARTHA LITTLEWORD, SMILING BENEVOLENTLY, SLIPPED THE black suede pump from her right foot and daintily tapped one polished red toe upon the dirty pavement of John F. Kennedy Airport's main entryway.

"And like that, we're back on American soil, Helen. Isn't it wonderful? How long has it been for you?"

Scanning the line of drivers waiting with name cards, Helen Ryes-Cousins, Martha's best friend and colleague, shifted her purse from one shoulder to the other.

"Too long. Something about this place makes me want to eat."

Helen raised her head and sniffed the air adding, "I'm probably going to put on ten pounds in three days."

Knitting her eyebrows, Martha considered the extraordinary idea of Helen wanting to eat. Since they'd met over six years ago, Helen's utter indifference to the temptations of food was a constant source of mystery to the comfortably curvy redhead.

"Well, this is my first trip to the States in a long time," Martha said, sliding her foot back into its shoe. "As soon as we're done with this meeting you conveniently squeezed into our vacation, I want to go eat slow smoked pork ribs. My mouth is watering thinking about it! In fact, what if we ate first, and then went to *your* meeting?"

"*Our* meeting," Helen said, still looking crisp and unwrinkled from their six-hour flight from London. "You'll survive the next three hours without wearing a bib. As for me, I'll never don one. Never! Not in this lifetime."

With a wicked smile, Martha murmured, "Better a bib, fussy-pants, than a blight on that suit."

"I heard that," Helen said, turning around with a grin. "Get a move on, Littleword. If you make us late, no barbecue for anyone tonight—because we won't be able to afford it!"

Martha rolled her eyes but stepped up her gait, following Helen through the tight crowd of people in the direction of a man wearing a black chauffeur's uniform and holding a sign reading 'Cousins-Littleword.'

Within minutes, their luggage was secured in the trunk, and they were comfortably ensconced within the quiet confines of the limo.

"Please help yourself, ladies, to the refreshments. We will be at The Plaza in about forty minutes. Traffic is good," the driver said as he pulled free from the curb.

Soon, the girls were watching the Manhattan skyline loom in front of them as they crossed over the Ed Koch Queensboro Bridge. Gazing through the window at the waves of people chasing after their lives, the two friends took turns pointing out landmarks, stores, and wonderful clothes being worn by New York's fashionistas.

"So many people," Martha said. "The world is such an amazing place, isn't it, Helen?"

With her neck bent to see the wondrously elongated skyscrapers jutting upwards into the sky like monstrous steel swords, Helen answered, her voice soft.

"Yes, truly amazing. Only a day ago, we were on the Brontë's moors. Today we're in the country of Capote, Wharton, Melville, and Salinger."

"And *Dickinson* ... the reason we're not soon to be elbow-deep in a pulled-pork sandwich," Martha added, sounding peevish.

Helen didn't have time to spar with Martha. They'd arrived. The Plaza was a visual feast for the eyes. One of New York City's most beloved and renowned landmark hotels, it was designed in the French Renaissance style more than one hundred years ago, and its location on the south-eastern corner of Fifth Avenue gave it not only a breath-taking view across Central Park but also put it at the heart of Manhattan's exclusive shopping district.

As Martha stepped free from the limo and came around the vehicle to join Helen, a bell-person approached.

"May I take your luggage, ladies?"

"Thank you," Helen replied, "everything but the two satchels. We'll need those."

The girls were to be the guests of one of their long-time clients, Mr. Hideto Kimura, an avid collector of all things Emily Dickinson, who lived part-time in one of The Plaza's private residences. He'd asked Helen to give her opinion on a collection of the poet's letters he wished to purchase at an upcoming auction. Concerned the letters were forgeries, he'd arranged to have Martha and Helen stay in one of the hotel's suites.

"We won't be going to our rooms at the moment," Martha said, smiling at the bell-person. "Our plane was late in arriving, so we'll be attending our meeting first."

"I'll take your things to your suite and have your things put away."

A zing of excitement tingled up Martha's spine. She'd traveled a great deal with Helen in the last five years and stayed at many lovely hotels and charming guesthouses, but The Plaza was a real treat. As for Helen, Martha knew she was excited, too; but being strung a bit tighter, Helen wouldn't relax until the initial meeting was over.

Walking up the blue carpeted stairs and into the Fifth Avenue

Lobby, they were greeted by a lovely woman, her age indecipherable, wearing a simple white suit with an exquisite black and gold silk scarf tied about her throat. Hints of chrysanthemums, maiden flowers, and butterflies swirled within the scarf's fabric. Stopping a short distance in front of them, the woman bowed and introduced herself.

"Good afternoon, Mrs. Cousins and Mrs. Littleword."

Both Helen and Martha respectfully returned her greeting with bows.

"Good afternoon," they replied in unison.

"Please let me introduce myself. I am Mr. Kimura's secretary. My name is Emiko Ikeda. We spoke on the phone yesterday. Luncheon is prepared upstairs. Please come with me."

Emiko turned and beckoned them to follow her with a shy smile. The three women wove their way through The Plaza's busy lobby and arrived at the elevators leading to the private residences. After Emiko pressed the call button, she asked about their trip.

"Was your flight comfortable?"

"Yes, it was," Helen answered. "Both Martha and I are pleased to be visiting New York and to see Mr. Kimura. It's always a great pleasure to work with him."

With a bow acknowledging the compliment to her employer, Emiko showed her agreement with another smile. The three women stepped onto the elevator.

"It is the same for Mr. Kimura. He is here to attend a reception for the McGee paintings he's loaning to the Metropolitan Museum."

"McGee?" Martha asked.

Emiko nodded.

"Jenny McGee. Mr. Kimura owns three. You will see them as we enter his residence. They are of exceptional beauty."

The elevator had been ascending for half a minute at the most and came to a stop, opening onto a private semi-circular, white and grey marbled foyer. A powerfully built man dressed in a black suit stood guard at the entrance to a double mahogany wood door. His facial effect was flat, barely acknowledging their arrival, but as they stepped free from the elevator, he moved to open the suite's door, making room for them to pass. As Martha walked through, she surreptitiously glanced over at him. Within the dark confines of his black jacket, she easily saw the gun and holster strapped next to the left side of his chest.

"Please wait here," Emiko requested, her voice soft as she pointed to two high-back wooden chairs. "I will let Mr. Kimura know you have arrived."

The two friends found themselves in an anteroom unlike any they'd ever seen before. White Carrara marble walls rose over twelve feet to a domed, ribbed ceiling playing host to a centrally placed cascading Chihuly chandelier of wiggling and writhing blue glass. Three tall, five-foot-wide niches lined the room, each housing a massive, luminous painting down-lit by a recessed light.

If the impression of the space was of unfathomable wealth, then the theme was how to lift the human spirit into rapturous bliss through beauty. These must be the McGee's Emiko spoke of earlier.

"I'm feeling a bit light-headed," Helen whispered, gazing up into one of the paintings. "It's like looking through layers of moving, blue-colored water to see another place, a place you want to dive down into and stay until all your cares are washed clean. They make you feel otherworldly like Alice when she went through the looking glass."

"For sure," Martha nodded, with a judicious air, adding, "they have an opalescence like you're seeing the inside of a seashell which makes me think these must have set him back a few clams."

A laugh burst free from Helen's mouth, causing her to go into a coughing fit, which made Martha giggle too.

"More than a few clams," a man's voice said behind them, "but worth every one. Don't you agree?"

In tandem, they swiveled around their expression like two surprised, bright-eyed owlets. An elegant older gentleman smiled graciously, if not a tiny bit mischievously, at them from the open doorway. With a sparkle in his eyes, he bowed.

"Mrs. Cousins, Mrs. Littleword," he said with dignity.

As an echo to his warm greeting, both Martha and Helen returned his bow, but with deeper inclinations.

"Mr. Kimura," Helen said after they both returned to an upright position. "It's a great pleasure to see you again. Thank you for inviting us to New York."

"Ladies, if you will"—he stepped to one side of the doorway and indicated gallantly for them to go through— "allow me to escort you to luncheon. As the Walrus said: 'The time has come to talk of many things: of books—and bards—and brilliant rhymes' ..."

Helen grinned at his playful reference to her remark about feeling like Alice in Wonderland and joined in quickly with, "Of poetry and dreams..."

They both turned and looked at Martha with smiles and slightly raised eyebrows.

"And will it be a Dickinson," Martha said, "or just a forger's scheme?"

Chapter Four

Briar Ridge Military Park
  Present Day
  Tuesday Afternoon

Special Agent Devon Williams of the FBI was tired of waiting for Briar Ridge's federal police agent, Lucas Hathaway, to acknowledge their meeting. He'd been sitting in the park's interpretation center on a wooden bench for over an hour, exchanging painful grins with Deb.

Initially, upon arriving at the Visitor's desk, he'd tried to engage the bottle-blond in conversation about the murder yesterday, but though pleasant, she claimed to know nothing other than what she'd witnessed.

Williams' presence at the military park yesterday wasn't coincidental. He'd come to Briar Ridge to talk with the Interpretation's Officer and to learn about this particular region and the many secret societies that operated here during the Civil War era. One group in particular had aroused his interest.

For over a year, he'd been investigating a group using a money-laundering syndicate operating out of Miami, Florida. The group, called the KGC, thought to be defunct since the Civil War, was now believed to be operating once more but under the guiding hand of Jesse Stacker from New Jersey. During the Civil War, the Knights of the Golden Circle were pro-slavery, pro-succession, and were possibly behind the assassination of President Lincoln. Stacker resurrected the organization but gave it a modern twist.

Today its rhetoric was authoritarian and promoted using violence. Though the group currently had chapters all across the United States, Canada, and the world, Jesse Stacker owned a vacation home on Beaver Lake where he wined and dined powerful politicians, lobbyists, and corporate CEOs in hopes of raising support for his political aspirations.

These legal fundraising schemes didn't hold a candle to his illicit ones. He'd been showing up on the FBI's radar for his anti-democratic rhetoric, but it was his connections to drug trafficking that focused their real attention on him. He had connections with mobsters all over the US.

When Williams and Deb found the murdered man in the display, Williams waited for Deb to return with the park's police officer. While she was gone, Williams had searched the man's coat for a wallet or any identification indicating who he might be. In an inner pocket, he found a receipt for payment to a motel. At the top was written the name 'Ricardo Gusman'. Williams barely had time to secrete the receipt into his own jacket's pocket before Agent Lucas Hathaway had appeared.

The Briar Ridge police officer seemed surprised to find an FBI agent standing over the dead man's body, but he rallied quickly and pointed out to Williams that because this was a federal park, it was under his jurisdiction. If he needed any assistance from the FBI, he'd let Williams know. It was a polite way of asking Williams to leave.

Later that evening, Williams had run a background check on Ricardo Gusman and found that Gusman had lived in Miami six years ago and was believed to be working as a low-level flunky with a crime boss. Stacker had been photographed dining with Gusman at an expensive hotel in New York only a year ago. Stacker's influence had long tentacles, and they reached to the highest social levels in America as well as the lowest.

Williams' investigation of Gusman also revealed he had ties to another more pacifistic organization, The Peace Party. This Arkansas group was born out of the Civil War as well, but with the intention to resist participating in the War. Wishing to be left alone and philosophically opposed to slavery, The Peace Party wanted nothing to do with succession from the Union or belonging to the new Confederacy. It was too coincidental that Gusman was straddling two highly opposed organizations and was now dead. Williams needed to learn more about these Civil War secret societies and Gusman's possible involvement with both organizations. He hoped that talking with Agent Hathaway today would enlighten him on both counts.

Deb's phone buzzed at the reception desk with an internal call.

"Hello?" she said, flicking uncertain looks in his direction. "Yes, I'll bring him back."

Hanging the phone up, he watched her apply more lipstick and check her hair as discreetly as possible in a hand-held mirror. Coming around from behind the waist-high desk, she adjusted her collar.

"Agent Hathaway will see you, sir. If you'll follow me."

Williams followed the freshly coiffed Deb down a narrow hall. He understood now why she was so reticent to talk with him. Her loyalty lay with the man he was about to meet—and not because he was her work colleague.

With a soft rap at the door, she practically cooed, "Agent Hathaway?"

The door swung open, and Williams caught the electric nonverbal exchange between Deb and Hathaway.

"This is..." she appeared to have entirely forgotten Williams' name.

"I'm Special Agent Devon Williams, Agent Hathaway," he said, putting his hand out for the man to shake. "Thank you for working with us on this matter."

Hathaway accepted the offered hand and shook it. His gorilla-like grip so ridiculously crushing, Williams chalked it up to a pathetic power-play move.

"Great," he thought to himself, "a weak ego. Fun times, fun times."

"Have a seat," Hathaway said, pointing to a chair.

"Thanks. So, how is your investigation going?"

Hathaway sat down and shook his head.

"We didn't find a wallet on him, and there wasn't a car in the parking lot. He must have either hitchhiked out here or gotten a ride with someone. Basic John Doe situation. I think he made someone mad, perhaps the person who drove him here. That person saw the knife, picked it up and killed him, then disappeared."

To Williams, Hathaway's narrative not only dripped with indifference to the gross crime acted out on federal soil, but it also sounded ridiculous and unprofessional. He clearly hadn't even identified the deceased yet. Williams wondered if he should throw Hathaway a bone or go for another angle.

"What about the note your docent and I found pinned to the man's shirt? Do you know anything about who must have pinned it there? Your docent was clearly upset by seeing it."

Hathaway smirked as he leaned back in his chair.

"If you ask me, she was scared, got emotional; not surprising because she's a woman, and blurted out the first thing that popped into her mind. A typical female reaction. She went and lost the note after I told her to put it in my safe."

Williams studied the man, half-wondering if Hathaway didn't expect him to commiserate in some way on the childlike ineptitude of women.

"So, the note is irretrievably lost?"

The man across the desk compressed his lips and slowly shook his head back and forth.

"Unless Deb finds it in her purse, her compact mirror, or her embroidery bag, she drags everywhere."

It was clear to Williams; Hathaway wasn't going to assist him or his investigation in any way. He wouldn't bother asking him about the secret societies either. Instead, he stood up, this time not offering his hand for the man to shake.

"I won't thank you for your help," he said. "You're mismanaging a federal crime, and you appear to be indifferent to the repercussions of that mismanagement."

Williams got up and turned to leave.

"You," came the low, snarling response from behind him, "your days are numbered."

Special Agent Devon Williams took his time turning around. The hate flashing in Hathaway's eyes as he sat still reclining in his chair almost made Williams want to laugh, but instead, he sighed.

"Agent Hathaway," he said, feeling like someone bored with the same old late-night reruns on TV, "get your affairs in order and clean up your investigation. If my days are numbered, then so are yours. We both work for Uncle Sam, and he's gonna outlast the both of us...guaranteed."

Chapter Five

The Plaza Hotel
New York
Tuesday Afternoon

MR. KIMURA USHERED MARTHA AND HELEN INTO A DINING room decorated with an art lover's touch. A long, lacquered Art Deco table surrounded by eight Ming dynasty-style horseshoe-back chairs sat under a spectacular lighting installation. The mid-air sculpture took center stage with its hundreds of golden orb-like fish swimming in the air between table and ceiling.

"You have been busy, Mrs. Cousins," Kimura said as they sat down to dine. "Stories of your adventures found their way to me through our mutual friend Count von Wallenstein. We met last December at The Albertina Museum during its exceptional exhibit of Albrecht Dürer's work. The Count and I bumped into each other in front of the German master's drawing, *The Field Hare*."

Helen finished a sip from her cup of mint tea and returned the delicate porcelain bowl to its saucer.

"Yes, it's been a rewarding partnership and friendship. Count von Wallenstein is a dear man, and his niece is working with a dealer in Vienna to bring a handful of rare Russian icons plus a substantial collection of illuminated manuscripts to auction sometime next spring."

Kimura's eyebrows shot up, and for a moment, his teacup hovered between his lips and the table. It was clear he'd been touched with a collector's fever at the mention of the manuscripts. Turning to Martha, he lowered the cup slowly to the table.

"Would any of these manuscripts be French in origin?" he asked.

"One book is," Martha replied. "It's a late fifteenth-century Book of Hours on finely worked vellum. We're waiting on a comparative analysis being performed at a lab in Lucerne, Switzerland, to tell us if it's from the workshop of Maître François."

Helen caught the delicate, barely noticeable tremor at the corner of Kimura's right eye.

"I know we're here to discuss your possible Emily Dickinson acquisition, but if you're interested, I would be happy to arrange for you to see the illuminated manuscript in London at your convenience."

Kimura's responding chuckle showed his natural good humor.

"Ah, Mrs. Cousins, you do know how to throw out the most delectable bait on your shiny, expensive hooks."

Shaking his head like a man accustomed to giving in to his material sins, he added, "Yes, please arrange it, if the manuscript turns out to be from the workshop of Maître François. I will be in London over Christmas."

Lunch was light and delicious. Hibachi Onion soup topped with shaved mushrooms, a smattering of fried onions sprinkled across the top, and garnished with finely chopped scallions. It was served with a steaming, tantalizing plate of moon-shaped dumplings filled with a minced mixture of cabbage, green onions, and mushrooms.

"I've had my chef prepare a curry rice stew for our entree," Kimura said as the plates were brought in and laid in front of them. "Curry is a loved spice in England, and with the cooler weather today in New York, I wanted to give you something hearty and warming."

A mouthwatering stew of carrots, mushrooms, potatoes, and tender pieces of beef sat before them. Poured over steamed white rice, the stew's taste was mild and savory. Taking a spoonful into her mouth, Helen's taste buds did a happy dance. For a minute, she wondered if Martha still pined for barbecue.

"Mr. Kimura, this is superb," Martha said. "I've never tried a curry stew before. I would love to have your chef's recipe."

With a slight bow of his head and a genuinely pleased smile at Martha's compliment, Mr. Kimura replied, "Thank you, Mrs. Littleword. I will have the recipe written down for you."

With their luncheon finished and the table cleared, Emiko appeared and announced the arrival of the auction house courier.

"Peter Broughton from Sargents is waiting in the library, Mr. Kimura."

Their host nodded.

"Thank you, Emiko."

Turning to Helen and Martha, "Shall we, ladies?"

Rising from their chairs, they followed Mr. Kimura through a door, down a hallway, and into a room appearing to be more like a vault than a library. Burnished stainless steel panels the color of charcoal encased a space the size of a typical bank's safety deposit room. In the ceiling's center, a domed-covered camera kept a vigilant eye on all those who came and went.

Waiting within were three men; two were security detail for the notebook, and one was a youth of no more than twenty-five years.

"Good afternoon, Mr. Broughton," Kimura said, greeting the young man. "This is Helen Cousins and Martha Littleword, the experts from England."

The boy-man, his hair curly, red, and extremely unkempt, offered Mr. Kimura a low bow and another for Helen and Martha. Wearing a fashionable three-piece, tweed suit with a bright blue plaid bowtie to match his blue Converse tennis shoes, Peter

Broughton was a true New York dandy, but Helen knew he wouldn't have been sent as Sargents' representative if he didn't have the razor-sharp acumen so important to the position of an auction house specialist.

"I've brought the notebook," he said, opening an aluminum briefcase that rested upon the only table in the room.

The group's gaze shifted as Peter lifted the simple, leather-bound object from the protective nest. An excited tingle in her stomach and an itchy twitch at the end of her nose told Helen she was in exceptional literary company. Compressing her lips to control her thrill at being so close to Emily Dickinson's genius, Helen took the magnifying glasses from her pocket and slipped them onto the bridge of her nose.

"The family we represent, Mrs. Cousins," Peter explained, "has owned this notebook continuously since the death of the poet's niece, Martha Bianchi. What you are about to see, except for the leather cover added in the 1920s by Mrs. Bianchi, is in its original form. The stitching is untouched making this notebook the only one of its kind."

Helen exchanged a fleeting wonder-glance with Martha. Too often in their work, the hype or the hopeful wishes behind a rare manuscript or art piece find resulted in a crashing let-down. But if what lay before her was the purest example of Dickinson's work, its worth was immeasurable.

Two experts had already weighed in on it and offered opinions casting doubts on the notebook's authenticity, but in the collecting world, this was typical of the trade. Disinterested posturing was a way to deflect too much interest by other competitors and keep the price within reach of whomever the expert was jockeying for in the high-stakes race.

Peter moved aside for Helen. Immediately she recognized the great care taken in maintaining the booklet's integrity. On one hand, the booklet's exceptional condition was a good thing, but on the other, its tidiness raised minor red flags.

There were many fakes produced by brilliant forgers who worked the rare manuscript market. They made fortunes off zealous, deep-pocketed collectors. To combat the cons and protect their clients, Helen and Martha used a combination of cutting-edge technology and painstaking research.

Provenance wasn't an issue with this book. The family was one closely attached to Martha Bianchi, the daughter of Susan Dickinson, Emily's sister-in-law. The story behind how they came to have the booklet gave perfect credence to it being the real deal.

Susan was the recipient of over two hundred poems by the poet. After Emily's death, Lavina, Emily's sister, asked Susan to put the poems into a cohesive group, but Susan's process was too slow by Lavinia's standards. As a response, she made a rather shocking decision and gave the job over to Mabel Loomis Todd, the woman who'd been Susan Dickinson's husband's mistress for years.

The outcome was well documented by Dickinson scholars. Mabel snipped the booklets apart, removing the red and white twine holding them together, and separated the poems from their natural order. Her loathing for Susan incited a terrible mutilation of a poem Emily wrote for her sister-in-law, only sparing a part of the verse because of a poem written on the page's verso.

Susan, for her part, kept the initial booklets Lavina gave her, plus a substantial body of poems Dickinson had written to her. After her death, Susan's daughter inherited her mother's cache but left everything, including the Dickinson house, The Evergreens, and its contents to her secretary when she died.

The sellers and the auction house believed this to be the last surviving, unmolested booklet. The poetry within was sublime. It was, for all intents and purposes, an unblemished example of Dickinson's talent and priceless in its purity. But was it the real deal?

Helen and Martha's job was to divine the truth for Kimura before he spent millions. Helen had spent a month studying with intense interest one of Emily Dickinson's other hobbies, needlework while Martha arranged for the book to be sent to Cambridge University for a battery of specialized laboratory tests.

It was well documented the poet made her booklets herself by punching tiny holes along the inside crease of each signature or section of folded stationery and deftly sewing the folded pages together into small packets with red thread or twine.

"Being a Victorian woman, Emily was taught needlework," Helen offered as she studied the bound packet's exterior, "and as we know, she mentions the skill often in her poetry. Sewing was important to her, and I believe she made the fascicles with great care. Binding them together was a second act of creation. Any artist, writer, or poet would understand the motivation to see their work produced, even if only for their personal appreciation. Sewing is an art, and every seamstress has a signature way of tying-off a knot, even Emily."

Gently opening the booklet's front cover, Helen pointed with the tip of her index finger at the homemade binding going down the inside crease between the flyleaf and the front cover.

"Here is the red and white thread she was known to use. The lab has confirmed it to be from the correct period and similar to other thread found in textile art in and around Amherst during the years Emily was still binding her packets."

Everyone around the table leaned in to get a closer look at the booklet's stitching.

"Emily was supposed to have tied off her thread or twine in a significant way and in a particular place. It is not possible to access the place where Emily tied the knot due to her niece's desire to give the booklet a cover, but I requested the use of an optical coherence tomography test for an up-close picture of what is going on inside the book's spine."

Turning away from the table, Helen took a folder being offered to her by Martha, who'd pulled it from her satchel. Opening it, she laid it on the table for all to see.

"This photo shows the exact place one would expect a careful seamstress to hide her tidy, finishing knot. Her work is fastidious. At this time in her life, she was beginning to suffer from weakness in her vision, and she pricked her finger, leaving a trace of the blood on the thread. With a second test using macro x-ray fluorescence spectrometry, we were able to see a trace of the blood and have it chemically assessed."

Helen took a bound document from her folder and laid it on top of the previous photo. It was a detailed laboratory analysis record showing the procedures and tests compiled upon the booklet.

"My colleague and friend, Sir Alex Barstow, requested similar tests from institutions owning one of Emily's handkerchiefs, the ink from three of her known poems, and a handwriting analysis from a renowned authority."

The room was quiet as the expectant group awaited Helen's verdict.

"The chemical and DNA samplings matched perfectly, and the handwriting analysis is spot-on," Helen said. "There is no doubt this is a booklet written, collated, and sewn by Emily Dickinson."

Chapter Six

Fortunata
　　Atlantic Ocean
　　1672

THE MEN HAD SEEN THE PALE, GHOSTLY WOMAN, TOO. WITH lightning speed, fear took hold of his crew. They whispered among themselves about ghost ships, vampires, and evil spirits who haunt the seas trying to entrap sailors or feed off the living. They quickly banded together and called for him to halt *Fortunata's* progress and to turn her away from the *Spiegel* before it was too late.

For Ian, though, the dye had been cast. The face he'd seen, her blue eyes like a winter's sky with long, wavy mahogany-colored tresses wrapping themselves like a quivering shroud about her fragile frame, had hardened him to his crew's concerns and superstitions. He would have the ship and know the woman. It was his privilege as captain.

"We stand to make a fortune from this ship's cargo," he'd argued back to them over the growing wind. "I am your captain, and I've pledged to our King to engage his enemies and bring him those spoils that are his due. We are at war with the Dutch. This ship is ours to take!"

"What about the shade? The ghost!" they demanded to know.

Ian turned away from them to look back at the *Spiegel*. The woman stood watching yet, unmoving at the ship's wooden railings, her hair slowly whipping and whirling about her head the same way the tendrils of sea plants will in the wave's undulating currents. Her beauty gripped him once again, holding his gaze and squeezing his soul in a way he'd never known before. The need to save her, to have her, to hold her seared itself upon his mind, and no sooner did he know this than a second idea arrived, sent fully formed from the same place.

"This ship," he yelled into the wind and pointing at the looming *Spiegel*, "belongs to England. For the men who volunteer to sail her back with me to Bermuda, they will receive double their normal take. Who among you fears no woman and wants to be a rich man?"

The crew appeared to consider his words. A few, goaded by his words to prove their manhood or enticed by the reward, stepped forward as recruits for his plan.

One man, however, was not moved by Ian's taunt and bribe. The boatswain, Harold, spoke up amid the crew's push to be the first to claim a place on the *Spiegel*.

"Don't bring the woman onto the *Fortunata*," he said, his voice strong and his eyes steady with conviction. "She'll do us no good, Captain. Keep her to her ship. It can hurt nothing to let her stay where she is."

Harold's warning riled Ian into a defensive anger. Inside, he knew he'd put this sudden infatuation for the woman before his men's safety and even naval protocol when commandeering a ship with a disease onboard; but to suppress his conscience and any questions lingering about his right to command, he turned back to face his men and called out, "I will captain the *Spiegel* to prove my conviction we have nothing to fear! Larkin will captain the *Fortunata*. Bring the two ships broadside!"

Within minutes the *Fortunata* was within fifty yards of the merchant ship. The able sailors neatly turned the sloop to come alongside the *Spiegel,* and they soon had a longboat lowered with men climbing down into it from the ladder. Ian was the last man to settle himself. The longboat heaved and rolled with the ocean's swells.

"Push off, men!" he called. "Put your backs into it! A storm is brewing, and we'll be tossed into the drink if we tarry long in these growing waves."

As they made their way, Ian maintained his focus upon the lone figure still riveted to the spot along the *Spiegel's* gunwales. Like a statue, she never moved. Then, once they were almost within reach of the ship's hull, she disappeared.

A momentary feeling of unease washed over Ian but was quickly dissipated when he saw her return and try to manage a rope ladder over the rails. Securing it, she withdrew, and Ian climbed up the ship's side.

Once aboard, he saw and smelled the carnage the plague had wrought upon the *Spiegel.* Bodies of the sailors lay where they'd fallen, but as he scanned the dead, he saw they lacked the normal Black Death signs. No blood pooled from their mouths, no buboes or enlarged glands were visible. A red rash and gangrenous sores on their limbs were the only clues to the disease that took their lives.

The woman, upon his gaining a foothold on the deck, had backed away, hurrying up to the aft deck where she slipped quickly into a cabin. He let her hide while they worked to prepare the sails. It wasn't until the first plumes of black smoke filtered up through the deck boards that Ian realized there was more amiss with the *Spiegel* than its torn riggings and dead plague victims. He sent a man down into the hull who quickly returned.

"It's a raging fire, Captain!" he yelled. "She's likely to blow. No telling how much tar and turpentine there is in her hull!"

Ian called for all the men to abandon the ship. As the smell of tar, turpentine, and burning human flesh filled the air, he made for the cabin's door, grabbed the woman, and wrapped her in a blanket. Picking her up, he made for the longboat, climbing down the ladder with her pitched over his shoulder like a sack of potatoes. The men pushed away and rowed hard, putting distance between their wooden craft and the enflamed *Spiegel*.

Once upon the safety of *Fortunata's* deck, Ian and his crew watched as their chance at riches went up into the air with the black, billowing clouds of smoke pouring from the ship's burning body. The wind whipped and intensified the fire until the *Spiegel* turned into a red and orange orb, careening and bobbing in the storm's white-capped waves, drifting ever further into the darkening distance.

Chapter Seven

Manhattan
  The Present
  Tuesday Evening

"Is it a dry rub on the ribs and the brisket?" Martha asked, her mouth watering with happy expectation as she perused the grubby barbecue menu. "I prefer my spare ribs done with a dry rub. I've never been a fan of the goo. Also, I see you have pulled pork sandwiches. Does that come with coleslaw on top?"

Martha was trying to buy everything she loved. It could be a long time before she was back in the States.

"We can leave it off, if you don't want it," the counter guy replied.

"Yes, please."

She scrunched her eyes up and pursed her mouth, scrutinizing the menu for hidden juicy gems she may have overlooked during the previous five reads. Overwhelmed with the smorgasbord of delicious decisions, Martha sighed and flashed the boy an ebullient grin. She'd held him captive; answering questions about side items, his opinions on beef versus pork, what kind of rubs the pit master used, and if the pies in the spinning display case were made fresh each day.

Her cup was running over. Going to a Southern pit barbecue restaurant, regardless of the fact it was in the heart of New York City, was like a pilgrimage to a girl brought up on Sunday afternoon post-church suppers where her uncles and daddy vied for supremacy in the grilling of all things meat.

Barbecue held a special place in Martha's heart, and she'd not had an opportunity to honor that magic-memory place (by eating copious amounts of the mouth-watering, smoky stuff) in over five years.

"I probably should get something with vegetables in it. Helen would like that. Please put a side of green beans in the bag, too."

The boy-man, his head shaved on all three sides with a swath of hair pulled up, looped, and secured into a bun with a purple scrunchie, lowered his eyelids in an annoyed feline way. He'd been assisting Martha for over fifteen minutes during a fairly busy dinner rush as she selected an array of barbecue delights for takeaway. A line was forming, and his minimum wage patience was wearing thin.

"Lady, does—this—complete—your—order?" he asked, his bun bobbing with pubescent irritation and his tone searing with impatience.

Fully satiated with what the menu offered, Martha turned a bright gaze back up to her saucy attendant.

"I think that'll do it. Wait! Add the peach cobbler, too."

After running a critical eye down Martha's less-than-sleek frame, Bobber-head pressed his lips together and rolled his eyes. His apparent judgmental boredom implying that all this food she was buying was surely for a party of hockey players coming off a weeklong detox cleanse. Martha knew she in no way resembled the glossy female ideals ever-present in fashion magazines and on television, but rude is rude.

"Let me see," he said, "you have...one pulled pork sandwich, a half rack of baby back pork ribs, two mashed potatoes with brown gravy, a side order of green beans, a side order of baked beans, a half order of fried mushrooms, one peach cobbler."

He took a deep, dramatic breath as if the recitation of her order had winded him.

"*Will* that be all?" he finished, pressing his eyes firmly shut and reopening them in an owlet-with-a-man-bun way.

It was the old "skinny man throwing shade at a woman with a healthy appetite" barb, but a quick, furtive assessment of the long human line behind her kept her quiet. People looked hangry.

Helen's voice cutting in kept her from answering.

"Wait! Add two pieces of coconut cream pie to that order and a side of mozzarella sticks."

Helen took up residence right beside Martha, adding, "It'll have to do, I guess, even if it is only the two of us dining tonight. The portions are kinda skimpy here."

Martha's face broke out into a huge grin at Helen's surprise arrival and cool handling of the man's fat-shaming intentions. He simpered but managed to collect the order in its entirety and hand it over to Martha, as Helen maintained a cold, steely focus on the cowed counter boy-man.

"Thank you, Helen," Martha said, peeking into the massive brown paper bag. "That guy needs to find another job. He's bringing bad mojo to an otherwise perfect environment. If I worked at a barbecue restaurant, I'd be so happy to hand orders out to people. How can anyone be grumpy working in a place full of joy?"

They walked along the wet sidewalk, as a cold drizzle filtered down from the grey cloud-hung heavens. Honking horns, hissing bus breaks, and sirens whining gave the urban nighttime the feeling of being in a darkening jungle. People moved in a hurried way around and past the two friends as they, too, picked up their speed to get back to their warm, quiet hotel suite.

"Here's the hotel. Let's get inside before it pours," Helen said.

Martha, her arms wrapped around her barbecue bundle of joy, breathed in deeply of its smoky aroma.

"This is so nice, Helen. It's like a bit of home—this bag, all warm, yummy smelling, and comforting. I might snuggle with this bag tonight or at least prop it next to my pillow."

"You're missing home," Helen said, as she pushed the button for the elevator.

She'd not realized it, but Helen's insight into her feelings was dead on.

"I am."

"Why don't you take a couple of weeks and go visit home? I bet your Aunt Tilda would be tickled to death to have you."

"I love that idea! Why don't you come, too, Helen? I'm sure your hubby would join us, if you asked. We'll have so much fun visiting family, seeing the old places, and eating all those yummy things you can't get in England like: fried catfish, pancakes, biscuits and gravy...BACON!"

As she pushed the hotel suite's door open, Helen was shaking her head and chuckling.

"You go. Piers would be too busy to leave England right now. I'm heading back tomorrow. I've got so much work to do, and Piers is expecting..."

Martha's cell phone erupted into song, stopping Helen's solid case against going with Martha.

"Would you hold this?" Martha asked, handing their dinner into Helen's empty arms. Fishing deep within her overcoat's pocket, she retrieved the singing phone and studied the caller ID. "Well, I'll be hanged. It's Tilda!"

Hands full, Helen headed to the table.

"Ask her if her ears are burning."

"Hi, Til! We were just talking about home...uh huh...well, yes... okay...of course, I mean *I* will, but Helen's going home...Oh, my goodness, Tilda, what have you gotten yourself into? Okay, I'll be there. I'll see you tomorrow."

Helen stood riveted to the floor beside the suite's small, round dining table. The two women locked worried gazes with one another as Martha listened intently to Tilda's instructions.

"Okay, Tilda. Please be careful. Wait! Don't hang up! How do I get ahold of you when I find it?"

Martha squeezed her eyes shut, trying to focus on Tilda's words.

"I'll do it. I promise, Tilda. Tell Jackie 'Hi' for me."

With all the earlier excitement for food and homebound travel sucked away like a power vacuum by Tilda's call, Martha stood with limp arms dangling from her shoulders and staring at the floor.

"Well?" Helen demanded. "What was that about?"

"You'd never believe it in a million years."

Helen nodded.

"It's Tilda. Try me."

Martha went over and plopped down on a bed. Raising her head to look Helen squarely in the face, Martha answered.

"Tilda and Jackie Boy have one week to raise fifty thousand dollars."

"What?" Helen squeaked.

Nodding like a bobble-head doll, Martha, her shoulders hunched and her hands limp in her lap, said, "Yep, otherwise, some guy named Ernesto's going to..."

She made the finger-across-the-throat gesture.

"Oh, my God!" Helen squeaked again as she dropped into one of the dining chairs.

"Yeah, Tilda says there's only one way to raise that much money in so short a time."

Helen and Martha locked gazes.

"How?"

Martha swallowed hard.

"I gotta go to Arkansas and find a necklace."

"A necklace?"

"Yes, and not just any necklace, Helen, but one worth a king's ransom. There's just one problem."

"I don't know if I want to know."

Martha nodded sagely.

"It's been lost for over a hundred and fifty years, and I won't be the only person looking for it."

Chapter Eight

Northwest Arkansas
  Present Day
  Tuesday Evening

RUBBING HIS HANDS TOGETHER TO WARM THEM, SPECIAL AGENT Devon Williams returned the binoculars to his tired eyes. He'd been in position watching the house since four o'clock that afternoon.

The location was excellent. Up behind the circle driveway and downwind from the westerly breeze, he had gone undetected by the four Doberman pinscher guard dogs running within the house's fenced perimeter.

Jesse Stacker's estate was palatial. Williams had requested yesterday, after his failed conversation with Hathaway, a complete location history and call history of Ricardo Gusman's cell phone. It showed that Gusman had been driving around the lake before he'd gone to Briar Ridge Military Park. Could he have been looking for Stacker's house? Williams wanted to know.

The mansion sat on a high promontory overlooking Beaver Lake, and Williams estimated the estate size to be at least forty acres of land and worth close to twenty million dollars. At any one time, he'd counted no less than four armed men located at different positions around the house.

"There sure is a lot of money in fomenting fascism and anarchy," he murmured to himself as he scanned the area with the binoculars.

The massive ironwork gates creaked into life and retracted. Williams saw a luxury sedan, its windows blacked out, coming up the private asphalt road on his left. As the vehicle entered the open gates, he focused his binoculars on the rear license plate.

"Hmmm," he said, using the binocular's photo capabilities to take a picture and a video. The car came to rest in the circular drive, and the driver's door opened.

Recognizing the tall, slim, middle-aged man, Williams made a few "tsk-tsk" disapproval sounds as he zoomed in for better clarity.

"Senator, senator, senator, you should choose your bedfellows a little better. Taking money from these guys makes you look like you have your hand in a very dirty cookie jar."

The house's front door opened, and a white-haired, extremely fit man in his late fifties stepped out, smiling broadly. Shaking the senator's offered hand, the two men turned to walk back inside. The hair on the back of William's neck stood up, as he snapped pictures of Stacker with his soon-to-be-bought senator.

"Whew," Williams whispered, keeping his binoculars zoomed in on the two men, "just another day putting chokeholds on senators, repressing the rights of others, and trying to bring down our Constitution—business as usual."

The men disappeared inside, and the two gunslingers returned to walking the perimeter. Special Agent Williams rolled off his stomach into a sitting position. Taking out his cell phone, he downloaded the photos and videos from the binoculars and emailed them via a secure server to his office in DC. With that done, he reached into his knapsack and pulled out a granola bar and a bottle of water.

"Breakfast of champions," he thought to himself and took a bite.

It had been one of his longest investigations, and he wasn't working alone. There were at least ten other agents in the field across the US trying to gather evidence against Jessie Stacker, but the agents were spread thin; and Williams had been working on his own for the last week.

When he'd been assigned to the case, it was because of his Jamaican heritage, and it was hoped he'd be able to work undercover to infiltrate a Cuban money laundering syndicate operating out of Miami, Florida. The investigation had taken two years and was successful in that they'd made over a dozen arrests and hauled in two of the organization's leaders.

After lawyers got involved, plea bargaining had taken place, and information came out about an organization operating in almost every state in the US. The People, as they sometimes called themselves, claimed to be the true progeny of an old Civil War organization, the Knights of the Golden Circle. Oddly enough, they had strong ties to the Cuban syndicate.

It was the typical trifecta used by most terrorist organizations: drug trafficking, the human slave trade, and the need to launder money. That's where the Cubans had come in, but until William's had read the rhetoric being slathered all over the KGC's social media sites, he couldn't have guessed at the terrifying power wielded by Jessie Stacker. The man would settle for nothing less than an autocratic dictatorship in America.

The sound of the gates creaking brought Devon's attention around. Raising the binoculars once more, he saw the senator's car pull out onto the road below and drive away. Three of the guards were standing together at the compound's entrance.

"That's odd," he thought to himself. "What are they all doing clogged up together?"

As if in a desire to answer his question, one raised his finger and pointed in the exact direction of where Devon was positioned. The agent's heart skipped a beat. They'd detected him somehow, even nearly a quarter mile away.

His brain immediately churned out his training protocol. Grabbing his things, he shoved them in the knapsack, and staying low, he got up and began moving down the hill toward the cove where he'd left his boat. Like being hit by a hard-thrown baseball, Williams pitched forward as a searing pain in his left shoulder brought him to his knees. Instantly he knew he'd been shot.

A heavy feeling coursed rapidly through his veins taking him to a relaxing, restful place. He forgot about the pain in his shoulder and the men coming for him. Rolling over onto his back, he looked up through the green pine boughs into a darkening blue sky, and as the sound of barking dogs and men calling to one another came closer, Agent Williams shut his eyes and fell into a deep, peaceful sleep.

Chapter Nine

Fortunata
  Atlantic Ocean
  1672

Ian's reverie from the last harrowing moments upon the *Spiegel's* burning deck instantly evaporated at the sound of Larkin's footfalls clunking on the stairs as he came up from the storeroom. The quartermaster had most likely been inspecting *Fortunata's* dwindling provisions and was on his way to tell him so.

"Captain," he said, saluting Ian. "I've done an inventory. I suggest we institute deeper economies. Also, the talk below is turning black. They're calling the woman a Jonah, or worse, a witch. Some are saying she sat fire to the *Spiegel* so to be brought onto the *Fortunata*. They want her thrown overboard and there's talk of the witch burnings in the Colonies."

Ian shook his head.

"She's been made simple, an imbecile, from her terrible experience, but she is no witch. I'll talk to the crew this evening. In the meantime, get her a meal in the morning and at night. She eats little. Give the job of getting her meals to someone you trust."

Larkin didn't move away but stood looking over the calm ocean with a hard countenance on his face.

"It wasn't the plague on that vessel, was it? You ever see that kind of sickness before?" he asked, his voice low. "Is it possible she's brought it to us, and we may all succumb to it?"

Ian didn't answer for a few moments. He wracked his brain for a memory or a conversation that might hold the key to what he'd seen that day on the *Spiegel*. Not one dead body showed signs of bleeding from the nose or mouth and no swelling of the glands, which would have been typical for plague victims.

The only survivor, Anne, as he'd come to call her, mumbled and seemed to see visions in the air. She behaved like an erratic, frightened child, and he often heard her plaintive cries from her cabin calling for her mother to come and help her. It was clear, the horror she'd seen and the illness she'd undergone still clung to her mind and body. She was an object of pity and shouldn't be feared or maligned as a witch.

"We don't know the ship's cargo," he answered, "but the *Spiegel* was returning from the Americas. The disease could be something we've never seen before."

"Whatever it was, the men believe she brought it," Larkin grumbled. "What will you do?"

Ian sighed. How could he blame his men when even he himself worried over the old superstitions? But Ian's common sense told him Anne wasn't to blame for *Fortunata's* predicament any more than a fickle, female wind was. The tides of nature were hard to understand, especially the invisible ones, but he'd not capitulate to the base actions of torturing a woman to appease some unseen god or frightened men.

"It is not so. I'm tired of women being burned at the stake because men prefer to take out their fears on the meekest in society. Besides, I have a plan to remedy our situation that should turn the crew's attitude around. Tell them tonight they shall have a feast. Pull old Shelby from his hammock and set him to cooking in the galley. Open up the stores and give him whatever he needs. Make sure he understands I expect his best efforts.

Two casks of rum are socked away under the floorboards of my cabin. I picked them up in Jamaica last time we docked. Have the men retrieve them and tell Garvey to bring his fiddle. I want a table set up on deck, and we shall commence our revelries at sunset."

Larkin's expression flitted from incredulity to concern.

"I hate to speak out of turn, Captain, but is this wise? We only have enough provisions to last a week."

Ian patted his quartermaster on the shoulder.

"The men need this to raise morale, and I must make amends to whatever gods rule the wind."

He smiled at his capitulation to those unseen tides.

"Do as I've asked."

Larkin nodded, saluted, and left to inform the crew who were below deck. Ian watched him disappear. With a smile on his lips, he strode down the deck toward the passenger cabins. He wished to check in on the creature who so terrified his men. When she didn't answer his knock, he let himself inside to find her curled up in her hammock, her face so peaceful it looked like a sleeping angel's.

He'd fallen in love with her in some strange way. They'd never talked or laughed the way lovers do, but a keen need to protect her never left him. Telling Larkin she was a simpleton was a way to deflect the crew's superstitions. Quietly, he watched as she dreamed and admired how the peacefulness of her expression was like the ocean which *Fortunata* rested upon.

"My lady," he said. "I need you to wake."

Chapter Ten

Grace, Arkansas
Wednesday Morning

THE DEER STAND WAS BUILT OF LUMBER AND ABOUT TWENTY feet in the air on solid timber poles. Its wooden shell, low roof, and position up against a thick-limbed ancient cedar tree provided the stand with almost complete concealment from human or animal eyes treading across the landscape below.

November mornings in southern Missouri can be bitter, but Terry, the deer stand's builder, and his wife, Ashely, were both well dressed for the occasion. Heavily insulated in camouflaged hunting attire, they kept quiet waiting for the sun to rise with their rifles perched upon the stand's window ledge.

Warm red and yellow rays broke over the eastern sky, giving Bob's Knob, the name for the singularly tall hill out Terry and Ashely's deer stand window—the impression of a having a halo. The day was breaking above and below. With it came movement.

Something crashed through the underbrush across the field to the deer stand's right. Both hunters, expecting at least a doe, but hoping for a buck, leaned in closer to their rifles. Ashley, the better marksman, used her gun's telescopic sight to scan the terrain much the same way a military sniper would survey her surroundings for enemy targets. Terry, using a night vision scope, zeroed in on the animal first.

"Oh God," he groaned.

Ashley, picking up on his unusual tone, lowered her weapon and looked at her husband.

"What? What is it?"

"A woman," he whispered. "She's running."

"What?" Ashley came back, her expression confused.

Terry pointed at a grove of oak trees where the sunlight hadn't pierced the twilight's gloom. Following his finger, Ashley put her eye to the telescopic sight, and with the instinct of a true huntress, she caught and found her target as Terry made a second low-voiced exclamation.

"Someone is chasing her!"

The two watched as the woman, her clothing inappropriate for running through a rough-cut field, continued to skirt the edge of the tree line. Every fifteen feet or so, she would steal a frantic glance behind her.

"The person chasing her has a handgun," Terry said, reaching up to his wife's shoulder and pulling her gently away from the open window. "We can't take any chance he might see us."

"Terry," Ashley said in a low voice, "if he's trying to kill her, we need to stop him."

Husband and wife shared a brief, tense gaze.

"I...I...don't know, Ash. He's armed. What can we do other than call the police? If he's crazy enough to chase a woman with a gun, he's crazy enough to start shooting at us."

"We can shoot over his head to stall him, so she can get away. If he comes for us, we can try and hit at his feet."

Terry's head shook back and forth.

"Are you crazy? You might kill him. He's a moving target."

"We can't wait..."

Ashley's sentence was snuffed short with the first cracking

gunshot blast shattering the bucolic dawn's perfect tranquility. Husband and wife instinctively ducked down.

Terry moved first. Raising the binoculars once more, he found the person still running in the same direction as before. Scanning the field for the woman, he found her crawling on all fours.

"I think she's been hit," he said. "Shoot over the gunman first. If he locates us, and raises his gun, try and hit his foot."

Taking her rifle, Ashley applied her right eye once again to the telescopic lens and moved the gun across the land below until she located the man moving toward his prey. Her first shot rang out over the field, bringing the man's progress to a complete stop.

"Be ready," Terry whispered.

They watched the human predator below study the wide field and come to rest with an eagle's accuracy on their semi-hidden stand.

"Yeah, that's right, buddy," Ashley said softly, her one eye still staring through the scope, "you're not sure if the first one was for you. Let me make it clear."

Compressing the trigger, the rifle expressed its pinky-sized but searingly lethal missile, causing the air to reverberate with a second great, deafening explosion. Ashley watched as her target hunkered down to the ground. Whoever it was, they had to know they'd been seen and the bullets were warning shots meant to slow him or stop him entirely if necessary.

"The woman is down and not moving," Terry said. "I can see blood on her back."

"Terry?"

"Yeah?"

"The killer is going into the forest. I'll lose him if I don't try now. What do I do?"

The air in the deer stand pulsated with indecision.

"Do you have a good shot at his feet, Ash?"

But they'd taken too long in weighing their moral dilemma.

"No, not any longer," she answered and sighed.

Shaking her head, Ashley pulled herself upright from staring down into her rifle's scope and took a deep breath, letting it out.

"He's gone."

Terry stood up. "We've got to get down to the woman. You cover me with your rifle. I'll call the ambulance and the police while I go to check on her. Watch the tree line where he went. When I get to her, I'll call your cell phone."

Terry climbed down the deer stand's ladder and Ashley watched as he ran across the field to where the woman lay face down and unmoving. He pulled his phone from his pocket and waved it in Ashley's direction. A second later, hers vibrated. Grabbing it, she breathed her question, "Well? Is she..."

"Dead. She's dead, Ash. You still have me covered, right?"

His wife had never removed her focus from the last place the killer had disappeared.

"I do, baby. I have you covered."

"Good," Terry said. "Don't take your eyes off that tree line, honey. I think I know why the guy was chasing her and why he killed her."

"Why?"

"Gold...coins, Ash. Really old gold coins are spilling out of her pockets."

Chapter Eleven

Fortunata
Atlantic Ocean
1672

IAN WATCHED FROM THE CABIN'S DOOR AS A TINY TREMOR AT
the corner of the young woman's closed eyes told him she was
swimming back up from her peaceful dream. He wished she might
wake in familiar, loving surroundings with those she'd lost still alive
to comfort her.

Since being brought on board, she'd not spoken to him and had
eaten very little. If he came to see her, she cowered, drawing
herself up into whatever corner of the room she scrambled to first.
A fever clung to her. Voices spoke to her, and he heard her carrying
on painful, tear-filled conversations in Dutch with people in her
dreams.

He guessed her age to be around twenty years, and the only
indication of her name was in the hem of the nightdress she'd
worn when she came aboard. Someone, perhaps the mother she
called for in her hallucinations, had embroidered 'Anne' in a light
blue thread. To make her comfortable, he'd made sure she had

water, food, and fresh clothing. Not once did she look at him with anything but fear.

Waiting until she was fully awake, he continued to stand in the doorway, not daring to go fully into the room. Slowly she pulled herself from the hammock, rubbed her face, and stood up. For the first time, her gaze focused on his face. Color blushed her cheeks, and her eyes were clear. Going over to where the food and water sat on the table, she picked up the cup, filled it, and took a long draught. Finished, she turned around. Her brow furrowed as she studied him.

"Thank you," her words sounding hoarse and whispery, "for your kindness."

He offered her a smile.

"You are welcome. You speak English. That makes things easier."

Sitting down in the cabin's only chair, she let her hand rest on the table, still holding the cup.

"Yes, I had a tutor who taught us as children. My father, despite the troubles between the Dutch and the English, believed we should know and speak your language."

Ian watched her face. It was devoid of any emotion as she stared through the round porthole. The sunlight streaming in illuminated her countenance with golden warmth. He nearly sighed out loud at her fairness but quickly swallowed it.

"I don't know why I'm still alive," she said, not looking at him.

"Do you remember what happened?" he asked.

For a few moments, she said nothing. Swallowing hard, she spoke.

"My father's business is in Leiden. He and my mother left six months ago from New Amsterdam, where we lived, but my sister and I were to follow once we'd returned from an extended visit at my uncle's home along the Hudson. Within two weeks of our ship sailing from port, a pestilence took hold. In time, everyone on board felt its effect. I, too, became sick, but my sister, Lysbeth, nursed me until she fell ill and…died."

She took another drink from the cup.

"Your vessel was adrift not four days from the Azores when we came upon it. You were off course if the captain's intent was Amsterdam. Do you have any recall of how long you were on the ship?"

Raising herself once again to a standing position, she turned and fixed her gaze on him.

"I've lost all sense of time. When Lysbeth died, there was no one able to help me. I remember a sailor bringing me a bucket of water and a bowl of mutton soup, but nothing afterward. The smell of the dead," she faltered, her face convulsed with disgust at the memory, "was horrible and the cries of the suffering..."

Putting her hands to her ears, she shut her eyes and shook her head. He didn't want to press her any further. It was best to tell her of their current situation and that she'd be confined to her quarters.

"I am sorry, but cheer yourself in knowing you have family waiting for you in Leiden."

Her hands slowly lowered from the sides of her head as her gaze pulled up from the ground to meet his own. In her eyes, the tempest subsided, and an ember of happiness glinted into life.

"Of course," she breathed. "Mama and Papa will be there."

Ian nodded.

"You will see them again, but for now, you must know this ship is caught in the becalmed latitudes. Until there is a shift in the wind, I will need to ask you to stay in this cabin. The crew isn't comfortable with a lone woman aboard, especially one who came from a plagued ship."

An expression of confusion briefly rippled across her face, but it passed, and she nodded.

"I will do as you ask as long as I may lock my door from within. I do not want to be imprisoned. I've had enough of that. Where are you bound for?"

"We hope to be in Bermuda in less than a week's time."

Fear crept back into her eyes.

"What will happen to me there?"

He took a deep breath. Since it was clear she was from a family of means, a ransom would be exacted from her father. It was in Ian's interest as well as King Charles' to see to her safety and wellbeing.

"I'll turn you over to the Governor of Bermuda. You will be taken good care of there, and once a ransom is agreed upon, your passage back to Leiden will be arranged."

Though this appeared to settle her, the loss of never seeing her again stung him deeply. She thanked him with a soft smile.

"May I ask you something?" she said, crossing the space until she stood in the middle of the room.

"Anything," he answered.

Their eyes locked, but she quickly looked away, a soft hue of pink creeping into her cheeks once more.

"I spent five years as a child in the company of an Englishman who was our tutor. He was the son of a nobleman, and his accent was similar to yours. What part of England do you call home?"

"My family is from Warwickshire."

She nodded and offered him another faint, but uncertain smile.

"I wasn't sure if you were a pirate," she said softly. "I heard your accent and hoped you were a gentleman."

Ian suppressed his reaction to laugh, resulting in a cough. Technically he was from the class who might call themselves gentlefolk, but he had rarely conducted himself as one. For her, though, he would gladly try to be one. With twinkling eyes, he smiled at her.

"There are two brothers before me to inherit my father's seat in the House of Lords. That's why I ran away to become a sailor. So far, I don't call myself a pirate, but if times become difficult, I'd rather work than beg a living from another man, even if he is a Duke and my brother."

Another quick nod and a hint of fear around her eyes, but he gave her a gentle smile.

"Do you mind answering one of my questions, my lady?"

She appeared to warm at the appellation.

"Certainly."

"What is your name?"

"It is Miss Anne van Houten."

"Well, Miss van Houten," he bowed, taking his hat from his head and sweeping it across low in front of him. "My name is Lord Ian Warwick, the third son of His Grace, Richard Neville, the 18th Duke of Warwick. You have nothing to fear from me, and I promise to do my best regarding your care. I am honored to make your acquaintance."

Her expression brightened, and she gave him a curtsy. Offering her hand, he took it and lifted it. With his gaze locked onto her gray-blue eyes, he kissed the back of her hand ever so gently, his heart banging in his chest.

"One more request?" she asked her words almost inaudible.

As she withdrew her hand, he answered, "Yes?"

"Would it be too much trouble to ask for bathing water? I would wash these clothes as well, and"—she lifted one of the long, loose mahogany tresses lying over her shoulder and gave it a quick, critical looking over— "if you might have a comb, I would be grateful."

"I will see to it, but your washing water will be from the ocean. Fresh water is being rationed."

Anne nodded and offered him another grateful curtsy.

He bowed, and when the door closed behind him, he heard the turn of the key in the lock. Being in her company had kindled a giddy, lightness in him he'd never known before in the company of any woman. For the first time since being stranded in the horse latitudes, he was grateful and overjoyed at his predicament.

"What a terrible yet wonderful plight I find myself in!" he thought to himself as he whistled down the short hall. "Caught between dying and living or loving and losing. I care not which as long as I might have her with me for a while longer."

Coming out into the sunlight, he stretched his arms wide like he wished to hug the world unto his chest and grinned broadly up into the blue heavens.

"Thank you!" he cried. "Thank you!"

As Ian hurried about his business, he'd failed to notice Larkin, along with two other sailors holding the rum keg they'd retrieved from his cabin moments earlier. Each man stood watching him with either bewildered, bemused, or skeptical expressions. Once Ian disappeared, Larkin looked back up into the sky, suspiciously scanning it for floating gods, his weedy eyebrows squeezing together in one long patch of perplexity.

"The captain's gone off his nut," mumbled the one sailor while shaking his head.

"Keep your tongues quiet. He's your captain. What he does is his business," Larkin growled.

"Nutty is fine by me," said the sailor smiling lovingly at the rum keg like it was his newborn babe. "The nuttier, the better. The nuttier, the better."

Chapter Twelve

Northwest Arkansas
  Wednesday Morning

SCREECHING LIKE A BANSHEE, THE JET'S TIRES MADE INITIAL
contact with the tarmac's wet surface sending up plumes of water
vapor hindering the passengers' views of a postage-stamp airport
nestled among sweeping farm fields. The plane continued to lift
and drop, trying to reconnect with terra firma multiple times like a
stone skipping across an asphalt pond before gravity's hold finally
and concretely was reestablished, much to the grateful, exhausted
relief of the people onboard.

The wind, for the last four hours, had bounced and shot the
plane through the air like a ball being passed between a seven-
hundred-foot basketball team. And the fun wasn't over yet. As the
jet whooshed down the runway, its backend took a detour, skidding
wildly to the right with the same force as a carnival Scrambler ride.
Passengers grabbed their seat arms and let out surprised cries (or
screams) depending on whether they subscribed to the worldview
of the glass being half full or half empty.

"That's it," Helen whispered through gritted teeth. "Someone, some brilliant mind out there in the world, needs to come up with a better way to move people around the globe. This feels completely uncivilized."

Martha, on her right, pulled her head up from her lap where she'd stuffed a pillow, her coat, and a bag of chocolate-covered peanuts. All were flattened or melted from a hot, fearful human pressing on them for two hours. She'd collected these last-ditch comfort items from her luggage somewhere over southern Indiana's air space and spent the rest of the flight clutching them desperately.

"If I'm going to die, Helen," she'd told her friend, "I'm going to eat chocolate on the way down."

The plane's airbrakes engaged, reducing the seventy-ton flying machine's speed from two hundred miles an hour to a mere thirty, thereby giving all onboard one last weightless Tilt-A-Whirl moment as the plane corrected its trajectory along the runway. Collectively, the brave, trusting, if not naive, passengers exhaled as the jet came to a jerking rest, each person's subconscious brain noting the faint odor of human terror permeating the cabin.

Air pumped from the vents above them, flushing away the last four hours of soul-searing horror and any residual fear-soaked air molecules hanging about their heads. But with herd nonchalance, those frequent flyers of the fiendish skies instantly forgot (or ignored) their near-death experience and prepared their personal belongings for catching their next flight.

"Sweet Jesus," Martha exhaled. "Thank you for getting us here alive."

"Who the *Hell* is flying this contraption?" Helen fumed. "Some sadistic lunatic with a thrill-seeking gene? At what point did it seem like a good idea to fly straight through a tornado?"

Martha's mouth went slack as her head swiveled to the left to look at Helen.

"Do you think we flew through one?" she asked incredulously. "It felt that way, but my brain feels like it's in sludge. It's hard to make a judgment call. I feel like I've got shaken-brain syndrome."

"Exactly!" Helen snapped, terse with internal rage and

righteous indignation. "I can tell you this: we will drive *back* to New York and take a *boat* home. This experience," she flung one hand into the air like she was swatting away all things airplane-related, "will take me quite some time to get over. I'm sincerely questioning this industry's customer service standards."

Martha nodded and released her grip on the pillow-coat-chocolate bundle. She stretched her tight, sweaty fists into normal-shaped hands as the flight attendant's voice came over the intercom.

"Welcome to Northwest Arkansas. On behalf of the crew, we'd like to thank you for flying with us today. Please be careful when opening the overhead bins. Some items may have shifted during the flight."

"Really?" Helen hissed under her breath. "Shifted luggage is their prime concern and whether we will be brained by it if we should open a cargo bin? What about the *shift* in our mental well-being? Where is the apology for almost killing us?"

With brilliant timing, a professional, upbeat masculine voice came over the intercom.

"Sorry, folks, for the rough ride. Strong storms were pushing up from the Gulf. The bright side is we've arrived six minutes ahead of schedule. On behalf of the crew and myself, I hope you have a pleasant stay and thank you for flying with us."

Helen made a harumph sound and sat staring at the back of the seat in front of her with lowered eyelids, her mouth puckered with anger.

"I'm so sorry," Martha said. "This trip isn't getting off to the best start."

Taking a deep breath and blowing it out, Helen reached over and patted Martha's forearm.

"No, no, no, don't apologize for anything. I wouldn't have let you come by yourself. This is a Tilda-escapade, and you're going to need backup."

She did another hand flick gesture in the direction of the pilot's cabin.

"Besides, we've already been manhandled by that psychotic

flying this plane. Surely, we can swing saving Tilda from the mob. Come on, they've opened the door, thank God. Let's get off this death trap."

In less than thirty minutes, they'd collected their rental car and were buzzing down a winding, tree-lined highway, the autumn colors bringing happy, grateful sighs from both women as the Ozarks' beauty filtered through the windows and into their tired, stressed-out beings.

"It's so good to be seeing this," Martha said as she maneuvered the safari-colored Volkswagen Beetle smoothly through the highway's curves. "This car is fun to drive, Helen. How do you like those heated seats?"

"Loving them," Helen murmured in a contented-cat way. "I might buy one of these Bugs when we get home. I like how people smile at us when we go by."

"There's the sign for Bella Vista. I've never been here before. My stomping grounds are much closer to Mountain View, but this community is nice, isn't it?"

Helen raised her eyelids to see a landscape not so different from southern England's in many ways. Soft, rolling hills covered with thick forests of oak, pine, sycamore, and maple interspersed with pastureland speckled with round hay bales and herds of cattle. Houses were tucked into valleys and perched against hillsides, overlooking lakes and streams.

"It reminds me of home. I mean where I grew up," Helen said.

Martha's phone rang, bringing Tilda's contact information up on the car's infotainment display. Pressing accept, she said, "Hi Tilda."

"Hi, honey! You make it to Grace yet?"

"No, but the GPS says it's only ten miles."

"Okay, listen up, sugar. There's something I haven't told you yet."

Martha and Helen exchanged looks—Martha's worried—Helen's dripping with mock surprise.

"You see, sweetie," Tilda went on, her tone sugar glazed with a hint of anxiety sprinkled in, "there may be a few of our family members also...for lack of a better word...*curious*, about the necklace as well."

"Curious?" Helen asked. "Would you please flesh that word out for us, Tilda? This necklace *is* yours to find and sell, right?"

"Helen?" Martha's aunt exclaimed, her southern accent stretching out the vowels between consonants like a taffy pulling machine in a candy store window. "Hi, Helen! I didn't know you were coming, too. Darling, I can't wait to finally meet you! This is so nice of you to come along and help Martha with this little errand of mine."

The two friends exchanged another set of expressions—Helen's repentant and Martha's pained.

"I'm looking forward to meeting you, too, Miss Tilda," Helen said with true warmth.

"Ummm," Martha jumped in, "this heirloom necklace, to whom does it belong, and where exactly do we go to find it in Grace?"

Semi-truck whooshing sounds on the other end of the line filled the background noise of Tilda's pregnant pause.

"Well...the good news is the necklace technically belongs to anyone who finds it first, but..."

"Technically?" Martha interrupted, but Helen jumped over her friend.

"If that's the *good* news, what's the *bad* news?"

"No, not exactly what I would call bad news, honey, and if I weren't hiding out right now and nearly seventy-three years old, I'd probably scramble down that little old hole myself."

Martha's mouth plopped open.

"*Little—old—hole?*" Helen squawked, each staccato word louder than the next. "*Where* is this necklace, Tilda?"

"That's the funny part, dear. The story goes that my great-great-aunt was being chased by bushwhackers when she made a daring climb up onto a cliff overhang and thrust the necklace into a cave. The family's been spelunking in every cave in northwest Arkansas for the last hundred years, but no one's turned up the necklace yet."

"Oh my God, Aunt Tilda!" Martha exclaimed. "You've got no real idea where it is, do you?"

"Well, yes and no. The last bit of gossip I heard was that it might be in a cave outside of Grace near a place called Bob's Knob."

"Who told you this, and were they sober?" Martha asked.

"No, your Uncle Butterfield wasn't exactly a teetotaler, honey. He liked his bourbon after dinner, but you've got to find the necklace! It's my only salvation!" Tilda begged into the phone. "Jackie and I are holed-up in this flea-bitten motel somewhere on the outskirts of Tampa, and he's a nervous wreck. You haven't known Hell, Martha, until you've been cooped up with a terrified, backbiting, neurotic drag queen who's run out of his high-dollar facial products and is having to use motel lotions on his delicate, sensitive skin. I'm nearly at my wit's end!"

"Okay! Okay! Tell me where you think this cave is? At least, that's a place to start."

"In all fairness, I need to tell you there might be a few family members and some other people searching for the necklace, too."

Helen dropped her face into her hands, imagining hordes of treasure-seeking fanatics, armed to the teeth with lethal weapons prowling the hills for the lost necklace of the Roller Clan.

"Tilda! Who?" Martha demanded.

"I know your Uncle and Aunt Butterfield have searched for years, but he's recuperating from a hip replacement, so he's not able to get around much, probably can't climb or scramble down holes with his cane. The one, in my opinion, you've got to look out for is Crazy Ricardo..."

"Of course, we do," Helen mumbled into her hands.

"He's married to your second cousin, Jelly, on your daddy's side."

"I don't remember ever hearing about a *Jelly*? Is the name like the stuff you put on toast?" Martha asked, weakly flicking a look at Helen.

"Yes, her real name is Jelinda, but when she was a toddler, her mama, Kari, married to your mother's brother, Lou Roller, found her chin-deep in a jar of blueberry preserves. So cute, don't you think? You both inherited that red hair from our side of the family. Anyway, the name Jelly stuck."

Tilda chuckled at the pun.

"Crazy Ricardo!" Helen cried. "Tell us about Crazy Ricardo!"

"Oh, yes," Tilda came back. "He's from either Cuba, or was it Canada, I can't remember, but he's a helluva dresser—gorgeous man with beautiful dark eyes and long lashes. I saw him at the last family reunion. All the women *and* your cousin Chase were enthralled with him, Martha."

"Why do they call him Crazy Ricardo?" Helen growled, leaning closer to the car's dashboard in a desperate attempt to be closer to Tampa Tilda and ring a direct answer from her.

"I suspect his real name is Richard or Ricky, but he's got the passionate temperament of his race...oh, maybe he is from Canada after all," Tilda mused. "Anyway, some say he killed a man over a car or was it he killed a man at a bar? My hearing is not what it used to be."

Helen slumped back in her seat, an expression of abject disbelief upon her face.

"The point is, Martha," Tilda continued. "Ricardo told Lou Roller, who told me, that he believed the necklace to be near a town called Grace, a toad's jump from Bella Vista. No one has ever been sure of the exact location of the Roller's farm simply because there weren't any land deeds to confirm ownership. You see, in 1862, the county courthouse was burned by Union troops. The Rollers never went back to claim their land. Ricardo told Lou he'd narrowed the search to a place called Bob's Knob. Get to Grace and ask if anyone there might know where the old Roller farm was and if they ever talked with Ricardo. Okay?"

"Bob's Knob? What does that even mean, Tilda? What if Ricardo found the necklace and is long gone?"

"No, honey, I don't think he did. Lou runs things, and he would've known. He told me Jelinda went to find Ricardo who is kinda missing."

"Missing? Exactly how is he *missing*?" Helen asked.

"Well, it's one of two things."

"Yes," Helen and Martha said together, leaning closer into the car's dashboard.

"He's out looking for the necklace, run off with another woman, orrr..."

Tilda dragged her 'r' longer than any Southerner's drawl normally dictated.

"Or what!" Helen chirped.

"Maaybe," Tilda drawled, "he's bit the big one."

Chapter Thirteen

Fortunata
1672

DAZZLING STARS IN WHITE-LIGHT FINERY CROWDED THE NIGHT time sky above the *Fortunata* as the ship floated upon a tranquil, dark blue sea. The heavens had the best seat in the house for the human drama or comedy about to take place on the floating stage below.

A great, long table constructed from unhinged doors stretched down the center of *Fortunata's* deck. Two silver multi-armed candelabras, their candles already lit sat regally among an amalgamation of poor crockery, battered tin tableware, and wooden utensils. Already each tankard or cup was filled with rum, and covered ironstone pots sat steaming down along the tabletop's center. Shelby, a cantankerous old cuss but amazingly gifted cook, had prepared a wonderful meal, its smell so enticing that both the gods above and the men below were champing at the bit for the feast to begin.

On the menu was boiled salted beef with cabbage and onions

along with a split pea soup, as well as bread, cheese, and a steamed suet pudding for dessert made with raisins, currants, and spices. The two kegs of rum sat near the captain's chair. It would be under his authority and goodwill that the sweet nectar would be distributed among his men.

Larkin had culled enough crates, stools, and even four chairs to give each crew member a place at the table. He went about his preparations like his life depended on the scrupulous execution of his duties. With a final survey, he adjusted his cravat, pulled on his jacket's lapels, and raised himself stiffly upright into a full military posture.

"Ahoy!" he bellowed in his best quartermaster's voice. "All men on deck!"

The crew, who'd been kept below deck until the final reveal, eagerly clamored up the stairs into the fresh night air. A look of wonder skipped like a stone from one face to the next as they each, in turn, bore witness to what lay before them. To be sure, it was an unusual departure from normal ship protocol, but as all gazes eventually fell upon the kegs of rum, even the naysayers in the bunch couldn't help a smile at the thought of the pleasurable evening festivities that lay before them.

"Stand to attention!" Larkin barked out, each syllable a staccato beat, in his baritone voice.

From the highest rank to the lowest, the sailors quickly found a place standing behind a seat, stool, or crate as Ian, coming out of his cabin, walked down the starboard side of the ship until he arrived at the head of the table.

"At ease," he commanded.

The men relaxed and turned their attention toward him. Ian's nascent love for Anne had inspired him to be a better captain and man, but first, he wanted to make things right with his creator.

"Tonight, we will dine together, giving honor to our maker. For we may only consider our lives worthy if we offer humbly our dutiful thanks. It is my opinion that the good Lord above must have been a great lover of the oceans, for he certainly put plenty of water upon this Earth."

His crew all nodded at the sagacity of this statement.

"Therefore, it goes without saying, he must have a special place in his heart for all sailors. So, men, let us eat, drink, and be merry, for as the crew of *Fortunata*, we must bring credit to all seafaring men and show his Lordship in Heaven we are courageous, worthy, and grateful for our lives. May we continue to sail the four corners of his creation!"

Ian raised his glass and the men, stirred by his speech, joined him.

"Hear, hear captain!" they cried, slugging down their first, bracing drink of spirit-lifting rum.

With the toast completed, the festivities ramped up into a full swing. Not a face around Ian's table was anything but cheerful and bright. Shelby's gastronomic endeavor proved to be a hit with not a scrap of bread or a spoonful of pudding left for the seabirds to retrieve once morning would arrive.

The first keg of rum was finished when Ian tapped into the second. Garvey lifted his fiddle to his chin and ran his bow over its strings. A tune known by all the men, *Saylors For My Money*, was his first choice, and no sooner did he alight on this well-loved ditty, than the men sang in unison:

COUNTRIE MEN OF ENGLAND
> *who live at home with ease,*
> *And little think what dangers,*
> *Are incident o'the seas,*
> *Give care unto the Saylor*
> *Who unto you will shew:*
> *His case,*
> *His case,*
> *How ere the wind doth blow.*

THE MELODY AND TEMPO WERE CHEERFUL, AND AS THE MEN sang, their enthusiasm increased. A general swaying on seats, toasting one another at each stanza's end, and clapping each other on the back were strong indications that Ian's crew were enjoying themselves heartily.

SOMETIMES ON NEPTUNES BOSOME
  Our ship is lost with waves
  And every minute we expect,
  The sea must be our graves
  Sometimes on high she mounteth,
  Then falls again as low:
  with waves,
  with waves,
  When stormie winds do blow!

AS THE REVELERS' SONG ENDED IN A CRESCENDO, THEY FAILED TO notice the change in the dancing movements of the candles' flames. The yellow-orange tips elongated, rising as if some invisible hand pulled their fiery tips upward until they resembled thin columns of light. Down the length of the table, Ian caught sight of a face peeking from the dark hallway leading to the cabins beyond. It was Anne. His heart smiled within his chest as his gaze caught hers, and in her eyes, he saw the power of her feelings for him.

THEN WITH UNFEIGNED PRAYERS,
  As Christian duty bindes,
  Wee turn unto the Lord of hosts,
  With all our hearts and minds,
  To him we flee for succour,
  For he we surely know,
  can save,
  can save,
  How ere the wind doth blow!

                        . . .

OFF IN THE DISTANCE, A MIGHTY CRACK OF LIGHTNING RIPPED through the Northeast sky as a gust of wind whipped across the table, extinguishing the candles and the sailor's soulful ballad.

A storm was upon them and Ian's prayer had been heard.

Chapter Fourteen

Grace, Arkansas
  Wednesday Morning

THE CEDAR-SIDED POST OFFICE WAS ONE OF THE THREE buildings occupying roadside space along downtown Grace's lone street. A longhaired pooch appeared to be the town's sole inhabitant, and he'd decided to take up residence in the center of the road, apparently his favorite midday napping destination.

Martha slowed the VW Beetle to a complete stop ten feet from the sprawled-out hairy heap. The only sign the fur had life was a shaggy tail limply beating the pavement.

"He seems comfortable. I guess he intends to stay," she said to Helen and sighed.

"Well," Helen replied, giving the quiet town a slow scan, "this *is* Grace, Tilda's supposed El Dorado. We should pull in there. It looks open."

She pointed to a building no bigger than an over-sized storage shed.

Martha peered through the windshield.

"Grace Water Department. They may know something."

"Good place to start," Helen agreed.

As they sat considering their next move, Helen said, "When we asked Tilda why she thought Ricardo might be dead, she said it was because no one had heard from him in two weeks."

Martha nodded.

"Yes, but remember, Aunt Tilda is a bit of a drama queen. Ricardo might have found something. It doesn't matter anyway. I've got to try to find the necklace whether Crazy Ricardo has it or if it's still in a cave somewhere."

Looking over at the Grace Water Department, Martha continued.

"Okay," Helen said with a smile. "Let's give it a try."

Backing the Bug up, Martha maneuvered it into the gravel parking area directly up against the tiny building's equally tiny front porch. The lights were on, so they got out and went inside. At the counter stood a statuesque woman, her name, Peg, written on a white tag stuck to her shirt.

If someone had asked Martha what animal best described the Water Department woman, she would have blurted out, "Bald Eagle!" For many reasons, Martha would have been dead on. With grey locks cut stylishly short and a lavender highlight running in a swath up through the gelled, back-swooped hair, Peg was a stunningly pretty woman with wide shoulders and a strong-built body. She held herself with a cowboy's economical ease, giving the appearance of someone used to breaking stallions, castrating calves, or tossing hay bales onto flatbed trucks.

As Helen and Martha entered, she didn't look up but instead stayed fixated upon her work, not breaking concentration but moving the plumed head back and forth with military precision.

"I'll be with ya in a minute," she said, her voice sounding as rough and gritty as the gravel in the parking lot outside. She waved a hand at the wall behind them.

"Have a seat."

Peg's directive sounded more like a command than a greeting, so they sat down on the wooden bench along the wall. A momentary flashback of sitting in her primary school hallway

69

upon a similar bench popped into Martha's mind. She'd been sent to talk with Mr. Clement, the school principal, at the age of eight for stealing Barton Shell's pudding cup from his lunch box. Pudding and donuts had always been her downfall in some way or other. Waiting on Peg today felt like waiting on Mr. Clement all those years ago—tough, awkward, and slightly scary.

"Now," Peg stated, her tone brusque and business-like, "Whatta ya'll need?"

She had finished her mystery work and was leaning her tall frame over the counter, giving Helen and Martha the same critical assessment she might have given an untrustworthy horse trader offering to sell her a lame animal. The expression was shrewd and intelligent, indicating to anyone within the normal IQ range that she wasn't a woman to irritate, cheat, or waste her time...ever.

"We're from out of town," Helen began.

"No shit."

The reply was swift and good-natured, if not also meant to be an invitation to share a mutual laugh. Martha chuckled, but she knew Helen was taken aback. It had been a while since they'd rubbed up against good, old, rural American directness.

"We wondered if you might be able to tell us the location of a farm owned by a family named Roller in the 1860s?"

Helen's follow-up approach sounded even less confident, but Martha knew she was trying to prescribe to the idea that if you kept moving forward, you might land on solid ground.

The eyelids across the counter lowered until only half of the steel-blue eyes were visible. Never removing her hard-ground focus from Helen's face, Peg rolled her jaw to the side in a bored yet thoughtful grimace and pulled a Vape pen from her pocket. Taking a long drag and letting it out, in the same manner your 1970s father might have done if he'd caught you in a dumb lie and was contemplating how to mete out your fate, Peg appeared to be considering the best way to approach Helen's question.

Martha's instincts told her the rapid-fire question round was about to begin.

"Have you tried the county courthouse?"

"Well, no, because we were told it burned in 1862, and the records were gone."

Peg appeared pleased. Nodding, she pursed her mouth outward appreciatively with Helen's answer.

"True, true," she conceded, a sharp glint in the piercing blues, as she threw-out her next zinger.

"What's your interest in the Rollers?"

Martha immediately tensed. As she knew from growing up in a small town, no one ever offered information regarding fellow local people. Inquiring, out-of-town strangers might be from the IRS. Address transparency simply wasn't on the menu in a place like Grace. This last question put forward by the wily Peg was a trick, and how it was answered would determine whether they received any future help.

Martha jumped into the fray, knowing that the family angle went a long way in opening doors.

"My family on my daddy's side were Rollers. There's supposed to be a graveyard on the land. It may be hearsay, but my Aunt Tilda, who lives down near Mountain View, Arkansas, wants photos. Some family members are buried there. My friend and I," Martha indicated Helen with a head tilt and a modest smile, "came up to see if we could find the place."

Peg's rumpled mouth flattened down into a thin, cautious line. Her calculating mien showed signs of shifting in their favor, but though the ice might be thawing, it was still unmoving.

"Sure has been a good deal of interest in the Roller farm lately," Peg said, shifting her searing gaze sharply back and forth between Helen and Martha. A slow, sagacious smile stealing across her mouth.

"Had a guy in here about a week ago. He wouldn't be kin of yours, would he?"

The question dripped with cynicism, and if they knew what was good for them, they'd better be straight-up, Martha decided. This woman wasn't anyone's fool.

"Okay, I am here to find anyone who would be willing to talk with me about where the Rollers lived. I have an Aunt Tilda who's in a lot of trouble with an angry mobster living in Florida. She likes to play poker, but her friend, a dancer in a nightclub, may have lent her money to play craps. The money wasn't exactly his to lend. There is supposedly some sort of family heirloom...a necklace..."

Peg held up her hand, her mouth set in a hard but softening line.

"No need to go into all that. Everyone here," she pointed out through the one window at the dog still lying asleep in the street, "knows about the Roller necklace. Hell! Your people have been wanderin' up here every six months for a hundred years trying to locate the place. The guy who showed up a couple of days ago got his face in the Briar Ridge newspaper. My twin sister, Deb, volunteers at the military park and was the one who found him. If I were you, I'd hightail it back to wherever you're from and count yourself lucky if you don't end up like him."

For a tense four or five seconds, Helen and Martha exchanged a confused expression with Peg's sour one.

"Your sister found a man? What do you mean by *end up?*" Helen asked.

"Nice looking fellow, too. She found him curled up like a baby behind a pile of ammo in an exhibit at the Briar Ridge Military Park with an Arkansas Toothpick run through his back."

Chapter Fifteen

Fortunata
1672

THE STORM BROKE ACROSS THE DOMED HEAVENS SENDING THE sails, men, and Ian into a flurry of excited seamanship work. A massive cloud bank blocked out the stars in the East, and it was moving fast toward them. Strong rain hitting the ocean's surface rumbled in the distance.

With a glance back in the direction of where Anne had been standing, he saw she'd disappeared. Every man was up and hastening to bring *Fortunata* up to speed for the voyage ahead. Each face registered happiness and intense focus. Spirits had surged, and the entire crew sprang into action with the wind's first rushing blast.

"Larkin!" Ian bawled over the growing wind, his face alight with pure joy. "Get two men to clear this spread from our deck!"

In no time and with all the crew working, the great sloop moved through the rolling waves. *Fortunata's* destination was northwest to Bermuda, and if they used their skills correctly, taking advantage of the storm's power, they would arrive at St. George in three days.

With all the sails hoisted, Ian helped to free the deck of any remaining articles from their feast. As he worked, a powerful truth dawned on him. His act of gratitude and honor toward something greater than himself had offered him and those who depended on him a second chance at life. He resolved to use it wisely.

"Take command of the deck," he told Larkin. "Put Hodgson at the wheel. He's my best helmsman. I've got to check on something."

Larkin never batted an eye. He saluted and hurried away to find Hodgson as another crack of lightning snaked across the dark sky. All hands were busy as Ian slipped into the passageway toward Anne's cabin.

Finding her door, he knocked. With its opening, thunder exploded, sending shock waves through the ship's skeleton. Anne's face blanched with terror, and she rushed at Ian, giving him no option but to embrace her.

He didn't move but held her quivering form tight within his arms next to his chest. The smell of the rose tinctured soap he'd brought for her to bathe with earlier floated up to him. Unconsciously, he breathed deeper, feeling a sense of intoxication take over him at the closeness of her ... the perfume of her.

The ship rolled in the mounting waves as she clung to him. His calm took its effect on Anne. Soon she pulled herself free from the safety of his arms and cast a timid gaze up into his face.

"Will we be safe?" she asked. "I don't want to be alone anymore."

A great desire to pull her back into his arms and protect her welled up in Ian, but fighting off the impulse, he offered her succor of a better sort. Anne needed courage, not cosseting. Taking her gently by the shoulders and looking down into her eyes, he smiled.

"This storm is our salvation," he said with real pleasure in his voice. "We will make Bermuda in only a few days. You'll be that much closer to seeing your family."

Uncertainty flashed across her face. As the storm lashed the outside of the ship, she looked down into her upturned hands and was quiet for a moment. With a timid glance back up into his eyes, she asked, "Would I be able to travel with you when you go back to Europe?"

There was no missing the emotion behind her question, and he had not the power to resist the electricity between them anymore.

She lifted her hand timidly to his face and lightly touched the curve of his jaw, sending shock waves through his body. No resistance was left in him. Reaching out, he grasped her once again, pulling her into his arms, kissing her soft, willing mouth.

When they broke, she took his hand and, turning it over, appeared to study the palm.

Not returning her gaze to him, she said, "I will not go on any other ship but yours back to Europe. You must take me."

Her words were without guise, and they were spoken so softly they were barely heard over the sound of the rain lashing the ship. He was transfixed by her. If she'd asked him to fly her to the moon, he would have simply nodded and sold his soul to the Devil to find a way to get her there.

"I'll take you," he whispered.

Before he realized it, words rushed from him.

"Only if you'll be my wife."

Anne's lovely face turned up toward him, a radiant joy illuminating it as a dazzling smile cleared away all fear from her countenance. If all the stars in the night time sky were set on fire by God's hand, Ian would have found them poor, dismal creatures indeed. For to him, nothing would ever compare to Anne's brilliant beauty.

She nodded and wrapped her arms once more around his neck. He lifted her off her feet and kissed her. Come raging storm, horrific Hell, or a grueling death, nothing mattered. Ian had found the meaning of life; love for someone besides himself.

Chapter Sixteen

Grace, Arkansas
  Wednesday Morning

HELEN'S KNEES WERE WEAK. BACKING AWAY FROM THE WATER department's counter and Peg's penetrating gaze, she felt for the wooden bench with her hand and sat down.

"You have any water?" she croaked.

"Sure," Peg replied and pulled two bottles from under the counter like a bartender in an old Western movie. "That'll be a dollar. Best prices in town."

Martha opened her purse and dug around in its depths until she managed a menagerie of British coins.

"I'm sorry," she said. "I don't have any American money."

"That explains a lot," Peg said with an easy shrug. "Keep the water, sit down, and give me the rundown on what's going on with the Roller farm. We've had more crazies showing up here, present company included, and fill me in on what you gals are up against with this Aunt Tilda person and her mob problem. The day's kinda slow, and I'm an enquiring mind, you might say."

Helen watched Martha pick up the bottles.

"Thank you," she said, sounding sheepish, and handed one to Helen, "that's very kind of you. It's been a weird two days."

Taking a long swig from the water, Helen sat, thinking it might be best to let Martha handle the story.

"Let me explain. My name is Martha Littleword, and this is Helen Ryes-Cousins. We both grew up in Arkansas but met about six years ago in England. I'd lost my husband, and Helen's had run off with a twenty-year-old."

Peg nodded, her blasé expression indicating she'd heard this kind of tale before. Making herself comfortable, she leaned casually over the counter, resting one elbow on its wood surface while using her other hand to occasionally pull on her Vape pen. Martha continued.

"My Aunt Tilda is in her seventies, and she plays the poker circuit. For the last ten years or so, she's had a wig designer out of Miami, Florida, named Jackie. His creations are fabulous and give her confidence. Aunt Tilda wears the wigs everywhere, but during poker games, she believes they give her an edge. They usually have rhinestones and ribbons and come in colors like pink, silver, lime green. They are simply amazing..."

"Distraction technique," Helen added.

Another low-lidded head nod from Peg.

"Yes, that's for sure," Martha agreed, "but Tilda has quite a following, and people love her."

Peg took a drag from her Vape and let it out.

"I take it this Jackie is the dancer who loaned your aunt the money? And he likes to dress up a bit?"

"Yes, Jackie Boy Divine, that's his stage name, has won many drag competitions, and he's like a son to Aunt Tilda. They fuss at each other, but last year Jackie nursed Til through the flu. They're simply devoted to one another, and I think that's why Jackie must have taken the money from the nightclub he manages. He wanted to help Tilda. They're in trouble, and I've got to find that stupid necklace."

Martha sat down beside Helen with a sigh. No one spoke for a few seconds until Peg put down her Vape pen, cleared her throat and said, "I got a brother, Jaime, who started out as a band majorette. Best one our high school ever saw. He lives in Dallas now and runs a dance studio."

Helen wondered if the mistiness in Peg's eyes was steam from her Vape pen or something stronger.

"I'll be honest with you girls. There's only one old-timer around here who might know where the Roller place was and be able to take you to it. He's practically a hermit living up near Bob's Knob and will shoot you if he finds you trespassing on his property, but Ned Potter, they also call him Tater, would be my best guess for someone to help you."

Helen's jaw went slack.

"How do we contact him?" Martha asked, sounding hopeful.

Peg scrunched up her face and pulled her mouth into a side pucker. She appeared to be weighing the pluses and minuses of enlisting this Tater person in the cause of two fancy-pants out-of-towners.

"Can't make ya any promises, but I'll be done at five o'clock. You come back here, and I'll drive ya up to Tater's. He's more likely to let us in if he sees my truck."

"Peg," Martha said, rising from her bench. "Thank you, thank you so much!"

This outpouring of gratitude appeared to momentarily rattle Peg's tough outer crust, but she rallied to resume her comfortable grumpy-like demeanor.

"I can't make you any promises," she declared, scanning them from head-to-toe and perhaps finding them shockingly inadequate for a visit to Tater's. She added, "You better find yourselves some clothes. I can't take you like that."

Helen's gaze dropped to her Chanel suit and exquisite Jimmy Choo suede high heels. She imagined tottering over rocky ground and having to run for her life in case Ned 'Tater' Potter should take a disliking to his mountain solitude being interrupted.

"Drive up the road," Peg pointed to her left, "and go to the *Farm and Feed* out on the highway. They've got a whole section of outdoor clothes and shoes. Don't show back up here unless you've got the right stuff on. If Tater decides to take you up into those hills," she pointed to her right this time, "he'll want to go tonight or early in the morning to not draw attention to your movements and *those*," she pointed at Helen's shoes, "won't even make the hike to Tater's front door."

Chapter Seventeen

Bermuda
  St. George
  1672

THE SUN BROKE THROUGH THE FILMY, COTTON CURTAINS OF Anne's bedroom, waking her from a sweet dream. For a long moment, she lay quiet, her eyes shut remembering it, the smile on her face a whisper of its memory.

She'd been the mistress of her own home in a faraway land called Carolina. Ian was by her side, and their family was healthy, strong, and generous. Her parents were there. A sense of longing and sadness touched her heart at the thought of them so far away and the loss of her sister, especially today, the day she would be married.

Anne was a sensible girl. There was no sense in brooding over what wasn't. Instead, she would appreciate the wonderful people she'd been given and who were treating her so kindly.

Sir John, the present Governor of Bermuda, and his wife, Catherine, had for four months given her a home under their roof as she awaited Ian's return with her dowry. At the time he'd left, he determined to not to take Anne on the voyage. The war between the English and the Dutch was still raging and Ian refused to put Anne's life again in danger. Fortunately, Sir John and Catherine were delighted to have Anne's company and they'd treated her like their daughter.

Ian's and Anne's wedding would be an intimate affair, taking place in the private gardens of the Governor's house. Only a few dignitaries, friends, and Ian's officers would be in attendance. Anne's parents could not join her until it was safe to sail once more.

Everything was ready, including a dress loaned to Anne by one of Catherine's younger friends. It would all be happening in a few hours, and Anne was like any bride: nervous, giddy, and utterly elated at the thought of being her new husband's wife.

Pushing herself up from the pillows, she looked out through the long window, which had a view of the great port of St. George. Tall masts, sails, and flags flew from the sailing ships floating in the cerulean blue waters of Bermuda's largest port.

Somewhere down in all that hustle and bustle, Ian's ship waited to take them to their new home. He'd only arrived yesterday from his voyage to England, and the news of his father's death, though sad, had also brought a generous bequest by Ian's older brother, Edward, the new Duke of Warwick.

Ian and Anne would manage Edward's vast lands in the Province of Carolina along the Southeast coast of the North American continent. Ian had spent hours last evening telling her fascinating stories. It was a wonderland of lush valleys, enormous pine forests, and indigenous people whose culture was noble, intelligent, and honorable. The adventure of a pristine wilderness to explore naturally appealed to Ian, while Anne's Dutch nature saw the potential of building a community.

Shaking her head free of all the thoughts of the future, Anne slipped free from the pretty canopied bed. A soft knock on the door announced Lizzy, her chambermaid, was waiting to bring in breakfast.

"Come in, Lizzy," she called, trying to hurry across the room to her wardrobe. "I'm putting on my dressing gown."

A sturdy redheaded girl about the age of fifteen poked her head around the bedroom door and gave Anne a dimpled smile. She had the kind of face that was always aglow with natural happiness. With round, elven-like blue eyes and a sprinkling of freckles across the bridge of her nose and cheeks, Lizzy was Irish through and through.

Since her arrival in Bermuda, Anne and Lizzy had become fast friends. Although Lizzy fulfilled the duties of a chambermaid by helping Anne with her dressing, and her hair, she was also much more. Because Lizzy moved about the entire house, she also knew all the gossip, both upstairs and down—an entertaining, if not valuable, asset Anne greatly appreciated.

"I brought you something new, Miss Anne," she said, with a pretty smile lighting up her face. "It's a drink brought by Captain John Smith to the Virginia colonies from Turkey many years ago. We've enjoyed it in Bermuda for some time. I think it will do you good today. We drink it with hot milk and sugar."

Lizzy, picking up a pot-bellied silver teapot, poured a steaming, black liquid into a delicate Delftware saucer. Lifting a silver pitcher, she poured an almost equal portion of milk into the saucer. From a silver bowl, she added sugar to the mixture and stirred.

"You'll need energy, Miss Anne, since it's your wedding day. Sip it slowly. It's called coffee."

Tentatively, Anne picked up the saucer, studying the caramel-colored concoction and breathed deeply of its nutty aroma. It smelled enticing. Taking a sip, she immediately liked its strong, slightly bittersweet taste.

"Lizzy, this *is* good."

With the saucer still in her hand, Anne crossed the room to a tufted chair in front of a mirror and sat down.

"Will you come help me, please? I need to do something special with my hair."

Soon, Anne's long tresses were wound and pinned in a most

becoming way for a young lady's bridal day. Lizzy had brought tiny white and yellow star-shaped flowers from the garden to adorn Anne's hair.

"You're gifted, Lizzy. I don't know what I'll do without you. I will miss you," she said, taking Lizzy's hands in hers.

With a lowered gaze, the younger girl, her voice faltering with emotion, answered, "Since you've been here, Miss Anne, I've enjoyed waiting on you. I hope you'll be happy. Is it true you'll go to live in the Province of Carolina?"

Lizzy looked worried, and Anne squeezed her two hands affectionately.

"It's going to be fine; and yes, Ian's brother, the Duke of Warwick, wishes us to take up and manage his lands there. My father is pleased and is offering to build our home for us. Ian wishes to offer homesteads to English families who will settle there."

"My family was from Ireland," Lizzy said. "We came here as indentured servants, but as you may have learned, the Irish have been banned from coming to Bermuda henceforth."

"Is your family here?"

Lizzy shook her head. A sudden tightness at the corners of her mouth told Anne the girl, but for the family she served, was likely to be alone in the world. She wondered if Catherine would let her pay Lizzy's debt and take her to Carolina as her companion and maid. It was worth asking, but later after the celebrations.

A knock made both young women jump.

"Anne?" Lady Catherine's muffled voice called through the door. "I've been given something by your husband-to-be. He wishes you should wear it today at the wedding ceremony."

Anne gave Lizzy's hands another excited squeeze, bounced up from her chair, and went to the door. Lady Catherine, a woman in her late thirties with the gentle nature and true warmth of a kind soul, stood smiling in the hall. She was wearing a lovely gown of pearl-colored silk, and her blonde hair was pulled up into a bun at the back. Along the sides of her face, long corkscrew ringlets hung with wispy curls framing her forehead.

In her two hands, she held a gift. It was wrapped in fabric and tied with a ribbon bow. Giving her hostess a curtsey, Anne bade her come inside.

"Captain Warwick intended to offer this special item to St. Peter's church out of gratitude for the salvation of his crew; but instead, he made a substantial donation of twenty gold Florins. He gave this to me asking that I should bring it to you," Lady Catherine said. "It was his mother's, and now it shall be yours."

All three women exchanged excited, bright-eyed expressions. Taking the gift, Anne went over to the stool once again and sat down. With a delicate touch, she carefully unwrapped the present and opened the flat hinged box. As her gaze fell on what the simple case held, she let out an astonished gasp.

Lady Catherine hurried around to Anne's side while Lizzy, standing on tiptoes, peeked over her mistress's shoulder, her eyes growing round with amazement.

"Anne, it's...lovely!" Lady Catherine gushed. Laying her hand gently on Anne's shoulder, she added after a few moments, "I've never seen a setting so remarkable. It truly is a great treasure and will grace your day as well as your beauty."

Anne's mind went blank as she stared at the extraordinary choker lying within its velvet bed. Comprised of three strands of exquisitely white, uniform pearls, the choker was held together by a doubloon-sized, octagonal-faceted sapphire brooch. This, in turn, was encircled by round diamonds, all of which were set in gold filigree. The brooch would lie at the back of the wearer's neck, while at the front, hanging free from the lowest strand of pearls, was a sapphire pendant surrounded by diamonds. This pendant acted as an anchor for a perfectly formed teardrop-shaped pearl the size of an almond.

"It's exquisite," Anne finally breathed. "Please, Lizzy, help me put it on."

With trembling hands, Lizzy secured the necklace around Anne's neck. Going over to her dressing table, Anne took full measure of herself in the looking glass. The necklace, she promised herself, from this point forward in her family would always be passed down from mother to daughter.

"It's much too grand for me, but today I'll happily wear it for Ian."

Turning around to the other women, she said, "I believe I'm ready."

"Then follow me," Lady Caroline said. "Your groom waits for you in the garden."

As they left the room, Anne turned to cast a bright smile back at Lizzy, who returned it with a quick curtsey and a happy smile of her own.

"Thank you," Anne said and blew her a kiss.

"May God be with you, Miss," Lizzy said, "and bless you both on this happy day!"

Chapter Eighteen

Beaver Lake, Arkansas
Wednesday Mid-Day

SPECIAL AGENT DEVON WILLIAMS AWOKE WITH A MIND-numbing headache and a left shoulder inflamed with pain. The concrete floor on which he found himself was freezing, but at least he'd not been bound in any way.

"That's a lucky break," he mumbled.

His eyes adjusted easily to the dark. The room had a cot against the wall with two embroidered pillows on it. Lit only by a weak ray of light coming in through a ventilation screen above the door, he moved to sit upright. The pain in his shoulder brought back the memory of being shot. Reaching his arm around, he touched the spot. No significant amount of blood was on his shirt.

"Was I shot with a bullet?" he asked himself.

The muscles in his back were sore, but upon feeling his shoulder, he could only find a raised area the size of a half-dollar with a puncture wound in its center. A dart gun had been used. Some blood had seeped out and dried, but nothing like what would have been there if he'd been hit with a bullet.

Noise coming from the adjacent room made him quickly resume his prone position on the floor with his eyes shut. Someone was coming.

"He was still out when I checked before work," the man's voice said. "We ought to go ahead and kill him. Get rid of him—bury him. No one would ever find him."

"Lovely, lovely people," Williams thought as he quickly changed his mind and pulled himself into a bi-pedal stance.

Looking around the room for something to hit the man with, he saw nothing but the embroidered pillows.

"Unless I'm gonna have a pillow fight, those are useless. I hope he's not too big," Williams grumbled, trying to stretch his left arm and work the stiffness out of his shoulder.

"I get it...not yet," came the voice. "What do you want me to do?"

There was a long pause before the man spoke again. Williams wondered if he'd heard the voice before but quickly put any mental gymnastics aside. Getting the jump on his jailor was priority number one.

"Okay, I'll bring him to you. Give me about an hour to get there. I need to call my superintendent and tell him I'll be out for the rest of the day."

Williams soon heard fumbling at the door's lock followed by a dog's low growl. The memory of Dobermans prowling Jessie Stacker's compound came back to him.

"Crud," he thought. "There's no way I can take 'em both."

The dog barked out its warning to his master. Williams simply walked free from his dark corner and waited in the middle of the room. The overhead light came on, almost blinding him.

A man, probably in his early thirties, heavily muscled but wearing a full-face mask, opened the door. At his heal was a Doberman pinscher.

"Well, at least," Williams thought, "it's on a choke chain."

The masked man reached under his left arm where a semi-automatic gun was holstered. Pulling the gun free, Williams saw a triangle with numbers in each corner tattooed on his arm. It was the same design as on the note pinned to the murdered man at Briar Ridge.

The man waggled the gun at Williams. "You go first. Straight down the hall and out through the door. There's a van waiting."

Williams did as he was told. On his way out, he went through a living room and caught sight of a sampler hanging on the wall saying something about home sweet home. His first thought was that someone was truly deluding themselves, but he continued walking until he passed through the house's front door. Coming out into the midday sun, his head pounded even harder with the light's intense brightness.

As his eyes adapted, he took note of his surroundings. A simple, almost dilapidated house with a dirt road running about fifty feet in front of it sat back against a row of cedar trees. The landscape was similar to the area near the lake, but its terrain was flatter.

"You get in the back," the man said.

Opening the van's door, Williams frowned. The van had no windows. He climbed in and sat down on the ribbed floor. The door slammed shut. Noting no handles on the inside, Williams scooted close to the van's exterior wall and listened as the doors were firmly secured with a chain.

Forty-five minutes later, the van stopped. The back door swung open, and the same man motioned for him to get out. He was back at Jessie Stacker's mansion. Three armed guards kept watch on the tree line, the sky above, and the road as the man himself came out the front door.

"Agent Williams, I believe," Stacker said. "Come in. We have some things to talk about."

As he followed Stacker inside, he noted that only one guard followed and no dogs. Cameras were positioned at various positions within the house.

The interior decor, Williams supposed, was in keeping with the knight theme promoted by the KGC. Emblazoned on tall oak-paneled walls were heraldic shields, armored breastplates, and swords arranged in fan shapes. It was as if he'd stepped into Elizabethan England. Clearly, Stacker saw himself as a feudal lord, and he liked to live as one.

"I won't offer you a seat," Stacker said. "I don't like your people."

"The FBI?" Williams asked, sounding a bit snarky. "We don't like criminals, so the feelings mutual."

Stacker shook his head and waved his hand as if brushing the remark and Williams further away from himself.

"I don't like most of them either, unless they're working for me."

Williams nodded congenially.

"I guess you'd better tell me *who* you consider 'my people' to be. Otherwise, I'm at a disadvantage as to why you've brought me here and what you want."

The lord of the manor turned away from his floor-to-ceiling windows overlooking the lake below and gave Williams a cold appraisal.

"I think you know who *your* people are, but that's beside the point. What I want from you is the name of your supervisor in DC."

"So you can buy her off, or so you can see if she is already in your hand?"

A fleeting look of confusion tinged Stacker's face.

"I hardly believe a woman is your supervisor," he sneered. "If that's the case, I'm sure she was only appointed to her position out of pity or because she slept her way into it."

And there it was. The true color of the man. A bigot, a misogynist, an entitled elitist, whose real agenda was to promote hate, mislead the fearful and the politically disenfranchised, and squash anyone who opposed him—all for a grab at absolute power.

"Well, my supervisor may or may not be a woman, and he or she might even be black, Hispanic, or a Martian for all I care; but I can see it bothers you, so I think I'll keep his *or* her name a secret."

"Stupid move, Williams," Stacker said, coming towards him, his face reddening with anger and disgust. "You're useless to me now. You might have saved yourself, if you'd told me who your supervisor was, but as a bargaining chip, you're useless."

He barked at the guard.

"Give him back to Hathaway. He'll take care of it."

Williams noted the name of Stacker's favorite flunky and waited for the guard to get within three feet of him.

"You probably shouldn't kill me right away."

Stacker's jaw clenched so tightly, Williams saw the facial muscles flex under his skin.

"Why?" he snapped.

"Because before you shot me with a stun dart, I sent my location and photos to my supervisor and my partner. And, if you didn't toss that knapsack about three hundred miles from here, they're gonna come asking questions, and it won't be one or two agents—it's gonna be a healthy, well-armed SWAT team. It would be better, for you, if I was still alive."

Jessie Stacker looked like he would enjoy wringing Williams' neck with his bare hands. Instead, he walked over to the fireplace and, taking the iron poker from its stand, beat repeatedly the massive, heavy oak mantel built into the stone wall.

Agent Williams willed his facial expression to stay completely calm, if not bored. Raising his gaze upward above the increasingly disfigured mantel, he saw the KGC's emblem or symbol.

It occurred to him as Stacker slaked his rage against the fireplace that throughout history, every political megalomaniac had promoted a flashy logo and an exciting, usually empty, motto.

"Get him out of here!" Stacker raged and flung the poker down. "Take him downstairs and lock him up."

He gave Williams one last look, filled with revulsion, frustration, and utter contempt.

"Don't kill him...yet."

Chapter Nineteen

Grace, Arkansas
   Wednesday Afternoon

THE *FARM AND FEED'S* PARKING LOT WAS JAM-PACKED WITH A fascinating array of massive super-duty pickup trucks. Duallies with their chunky saddle-bag rear-wheel fenders, along with regular 4 x 4's with running boards and shiny steel grill guards attached to their fronts, and even a few diesel flatbed trucks carrying bales of hay, farm equipment, or stacks of feed bags were pulled up and waiting at the front of the building like colossal, metal horses in a futuristic western movie. It was clear—this was a store for ranchers and farmers, not the average Joe and Jill's retail experience.

Into this mega-metal monster roundup drove the Lilliputian Beetle. Martha squeezed the VW into a space between a Ford F-150 and a Dodge Ram 3500 as the two women's conversation dried up. After leaving Grace's Water Department, they'd worked out that the man killed at the Battlefield Park must have been Crazy Ricardo. Had he already found the necklace? Had he been killed for it? Or was he on some sort of cultural side trip and murdered by another treasure hunter not willing to suffer competition? Either way, Ricardo was dead, and nerves were running high in the Bug as Martha turned off the engine.

Gently elbowing Helen, she said, "We're snug as a bug between two lugs."

"Good one."

"Helen, I think you'd better go back to England. This is my crazy family problem and..."

"Stop," Helen said, raising her hand. "I won't let you go on, especially by yourself. I was a bit scared when Peg confirmed what Tilda suspected, and I realized the real danger of the situation."

She was quiet for a moment as she inspected and fiddled with an invisible piece of lint on her jacket. Reaching over, she laid a reaffirming hand on Martha's arm.

"We've faced all sorts of crazies together. We'll be okay dealing with this."

"Thanks, I think," Martha replied, her tone unsure but also grateful.

"Come on," Helen said, patting the arm once more, "we'd better hurry. It's already four o'clock, and we promised to meet Peg at five. She's not a woman to keep waiting."

"That's for sure. Okay, lead the way."

Grabbing their coats against the oncoming evening chill, the two friends walked across the parking lot and entered the building through the sliding glass doors. Curious gazes following their trail. Inside, they headed toward a sign reading, "Hats, Boots, Clothes," which dangled from chains wrapped around the ceiling's overhead crossbeams.

Stepping over intermittently strewn remnants of straw and mud debris, they inhaled the store's earthy aroma of fertilizers, leather goods, livestock feed, and medicinal items. All were fresh, pleasant smells, and though Martha and Helen were dressed for Bond Street in London or New York's Fifth Avenue, the natives did not snub them but instead offered them amiable nods, warm smiles, and index finger touches to the brims of their caps or hats with the gentleman-cowboy greeting of "Ma'am."

They were soon intercepted by a bright-eyed, pretty teenager, introducing herself as Ruthie.

"If you need any help," the young girl said with a warm smile showing off a mouth full of orthodontics, "just yell. We have a ladies' bathroom if you want to try on clothes. It's real clean."

"Thank you," Helen replied, returning Ruthie's warm smile and greeting with one of her own. "We do need some assistance picking out the proper things for..."

She turned to Martha, "What would you call it? What we're doing with Peg?"

"Well," Martha said as she dug through a table of flannel shirts and her tone showing she wasn't sure either, "I think we might be going into a cave and walking in the forest. There might be some climbing, too."

Ruthie's eyebrows knitted as she appeared to weigh Martha's words.

"You're going to need waterproof, insulated clothing. It's getting pretty cold at night, and I think the weather has called for rain. Do you need boots?"

"Definitely," Helen said with a ring of excitement to her voice. "What kind do you have?"

Ruthie went over and pulled out two types of thick-tread work boots with heavy leather and canvass uppers. She handed them to Helen.

"Whoa," Helen said, admiring the rugged-looking boots. "These are amazing. Do you have them in black?"

"I'm glad you like them," Ruthie returned, her face lighting up with salesclerk pride. "Let me find them for you."

"Should we try some of this camouflage stuff?" Martha asked, holding up a bulky fleece-lined jacket. "I like the idea of being invisible out there, but I don't want to get shot. I heard one of those men say, as we came into the store, that this is deer season."

"Yes, it is deer season, and before you leave, we can get you both an orange safety vest. The jacket you've selected is for hunting, but it's multipurpose as well," Ruthie explained. "It's insulated and waterproof. If you want, I'll show you the bibs that go with the jacket?"

Martha looked up at Ruthie, her expression perplexed, "Bibs? What is a bib?"

Going over to a tall rack, the perspicacious outerwear guide pulled a one-piece garment resembling overalls from its metal hanger. The entire item was covered with splotches of brown, green, and hints of white colors.

"These are bibs," she announced, peeking out from under the shoulder straps. "They're great for everything."

"No way," Helen mumbled, giving her head a shake. "Not for me. Do you have something in a size four pair of pants and all black?"

"Sure," Ruthie answered. "Let me find them for you."

"Are you going for all black, Helen? Where's your sense of adventure?" Martha asked after picking up the camo bibs Ruthie laid down. "I kinda like these things. Makes me feel tough. Where is the ladies' room, Ruthie?"

Martha headed off in the direction of two signs reading, "Heifers" and "Bulls."

"Here, ma'am," Ruthie said and offered Helen a pair of slim-cut black pants, a black insulated jacket, adorable fur-lined gray and white hunters cap, and work boots to match. "Try these. I think you'll like them. The pants and jacket are cut to fit a woman's figure."

"Thank you, Ruthie. If you'll show us the dressing room, I think we're ready to try these on."

Five minutes later, Helen stood fully attired from head to toe in her new togs, but Martha was still wrestling with her bibs.

"Oh my Gosh!" Martha exclaimed. "You look awesome, Helen, like some sort of cool ninja chick wearing combat boots. Help me with these straps," she mumbled as she tried to finagle her bib ensemble up around her bottom, "and tell me I don't look fat once I'm fully encased in this thing."

Taking the flapping suspender straps hanging down Martha's

back, Helen flipped them over her friend's shoulders and snapped the plastic buckle ends together.

"Okay, let me help you into your jacket."

Finally, completely attired in her bibs and boots, Martha spun around grinning and announced, "Ta-Da! What do you think?"

Her fashion reveal was met by Helen's frozen expression of determined, bright optimism.

"Weeell," Helen said, "I think we need to go back out and ask Ruthie to bring us something less...," Helen scrunched up her nose as she continued to run her gaze down her best friend's getup, "bulky."

Scooting over to the three-quarter mirror affixed to the wall over the bathroom sink, Martha's gaze fell on her well-padded persona.

"Oh my God!" she cried. "These things must have been made for Arctic endurance competitions. I look like the Michelin Man's redheaded honey!"

Martha pulled at the bibs' shoulder-strap buckles. "Help me get these things off! I wanna be a sexy ninja chic, too."

In fifteen minutes, Martha's costume was reassembled by the efficient Ruthie, and she emerged from the Heifer's bathroom looking outdoor-ready and extremely chic for her night in the Ozark wilderness.

The girls were ready for whatever Peg and Ned Potter threw at them. As they exited the *Farm and Feed*, Helen and Martha handsomely compensated Ruthie for her help, smiled back at the approving nods of the staff, and even remembered to give the gracious, friendly index-finger tap to the brims of their hats. It was good to be home.

Chapter Twenty

Territory of Tennessee
May 1804

SEREPTA GUYON WATCHED WITH A MOTHER'S INTENSE FOCUS
and unease as her daughter, Eliza, navigated the boulder-strewn,
raging creek. Spring's thaw high up in the Appalachian Mountains
had engorged the lower riverbeds making Bear Hollar's creek a
rushing storm of dangerous whitewater only traversable by those
practiced in the arts of balance, rhythm, and fearlessness. Barely
five years old, Eliza was already good at all three. She'd been
playing in and along the creek since she'd learned to walk.

Serepta, on the other hand, pregnant with her second child and
due in a few months, must take each transition with studied care.
Fortunately, mother and daughter were traveling light. They had
little to weigh them down except for the unborn baby in Serepta's
belly and the carpetbag she carried over her shoulder.

Earlier that morning, they'd left their cabin before dawn,
slipping out the door after Serepta was sure Jacob was gone. He
was going bear hunting, which meant he would head for higher
ground this time of year, and if they hurried, she and Eliza would

have at least six hours on him before he returned and found they were gone.

Stationary on a massive rock, Serepta watched Eliza hop neatly from one boulder to the next despite the torrent rushing between them. A bruised wound on her daughter's sparrow-like leg appeared in no way to hinder her natural agility. Sunlight filtered down, illuminating Eliza's long, fine strawberry-blonde hair, creating a halo effect about her head while invisible air currents lifted each fine strand the same way golden ears of wheat will lift on heated currents of air in the hottest part of July.

For a brief moment, a smile brightened the young mother's face at the beauty, courage, and strength her daughter possessed. But like a cloud moving over the sun, last night's dark memory shifted back across Serepta's mind, melting away all the warmth from her face. Paused on the rock with the roar of the creek's water drowning out other sounds, uncertainty again pressed in on Serepta about leaving. As if in answer to unsteady resolve, her gaze fell on the blue bruises marring Eliza's leg, and her mind went back to last night.

Jacob had come home drunk. Lately, his anger over the difficulties they'd faced trying to scrape a living from life in the mountains had caused him to seek out any opportunity to drink with the logging men down along Sawdust Creek. In a drunken rage, he'd pushed Eliza as the little girl, eager to be helpful, tried to fill her father's pipe and, in her haste, spilled Jacob's precious tobacco.

This simple mistake riled Jacob's whiskey-soaked brain, and he lashed out, shoving Eliza out of the way and sending her across the room where she fell against the cast iron stove, hitting her leg. Reacting quickly, Serepta had hurried to the child and lifted her from the floor while Jacob bellowed over the wrong done to him.

With Eliza in her arms, Serepta had stayed calm. Something told her it was the only way for Eliza and her to survive his demon-driven anger. Any rebuttal would only inflame him more. This was the first time he'd laid a hand on one of them. The blow to Eliza had stunned Serepta, and an icy coldness had sifted down upon her as she realized any love for Jacob was stripped from her heart with this brutal action toward her daughter.

Hate kindled within her breast for him, and though her gaze flicked to where he'd leaned his rifle against the wall, she already knew she'd never get it loaded in time before he would be upon her. Instead, she bent over Eliza and kissing her, she set her on a stool near the cook stove and brushed the fine hair away from her forehead.

"Stay here, baby," she whispered and went to prepare Jacob's dinner.

As she moved about the space cooking his meal, her mind chewed on how to rid herself of him. An instinct inside told her to play the dumb animal, the subservient woman, until her mind was clear. She needed a plan. Staring down into the stew, she stirred an idea into life. Soon Serepta knew exactly what to do.

Going to Jacob, she smiled, handed him his plate, and filled his pipe laying it down beside his arm when she was done.

"I'll feed the fire," she said and did so.

Stoking the flames until the wood crackled and hissed, she brought the room's temperature up. Warm, Jacob settled deeper into his chair and stuffed the stew into his mouth while Serepta went to Eliza, picked her up, and carried the child into the side room where they slept.

"It's going to be okay, baby," she said softly, kissing the petite girl and smoothing down her downy-like hair. "You know Mama will take care of you, right?"

The child nodded and looked deeply into Serepta's eyes, seeming to search the hidden truth and promises made by her mother.

"You go to sleep, sweet one. Don't fret anymore tonight. Tomorrow I'll take you to the river, and we can catch a nice fish for dinner, understand?"

Again the nod, but this time a tiny light of excitement glittered in the round, tear-pooled eyes. Tucking Eliza under a quilt, Serepta kissed her once again and got up. As she left the room and passed through the door, her mind also crossed its own threshold. Never again would her child ever be touched in anger, and she wouldn't stay where her children weren't safe, even if it meant going into a harsher world to find a better place. She and Eliza would go to the river tomorrow, but they weren't coming back.

A crow cawed up above her, calling Serepta back from last night's watershed moment. Looking to where Eliza had been, she saw her daughter had made the other bank. With one last scramble, almost on all four limbs, Serepta managed to cross the swollen creek and land safely beside Eliza. They were wet and cold, but at the Cadmen's cabin, they'd have a chance to warm themselves by Miss Paralee's fire.

A rifle shot higher on the mountain echoed through the valley. Serepta turned and scanned the dense fir and oak forest stacked behind her. Somewhere up along the ridge, Jacob was closing in on his prey. Instinct coupled with intelligence dictated it was best to get moving. Grabbing Eliza's hand, she quickly headed down the path.

"Mama?"

"Yes."

"We're not going fishing, are we?"

"No."

"Where are we going?"

"Going to see the Cadmens, Miss Paralee and her brother, Edward, further down in the valley. We're going to see Uncle Joe and Aunt Sue Roller in Arkansas Territory. Your papa has fallen into bad company. Let that be a lesson to you. You become who you take up with, and those men with their drink have a hold over him. I'll not stay with him any longer. It's safer to go live with our kinfolk far away. Jacob needs to learn more about being a man and less about being an animal. Only then, will you and I have something to do with him."

Serepta flashed a brave, regal look down at her daughter, who returned it with a bright one of her own.

"I'm fine with that, Mama. He's been much too cross. He needs to learn better manners."

"That's true," Serepta said firmly. "You and I have a long way to go," she pointed down to her belly, "and a short time to get there. I'll need you to help me, Eliza, so let's make a pact."

"Okay, Mama!" the child said, skipping along the path. "I love making pacts. Can we spit on it?"

Serepta smiled and shook her head.

"What have I told you about spittin'?"

Eliza's shoulders showed hints of a tiny shrug.

"No spittin'!"

"That's right; listen to my words and tell me if you're grown enough to fulfill your end of the bargain."

Coming to a dead stop in the path, Eliza turned around and faced her mother, a serious expression on her small face.

"I'm listenin'," she said.

"Eliza May Boxly, will you be brave, helpful, and do exactly what I ask all the way to Uncle and Aunt Roller's home?"

The child nodded, her expression registering the seriousness of her stance on the subject.

"I will, Mama."

"Okay, let's start this minute. You remember the way to Miss Paralee's cabin?"

Serepta knew the way, too, but she wanted to bolster the child's confidence, especially after last night's experience.

"I do! You follow me, Mama! I'll show you how to get there."

In less than an hour, Eliza had made good her promise. They were heartily greeted by Miss Paralee and her older brother Edward, who took them inside and heaped upon them biscuits and gravy, scrambled eggs, smoked bacon, and steaming cups of coffee for Serepta and a cup of fresh milk for Eliza.

With a knowing nod to Edward, Miss Paralee indicated she wanted her brother to take Eliza outside. First, the older woman held out her arms for Eliza to crawl up on her lap.

"Would you like Mr. Edward to whittle you a pretty dolly, sugar? I've got a piece of calico and some yarn. We'll make your dolly a dress and glue some hair on it."

Turning to Edward, who was already digging for a good piece of soft pine in a basket by the fireplace, Miss Paralee said, "Use some of my special ink, George, and draw real pretty eyes and a mouth for Eliza's dolly."

The tall, old man, a sweet smile on his face, held out his hand to the child who ran across to him, eager to have something as wondrous as a doll made for her. She took his outstretched hand, and together, they went outside to the front porch.

As the door shut, Miss Paralee turned to Serepta.

"You're leaving Jacob."

It was said with simple truth.

"Yes, I am. He pushed Eliza. He's drinking more and more. I want to get to Arkansas Territory where my mama's sister, Sue, is living, and I have a way to pay for our passage."

Miss Paralee's eyebrows lifted and pulled together again before she spoke.

"How so?"

Serepta rose and, going over to the one bag she'd packed, pulled out a box. Miss Paralee and George were trustworthy, or she wouldn't have come straight to them. Taking the box, she headed back to where the older woman sat by the fireplace.

"Cause I'm gonna sell one of these stones. It's the only thing I have left from Papa and Mama. She always kept it hidden, saying it was not for selling, but she'd understand if I had to part with one if it meant getting us to a safer place. Would Edward take me down to Jonesborough? That's where I'll barter for a river guide to take us to Georgetown in Arkansas Territory."

Miss Paralee shook her head the way an older woman will do when she sees a lot of trouble coming.

"Honey, that's a long way, especially when you're carrying a baby and have a little one who's not used to walking far. It might take you a month or more to get to Georgetown. Are you sure about this?"

Serepta nodded once and let her gaze drop down to the still unopened box.

"Yes, I don't see it going anywhere but bad if I stay with Jacob.

He's half-mad already, and my Aunt Sue always did want us to live closer to her. I'd like Edward to arrange the guide if he would."

The crackling fire was the only thing left talking as Serepta finished. Miss Paralee rocked gently in her well-oiled rocking chair, seeming to consider the glowing flames inside the wide, stone fireplace for the ancient wisdom inherent in an element at the heart of all life.

"I have a better idea, Serepta," she said finally. "Two miles from here is my nephew, Ralph's cabin. He's a good sort but likes his privacy. His wife died three years back from fever, and he's got no children. With all the new settlers filling up these hills, he's wanted to go out to the western territories but hasn't had the right inclination. Taking you and Eliza will be that inclination. He's rough, loves to play on his fiddle, and cusses like the devil himself, but Ralph is at his core a good man. He'll take care of you and get you safely to your Aunt Sue. You keep that necklace under wraps, Serepta. Ralph will take you to your kin without pay. There will be land out there, and he can start a new life on it."

Serepta pulled herself up from the stool and went over to the gentle, good-hearted woman, wrapping her arms around her shoulders.

"Thank you, Miss Paralee," she said. "Thank you from the bottom of my heart."

Until that moment, she'd not allowed herself to think about how desperate their situation was. A wave of relief mixed with the fear of Jacob finding them rolled over her, and she cried like a child on Miss Paralee's neck.

"Now, now, now," the older woman soothed as she patted Serepta's back. "You're gonna be fine, sugar. We need to get Edward to take you down to Ralph's cabin. It's at least an hour away. We need to work fast. Somethin' tells me old Jacob'll be wishin' to visit with me soon. I'd like to be ready for him."

Serepta lifted herself from where she'd knelt by Paralee's rocker, a look of fear pinching at the corners of her mouth and eyes.

"He'll come here, all right. He'll ask where I've gone. He might think you helped me."

"Don't worry yourself. I'll be neighborly and tell him you came by," Paralee said, lifting herself from her rocker. "I'll invite him in for some pie."

"Will you tell him where I've gone?" Serepta asked, the worry setting in once more.

"I won't lie," Paralee vowed, putting her right hand over her heart. "Won't put that sin on my soul even for you, darlin', but I'll say I remembered you were from Boone over in the Carolinas as I pour him a cup of strong chicory coffee. I'll be helpful and hand him a delicious piece of apple pie. I'll say I wonder if that's where you got off to, back to your kinfolk."

A smile crept back over Serepta's face.

"I've no kinfolk left over there, but he might think I've gone to his mama's house. You're what my gramma used to call a 'caution,' Miss Paralee. Thank you. I do hope he heads off toward Boone. Maybe his mama can talk some sense into him."

"Now, go get that young'un and bring her in here. We have a doll to fix-up, a mountain man to convince that a change of scenery is what he needs, and some victuals to pack on that old mule's back. Time's a wastin', Serepta. Let's get a move on."

Chapter Twenty-One

Grace, Arkansas
  Wednesday Evening

THE ROAD, IF IT COULD BE CALLED ONE, SCRAMBLED LIKE A GOAT path up a cedar-covered hillside, skirted ribbons of limestone bluffs, and squeezed through scraggy bramble bushes before it emerged upon a low valley tucked among tall oak-covered hills. Peg's nonchalant attitude to four-wheeling in a vertical direction was clear by her one-handed handling of the steering wheel. The other hand was for shifting the gear stick to her right and swiveling the radio dial between various country-and-western stations.

A country rock song about a tough woman blared from the car's speakers as Peg pointed through the windshield at a bend in the goat path.

"Gonna give you some advice before we get to Ned's."

It wasn't a conversation starter. It was a military briefing.

"He's fond of shotguns, and he likes to shoot first and ask questions later. Once he sees it's my truck, he'll call off his dogs.

Hopefully, they won't get a chance to bite my damn tires this time. If they do," she reached down under her car seat and retrieved a .45 pistol, "I need one of you to fire this out your window, but for God's sake, don't shoot one of Ned's dogs. That'll get us all a shallow grave. Understand? Fire this pistol straight out the window and up into the air. Works every time. The sound scares 'em, and they'll skedaddle back under Ned's porch. I'd do it, but with all this jumping around, I can't take any chances I'd hit one of 'em. Whichever one of you knows how to handle a gun, take it. The safety is on."

With the gun being waggled at them over the seat and Helen doing her best impression of Edvard Munch's *The Scream*, Martha tentatively reached up and took the gun. After all, she'd had the most experience wielding one but nearly dropped it when Helen elbowed her in the ribs with a powerful jab and whispered, "Oh, my God! A gun? Wild dogs?"

Martha returned the question with a nervous grimace and a shrug.

"We've got to do what she tells us. This Ned Tater person is our only chance of finding the place."

Helen compressed her mouth into a tight, grim line at Martha's statement, but all backseat conversations were brought to a dead stop with Peg slamming on the brakes and crying, "Holy Hell! Tater's chicken house is on fire!"

Like two ostriches craning their heads up over the truck's backseat, the girls' gazes, eyes wide with mouths in the shapes of 'o's, locked on the flaming spectacle in the valley below them.

"Come on," Peg said, throwing the stick shift into first gear, "let's go save what we can of Tater's livelihood."

The heavy-duty diesel truck shot toward the red and yellow beacon of flames, and as the gap shortened, a concert of barks, howls, and growls kicked off along the truck's two flanks.

Peg, obviously not one to shun a showdown, rolled down her driver's side window and addressed with gusto her four-legged attackers.

"You dumb, mangy, flea-bitten mongrels! If you bite even one of my tires, I'm gonna get out of this truck and bite you back! Ya hear me? I'll use your worthless hides for tire patches!"

Peg turned her head in the direction of the two cowards quivering in the back seat and yelled at Martha.

"Squeeze off a few shots, Red! Don't let 'em get too close!"

The truck's speed doubled in the direction of Ned Potter's calamitous conflagration, outpacing its canine pursuers, taking every rut, rock, and ripple in the road like a downhill skier fond of moguls on a Black Diamond run. The girls, tossed about in the truck's back seat, bounced off each other with the buoyancy of popcorn kernels in a sizzling hot cast iron pan.

Martha, finding her balance, rolled her window down and did her best to aim the gun up at the tree line.

"Helen, brace me!" she called over her shoulder. "I can't shoot the gun with all this bouncing!"

"Oh, my God, we're gonna die," Helen moaned but managed to grab Martha about the waist, hugging her tightly.

With eyes wide open and both hands gripping the .45, Martha pulled back on the trigger releasing out through the window three great explosions in rapid succession. The blasts hurled the human composite of Martha and Helen backward with such force that as one last bullet erupted from the gun, it exited not through the window but up through the truck's roof.

"You shot through my roof!" Peg cried. "Son of a..."

But Peg's expletive was cut short, for the dog pack would not be so easily thrown off its game. One particular burly monster continued to leap high in the air much like an antelope might on some wide-sweeping African plain, baring a set of gleaming sharp choppers any shark would have envied.

"Give me that gun before you shoot my head off!" Peg yelled back at the girls. "I'll settle up with you later. Right now, we're coming in hell for leather! Be ready to jump! Looks like Tater's down to half a house!"

"Jump?" Helen squeaked. "What about the dogs?"

Peg flashed a sour look in the rearview mirror but returned her focus quickly to the cow path she was currently soaring across on two wheels. Martha feebly handed the gun back over the seat to Peg's waiting paw.

Encircled by a stampede of barking dogs, the rumbling diesel truck traversed the last four hundred yards of rocky pasture and screeched to a stop twenty feet from Ned Potter's inferno.

Peg jumped first, and the minute her feet hit the ground, all barking ceased. A grizzled man wearing John Deere pajamas, his grey hair wild about his head, came running toward them. Ned 'Tater' Potter, as Martha assumed him to be, arms high in the air, rushed the tall, blonde Peg like she was his white knight come to save him from a dragon's hellish breath.

"Peg!" he cried. "My chicken house! It's almost gone!"

The dog activity, having wilted into whimpers and whining, gave Helen and Martha the courage to get out of the truck.

Introductions would have to wait. While Ned froze into helplessness, Peg and Martha ran over to a stock tank full of water, grabbed buckets, and tossed water onto the flames. Seeing a hose attached to the main dwelling, Helen wormed her way through the affectionate pack of mutts, loosened the spigot's valve releasing the water, and began dousing the metal building with its rushing stream. With the arrival of reinforcements, Ned grabbed a feed bucket and joined the fire brigade. They fought the good fight side-by-side until after an hour, the only remnants of the mountain man's chicken house were a sizable patch of charred ground and a sad, blackened skeleton of metal posts, joists, and hanging, corrugated panels.

"She's been brought real low," Ned said with a sigh as they put the buckets down, and Helen went to tighten the spigot's valve shut. "I built her ten years ago with my son before he left for Alaska. I owe you girls a mighty big thank you for helping me save what we did. Come inside. I've got something to wet our whistles. Don't know about you, but mines chock full of ash and smoke."

With slumped shoulders, Ned and his menagerie of mutts turned and walked toward his house. Exchanging looks with Peg, Helen, and Martha followed him up onto a wooden porch.

"Tater," Peg said, "I've brought these ladies to ask you a favor.

This is Helen Cousins and Martha Littleword. They'd like to talk with you."

Ned motioned for them to follow him inside.

"Nice to meet you. I wish we could have met under nicer circumstances. I appreciate your help, ladies. Have a seat," he said as they came into the kitchen. He indicated a round oak table with its accompanying four chairs, and they sat down.

Reaching up, he opened a cupboard and pulled down a glass jug.

"I'm bringing down Cooter's Reserve tonight. It's strong medicine for when you lose something. Some men drink to lost wives, lost jobs, and even lost wars, but losing a chicken house is..."

Ned's voice cracked with emotion, and he fell silent. Going to the kitchen cupboard, he took out four glass jelly jars and put one down in front of each woman. A large mason jar filled with a clear liquid was retrieved from the back porch, whereupon Ned poured each glass three fingers full.

"Better sip it," was his only instruction, "otherwise you'll find yourself sleepin' it off in the back of Peg's truck and headin' back into town. I don't hold with sloppy drinkers under my roof."

Martha lifted the glass and breathed in the powerful fumes from the clear liquid. Over the rim of her glass, she watched Helen do the same as Ned took his seat opposite Peg.

"Here's to my chicken house. She was a good one," he said, lifting his glass. "And here's to people who show up when your world is falling in and lend you a hand."

He offered Peg, Martha, and Helen a crooked, stubble-rimmed smile, as they took their first drink.

"Oh, my God," Martha wheezed once she was able to catch her breath. "That has got one heck of a kick to it."

Instead of a chicken house, it was her esophagus and her stomach that was on fire. Ned grinned brightly at Martha's surprise.

"Truer words were never spoken, lady," he said, taking another drink. "Cooter's Reserve is for givin' yourself a kick start after life's taken a bite outta yer back end."

108

"Or for removing rust or paint from metal," Peg added. "It's like most things in these hills. It's gotta do double duty if it's gonna earn its keep."

Helen's face betrayed nothing of her inner mind or gastric system, and Martha wondered if she'd only faked taking a drink to be polite. Putting her jelly jar down on the table, she asked, "Mr. Potter, I'm sorry to ask you this right after losing your chicken business, but we did come up here for a reason."

"Go ahead," he said, refilling his jar. "I figured Peg had you in tow for some reason other than fighting chicken house fires."

"Have you ever heard of a cave in this area not far from where a family named Roller once lived in the 1860s?"

Martha saw Ned's quick look at Peg. Setting his glass down on the table, he said, "Honey, every old boy, and his brother have been looking for that cave over the last hundred and forty years. I, myself, have wandered these hills for darn near eighty, and I've come across only one cave that's not been plundered or dug up by all the Toms, Dicks, and Harrys looking for the Roller treasure. It's too small, and that's why no one has ever bothered with it."

"Will you take us to it?" Martha asked. "I've got to at least look. My aunt is in a mess, and she's asked me to see if I can find it."

Ned's mouth compressed into a sour, crinkly line. It was clear he thought it was a ridiculous request, but hill people believe in honoring a debt of assistance, and Martha had fought valiantly for over an hour to save his chicken house.

"Okay," he said after taking a deep breath and heaving a sigh. "I'll take you up there, but not until first light in the morning. You can have the loft to sleep in."

He pointed to a second level directly above where they sat. Taking a slow sip from his jelly jar, Ned scrunched up his mouth and crinkled his bushy eyebrows. It was clear he had some deep concern itching the back of his mind.

"It'll be dangerous to go up there. That chicken house burning out there was no fault of mine. Last week I saw somethin' I shouldn't have. You have to understand; if we go, the trip has its risks."

"What'd you see, Tater?" Peg asked, putting her jelly jar glass down firmly on the wooden table.

Ned shook his head and cleared his throat.

"Peg, it's shameful business The People are doin'... They're using abandoned houses to brew their drugs and moving the stuff by boat. The Missouri Creek connects to Beaver Lake, and it runs down The White River. I took a misstep last Wednesday when I went up on Bob's Knob to deer hunt. Ran into some scary critters, and they told me to forget what I seen. I said I most certainly would, but..."

Ned sighed, took another sip from Cooter's Reserve, and gestured with a head nod in the general direction of the burned-down chicken house.

"Guess you're seein' their insurance plan to keep me quiet."

Peg banged her fist on the table.

"I'm so sick of those criminals running the show around here. Good people have been run off, bullied, and killed by those no accounts."

She turned an eagle eye on Martha, who swallowed hard.

"Tomorrow won't be a pretty hike in the woods, ladies. Best keep your wits about you, and if they stop you, tell 'em you're Jesse Stacker's cousins. That's the only way they'll let you alone."

"That brings me to another concern," Ned said, his eyes narrowing and shifting back and forth between Helen and Martha. "You tell me who's gonna crawl down in that hole? It's gonna take a person of slim girth, that's for sure."

Ned, Peg, and Martha didn't miss a beat. They turned in unison to look at Helen, who'd been nervously brushing away stray ashes or sticky dog fur from her Ninja duds.

The lag in chatter brought her attention up to three sets of eyes focusing exclusively on her.

"What?" she cried. "Why are you all looking at me?"

Martha didn't dare speak her thoughts, but she didn't have to because Peg spoke hers.

"Your skinny butt should fit nicely."

Helen's mouth went slack as her eyes rounded.

"Fit *where?*"

Peg's smile was wickedly bright.

"Down a hole," she replied, "like that English guy wrote about."

"What English guy are you referring to?" Helen asked her tone snippy and defensive.

Peg's smile lengthened, and a sparkle lit up her eyes.

"Lewis Carroll, and you're gonna get to play Alice."

Chapter Twenty-Two

Missouri Creek Area
Missouri-Arkansas Border
November 1862

"WE NEED TO HURRY, MADGE. GLEN IS DONE LOADING THE kitchen things, so go to the root cellar, and pack as much food into baskets as you can."

Nella Mae Roller, a woman in her mid-forties, had been issuing commands to her children since dawn. The stillness of deep dreams under warm quilts was broken by a loud, demanding knock on the front door of their farmhouse. Mr. Simpson, a good friend, a member of the secret Peace Society, and farmer who lived two miles away on the southern side of Slate Gap Ridge, was standing in the lantern's light when Nella swung the door open.

"Pack your things, Mrs. Roller, and get your children together. There's word of bushwhackers coming up from the Briar Ridge area. They've been burning farms. You're welcome to head over to my place. Marie, my wife, is there and is expecting lots of arrivals. There's safety in numbers."

Nella thanked him, but said she'd collect her things and head to her father's home in Grace, a substantial town, about ten miles to the West. Simpson nodded, climbed back up into his saddle and rode off to warn others, the sound of his horse's hoofs receding in the cold November darkness.

Sleep was over. Nella rallied her children, Madge, Glen, and Coin, and with relentless focus and backbreaking effort, they loaded what they most needed into one wagon. With their safe harbor a half day's travel by foot, they must leave by mid-morning to outrun the human predators coming, but also the winter weather Nella expected to arrive by that evening.

For the last two nights, there'd been a white halo surrounding the moon, and the wind was blowing hard out of the Northeast this morning. A storm was on its way, and with the temperatures dropping, it might be snow, or worse, sleet coming before nightfall.

Nella told herself she would leave nothing of use to the murderous men who prowled the upper Ozark Mountains raping and taking what they wanted in the name of one government or another. In her mind, the bushwhackers, jayhawkers, partisan rangers, and military, both Union and Confederate, were brutal opportunists, mercenary capitalists, and she would give them a good run before they laid one greedy finger on anything or anyone belonging to her.

As she loaded chickens into a wooden cage, her oldest son, Glen, came out of the barn with two pigs tied together with one rope.

"Mama," he said his tone somber, "everything is out of the barn except the goats. What do you want to do with them?"

"I'll not leave them," she answered, looking up at him. "Get another rope and tie them, too. When you're done, bring the cow from the field, and that should be all. Madge has two more baskets to haul up from the root cellar."

Glen nodded, and though his mouth was set in a hard line, Nella saw him fighting to hold back tears.

"Mama, will we ever come back?"

He didn't look at her directly but out over the straw-colored, stubby field behind their house to where a barely visible mound of native stone rested low among tall cedar trees. There, under an early morning sun's clear light, two graves nestled together in an eternal embrace; one for a father, the other a child.

"Absolutely," she replied with firmness. "I'm only going, Glen, because I need to get us to safety. We can't fight the men who are coming. They'd kill us all or do worse. I'll not let them take you or hurt Madge. As for Coin and me, they'll kill us. I'm too old, and he's too young. We're useless to them."

Since the Union and Confederate armies had pulled out of the area, lawless guerrilla fighters on both sides had taken to preying on homesteaders by killing the men who fought back, plundering the farms of all their valuables, and sometimes doing unspeakable things to the young women and girls. Glen nodded and swallowed hard at the same time.

"Yes, ma'am. I understand."

"Go get the cow and the goats. We'll leave soon."

Barely fifteen years old and taking on the worries and responsibilities of a man, Glen hurried away as Nella turned around to scan her dwindling domain. Softly sighing at the loss of everything she and Thomas had spent ten years building, her gaze came to rest on the same place Glen had focused on moments earlier.

Even eight months later, it didn't feel real; the deaths of Thomas, her husband, and Geneva, her baby, a golden-headed toddler. Both were taken by influenza in early March as the battle at Steerhorn Tavern raged only ten miles away. The canons' relentless booming reverberated around the hills as she, Glen, Madge, and Coin laid Thomas and Geneva to rest.

Since that day, she was never warm, never really alive. Living was a duty, a moral responsibility, she'd honor. Nella was acutely aware of God's will. Whether he let her live to finish raising her children or not was his business, but in the meantime, she'd get on with the work that needed to be done. Sometimes that's all we had, she thought, was the work that needed to be done, which made her think of her youngest son.

"Coin!" Nella called, looking around the farmyard for signs of him.

Out of the two-story farmhouse came Coin, carrying Millie, their old barn cat in his arms. Nella shook her head ever so slightly and gave another sigh. Coin was her dreamer with a heart so tender he'd refused to eat meat after seeing a hog butchered at the age of five. He was thin, tow-headed, and probably going to take after his daddy and be the tallest of all her children.

"Mama," he said, walking slowly over to her, seemingly unaware of the urgency of their situation, "we are taking Millie, aren't we?"

Nella put her hands on her hips and surveyed in a long, slow sweep the remains of her day. Some battles were better than others to fight.

"Coin, if Millie will ride in the wagon, she can go, but if she takes off into the woods halfway down the road, I'll not let you go after her. Do you understand me, son? We must make it to your Grandpa Theosolus' tonight."

The young boy's mouth pulled together in a tight, serious bow, and he nodded his head in consent. He quickly raised his head, his eyes bright with a brilliant grin across his face.

"I'll put Millie in a basket, Mama, and tie down the lid with some yarn. She'll hate it, but she won't be able to run off."

"That's fine, but don't use my knitting basket."

Coin's fair eyebrows pulled together. No other basket in the house had a lid.

"Could we stuff the knitting in another basket, Mama? It'll be okay, and we have to make sure Millie is safe. She's too old to make it on her own here," he reasoned. "She needs to sleep with me at night. She told me so."

One thing Nella knew for sure. Coin might be a gentle soul, but he was a stubborn one. He'd be more help along the way if he wasn't mourning Millie's loss.

"That's fine," she said, looking down at him, "but once she's in the basket, I want you to help your brother with herding the goats."

Coin nodded, crawled up into the wagon with Millie, and dug for the sewing basket.

"Mama," he said, holding up a leather box he'd pulled from the wagon's depths, "what's this? I've never seen it before."

In his hands, he held a simple, flat box with a brass clasp. Nella's heart skipped a beat. Coin had dug in the basket holding her personal things.

"That's a special family heirloom handed down through your great grandmother, Serepta, on your daddy's side. Put it back where you found it and cover it up."

Within an hour, the compact Roller caravan covered two miles following a quiet trail running beside a dry creek known as the Missouri due to its closeness to that state's border. Nella chose the unusual route for its isolation from other well-traveled roads.

They were making good time when the sound of horses high along the ridge made Nella hold up her hand, bringing all movement to a stop. With the same focus as a cat listening for mice in a wall, she heard men's voices growing more distinct and cascading rubble as the horses maneuvered down the rocky hillside.

Turning to Glen, Nella said in a whisper, "We must hurry. They're coming this way."

Chapter Twenty-Three

Tampa, Florida
Wednesday Evening

"I'VE ALREADY TOLD YOU," TILDA EXPLAINED TO HER COUSIN, Lou, on the other end of the line, "Martha's got it all in hand. If she finds it, her friend, Helen, will get it sold, and the family can have their cut. If the old stories are true, there will be plenty of money to go around."

The traffic moving outside and the chatter from the stylists working on their clients made it difficult for Tilda to hear Lou's hoarse voice.

Communication options with the outside world were extremely limited. She and Jackie had decided to jettison their regular cell phones. A cell phone, even they knew, was a one-way ticket to a bad end if you were trying to stay under the mob's radar. Tilda had purchased a burner phone, but it was only used to talk with Martha. All other calls had to be cajoled from local merchants such as this hair salon.

Kiki, the owner, flashed a perturbed look in Tilda's direction. It was time to wrap up the phone conversation.

"I can't tell, Lou, where I am for your safety. You can trust me. Unlike some in the family, I'd never take more than my share. As for Martha, she's a peach and honest as the day is long. I'll call you when she has the necklace in hand."

Kiki laid down her sheers, gave her tigress mane a spritz or two of volume spray, and spoke to the woman in her chair. As Tilda watched, the salon mistress scanned her domain. Raising one turquoise-painted, bedazzled finger, Kiki drew it across her throat at Tilda. The meaning was clear: get off and get out.

"I've gotta go. I'll call you later."

Lou wouldn't be dismissed so abruptly.

"Don't you remember?" Tilda asked. "She's got the same hair color as her mother—your cousin Carolyn. Red. Martha's hair is red. That's a strange question, Lou. What made you ask it?"

In the background of Lou's call, Tilda heard a radio playing. An advertisement for a Springdale car dealership was promising 'no money down on all new sedans.' Tilda's brain noted the oddity but quickly refocused upon the incensed Kiki, toddling toward her on impossible three-inch-high platform wedges.

"Bye, Lou," she said, putting the phone in its charging cradle and headed out the salon's front door as quickly as her orange plastic flower flip-flops would carry her.

The busy street, its cars moving sluggishly in the Floridian heat, and people of every shape, age, and pedigree gawking at tourist-trap venues, enveloped Tilda, providing her immediate concealment from Kiki's eagle eyes.

As she scooted down the wide sidewalk, weaving in and about the brightly colored stands and human logjams, Tilda's brain meandered the opposite way in both time and place to that peculiar micro-moment when Lou asked about Martha's hair color.

"Why ask..." she murmured to herself, but as the question framed itself in Tilda's mind, she came to a dead stop, creating an unwanted obstruction for humanity's flow down Gulf Boulevard.

"Springdale?" she breathed, as a middle-aged man dressed in a light pink Polo shirt and khaki Bermuda shorts bumped into her, making her teeter to one side.

Not offering an apology or even a steadying hand, he growled, "Lady, you're blocking foot traffic."

Tilda watched the rude man steer a woman, younger by a decade, into a shop. Raising her eyes to the long awning above the door, her eyes came to focus on an illustration in the French style of two scantily clad chorus girls in different poses, clinging to an Eiffel Tower.

"Ooh la la," Tilda read softly the lingerie store's name.

As she stared at the awning, enlightenment hit her, and it came with a strong backbeat.

Lifting her hand, she laid it across her well-endowed bosom, feeling her heart thump like a bongo drum in her chest.

"Oh, dear Lord," she whispered. "Please watch over Martha. Nothing good ever came from Lou leaving Paris."

Chapter Twenty-Four

Grace, Arkansas
   Wednesday Evening

DEB SANDERSON SAT BEHIND THE WATER DEPARTMENT'S counter at her sister's desk sipping a fancy frozen coffee concoction. Her spirits were low, and she was trying to find enough energy to finish her work. She didn't want to be here tonight, but during the week she came in late after Peg was gone to do some light cleaning and some filing. Her sister paid her handsomely, and they didn't have to see each other. It was a good arrangement for them both.

Taking another drink from the caramel latte, Deb flipped through the first of two sales catalogs she'd picked up last week at the *Farm and Feed*. It was Lucas's birthday soon, and she wanted to buy him something special.

She'd hinted about giving him another item from her father's gun and knife collection, but he'd declined the offer. He wanted something new for his birthday, so she'd happily gone to the *Farm and Feed* to look at crossbows with him.

Deb had enjoyed looking at the variety of weapons with Lucas.

It reminded her of going with her daddy and Peg years ago to auctions. Her father had been fascinated with old knives and firearms. Over his lifetime, he'd spent a fortune on them; but for a single woman living on a tight salary, it would be a stretch for Deb to buy something as expensive as the crossbow Lucas finally picked out.

Shaking her head, she closed the gun catalog. It didn't matter. She was crazy about him and especially after today, making him happy was the most important thing to her.

It had been a rough afternoon at the military park. If she tried to make Lucas happy by bringing him lunch or doing his filing, he brushed her off with a new coldness. It occurred to her he might be thinking about ending their relationship after what happened with the man from Paris, Arkansas. Almost forty and with one failed marriage under her belt, Deb didn't want to lose Lucas. She was tired of being alone. The gift was more important than ever.

Sighing, she shifted her attention over to the next catalog. Christmas was coming soon and her mama wanted a new bedspread. Deb flipped through the needlepoint and embroidery quilt block options. A tender smile bent the corners of her mouth as she thought about how much she loved her mother; but lately, there had been some strain between mother and daughter. The faint smile faded away.

"Oh, I wish Peg got along with Mama. If she would make time for her, I wouldn't feel so guilty about wanting a life of my own."

When their father died, Mrs. Sanderson refused to do anything for herself. Peg and Deb, twins by birth, but utter opposites in every other way reacted differently to their mother's breakdown. Peg, married with two teenage children, kept working, staying involved in her many community clubs, boards, and hobbies, while Deb became their mother's nursemaid and companion. It had been a lonely life, and when she'd finally ventured out to work, the only thing she'd found was a volunteer job. That's where she'd met Lucas Hathaway. It was a wonderful time that followed. She'd fallen madly in love with him. Now, the only thing Deb wasn't willing to give up was Lucas or her part-time volunteer job at the military park. Mama would just have to understand.

Putting the catalogs away in her knitting bag, she stood up. It was time to tidy the office. A folder lying on Peg's desk caught her eye. It was marked *Benson County Historical Society and Civil War Loot*. Deb shook her head and opened the folder.

"Peg and those old gray hairs at the historical society are poking their noses again where it doesn't belong. Everything our daddy left to her she's given to that stuffy museum."

A photocopied Arkansas map lay inside, arresting Deb's attention. Across the state's upper northwest corner, tiny red stars denoted possible places where Civil War money caches might still be hidden. A wonderful thought popped into Deb's head. In her hand, she had something to trade on, something to buy back Lucas's good graces.

Lifting the map to see what was underneath, her gaze fell on a cut-out newspaper article about the Briar Ridge Park murder and a picture of the man found dead. Catching her breath, Deb's forehead crumpled into horizontal lines as she lifted the flimsy paper from the folder and read.

Slowly, a frost spread over Deb's skin as halfway down the article, her scanning came to an abrupt stop. 'Arkansas Toothpick' and 'murder weapon' underlined, with a red gash of ink, caught her attention. All earlier excitement at having something to give Lucas drained from Deb's being. She dropped the article, letting it float down like a feather on air currents until coming to rest on the open folder.

"Oh, Peg," she said, her words barely audible even to herself. "What have you done? What *have* you done?"

Chapter Twenty-Five

Missouri Creek Area
    Northwest Arkansas
    1862

GLEN QUICKLY TIED THE PIGS' ROPE TO ONE OF THE METAL RINGS along the wagon's side and grabbed the already loaded shotgun. Putting a finger to her lips, Nella pointed to a thick clump of cedar trees growing up against a high bluff line beside the creek's bed. She reached into the wagon's depths and pulled out a pistol.

With gentle stewarding, Madge guided the horse toward the place her mother indicated, and in a few minutes, the wagon was neatly embedded among the cedar boughs. They each followed, and once inside, Nella saw a rocky ledge about twenty feet up, invisible to anyone coming along the creek bed. Above it was a great bluff overhang creating a refuge impossible to see. Boulders and debris spilled down the rock face making it necessary to pick one's way up a narrow path to the ledge's floor. No doubt the Osage would have used this spot to camp due to its defensive value, and with any luck, Nella thought, it might serve her family, too.

Whispering to her children, she pointed to the ledge and said, "Climb up there and press yourselves against the ground. Tuck deep into the bluff's mouth, and I'll be right behind you."

Glen nodded, his hand still holding the shotgun, and heading up, helping Coin to reach the ledge. After tying the horse to a limb, Madge followed. The goats, naturally noisy creatures that they were, needed hay to stay quiet, so Nella grabbed the one bale of hay they'd brought along for such an emergency and quickly piled it down on the ground letting the animals eat. Taking feed from a bucket, she spread it evenly in the chicken's cage, giving them much more than they'd normally receive. The Rollers' safety depended on the animal's silence.

The riders descended into the narrow valley. Scanning the ledge to be certain the children were hidden, Nella's heart banged like a hammer against an anvil in her chest. Horse hoofs crunching on the dry creek's gravel declared the riders' rapid arrival.

Quickly, she grabbed a small bag holding her most precious things, scrambled up the bluff's tight, rocky path, and pulled herself up to the ledge. Surprised at its depth of at least twenty or more feet, Nella immediately saw a low, dark entrance to a cave sitting back against the limestone wall. Rock debris of various sizes, including boulders, lay strewn about the ledge. She prayed the overhang was stable, but there was no time to change locations.

Lying down flat on her belly between Glen and Coin, she pointed her pistol down in the same direction as Glen's shotgun already aimed toward where the wagon sat among the cedars. If the riders found the wagon, they'd have a devil of a time surviving the climb up to where her family lay. She didn't want to, but if she must, Nella was prepared to defend her children's lives.

The sound of male voices soon reached her ears. Their tone was conversational, and after a short time, Nella saw the five men clearly as they came around the bend right below where she and the children lay. No military caps donned the men's heads, but she knew the bushwhackers preferred wide-brimmed felt hats like the ones worn by these men. Each rode with a rifle in a scabbard attached to their horse's saddle as well as a pistol holstered to their belts. They didn't seem to be paying close attention to the ground, which, for Nella, was a good sign. They may not be tracking her, but deliberately traveling an isolated route, like herself, to go undetected by hostile parties.

Like a crack of thunder, the air overhead exploded with gunshots, ripping the cold atmosphere's static fabric with hissing screams. All who lay upon the bluff's ledge recoiled at the sound of the gunshots ringing across the valley. Nella frantically searched the valley's tree line for shooters.

"Children," she whispered, handing Glen the bag she'd retrieved from the wagon, "take this and slowly inch your way deeper into the crevice of the bluff line. If you can, squeeze into the cave and pull some of the boulders in to hide yourselves completely. If we're found, Glen, stuff the bag deeply into some hole. We can return for it later."

Turning around to peek below, Nella saw the riders were dismounted and taking up positions within the boulders below. They'd found the wagon and were scanning the area for its owner.

One man, his face covered with a beard, pointed at the ledge. Nella gripped her pistol and crawled on her knees back to where her children, who, like a clutch of chicks, sat almost one on top of the other in the deepest part of the bluff's rocky cleft.

"A man is coming. Get in the cave," she said softly, "Glen, lay the barrel of the shotgun on my shoulder and if the man shoots me —kill him. Give the pistol to Madge. Use me as a shield, and don't leave this crevice until you can all three walk away. Get Coin and Madge to Grampa's house. Do you understand me?"

A clarity came into the boy's eyes. Any youthfulness that may have been left over from the death of his father evaporated before her eyes. More gunfire crisscrossed the valley as they heard the rough scraping of boots as someone tried to find a foothold in the rocky limestone wall leading up to their rugged mountain keep.

Chapter Twenty-Six

Benson County Police Station
   Wednesday Evening

"Her name is Jelinda Rosemary Gusman. She was twenty-four, and her home address is in Paris, Arkansas. Yes, sir, a quick scan of the Holloway County Assessor's records shows she's the wife of the man killed at Briar Ridge Military Park. I should be able to give you more information once I talk with her parents. Her mama and daddy, Lou and Kari Roller, are on their way up to identify her."

Detective Ryder Towbridge waited for Sheriff Carmichael to respond. Jelinda Gusman's murder case had hit a snag, and it was because the federal police officer for Briar Ridge Military Park, Mark Hathaway, wasn't returning his phone calls regarding the connection of Jelinda to Ricardo Gusman. He'd been on the phone all day trying to finagle Mark Hathaway, the investigator for the murder Jelinda's husband, Ricardo Gusman, to share some of his information. It was seven o'clock, and he'd heard nothing back from Hathaway. The Feds were that way. They kept you in the dark until they either solved their case or filed it away for fifty years.

"Get on the horn," Towbridge heard Carmichael say through the phone, "and ask to speak to the park's superintendent. His name is Harold Peters. He's a good friend of mine. He'll light a fire under Hathaway's butt."

Towbridge heard his phone click as Sheriff Carmichael ended the call. Picking up his cell phone, Towbridge accessed the county's secure police server, intending to send his supervisor a follow-up email before going home to a frozen pizza and his dog. Tomorrow he'd call Superintendent Peters. Tonight he'd reread the coroner's report and watch a football game.

Ryder's phone rang. Looking at the display, he didn't recognize the number.

"Probably a telemarketer. Kinda late for trying to sell me something," he grumbled and let the call go to his voicemail.

The phone rang again. It was the same number. Telemarketers never rang twice.

"This is Detective Towbridge."

A man's voice cracked with uncertainty.

"Uh, hello. My name is Terry Lauderdale."

"Oh yes," Towbridge replied. "I'm glad you've called, Mr. Lauderdale. I have a question for you, but first, how may I help you?"

"Well, the property where Mrs. Gusman was murdered belongs to my wife and me. It's near Grace. This afternoon I was out with my brother-in-law after the police left, looking for a lost pregnant cow. We were half-way between the two locations, my house and the...place where the woman was killed. There's a creek close by and it runs right up along the side of Bob's Knob. We found the cow, but also something I think I'd better bring in for you to see before I give it to the rightful owner."

Terry Lauderdale's voice died away. After a brief pause, he cleared his throat and continued.

"It's a gold coin like the ones found in Mrs. Gusman's pockets."

Excitement surged through Detective Towbridge's brain and

heart. Cases always had a turning point. An idea popped into his head.

"Thank you, Mr. Lauderdale, for calling me and your honesty. Instead of you coming into the police station, what if I met you in the morning, say about eight o'clock? Would you be able to take me to the place you found the coin?"

"Yes, I don't think that's a problem. There are one or two things you need to know."

Tension sizzled through the phone line. Something in Terry Lauderdale's voice told Towbridge there was more than a gold coin at the root of this call.

"Okay," he replied, his tone encouraging.

"I guess you've had a chance to look those coins over. My brother-in-law is an amateur Civil War historian. Likes to do the reenactments over at Briar Ridge Military Park. He says the coin we found this morning was pretty valuable."

"Yes, I've had a local numismatic dealer look at them this afternoon. They're 1861 Liberty double eagles minted in New Orleans. Jelinda Gusman had some in her pocket at the time of her death. They're quite valuable."

"This new coin I found was not on my land, Detective Towbridge, and that's why it took me so long to call you today. It was actually on a friend's land that lets me run cattle on his place. I was going to wait to talk to him, but he wasn't up at his cabin today. I didn't want to wait any longer, so I'm calling you. I think you ought to know his name, though, and we'd better fill him in on the situation before we go tramping around on his land. He can be a tough old codger."

"What's his name?"

"Ned Potter," Lauderdale said.

"Oh Lord," Towbridge groaned. "Do you mean Tater Potter?"

"Yes, and that's not the worst of it."

"There's more?"

"Where we found the gold coin, my brother-in-law saw a rather unique carving like a pyramid on a low bluff face. It's similar to some symbols used by the KG C and the bushwhackers who sometimes worked for them."

Towbridge wasn't sure he'd heard Lauderdale correctly.

"K.G.B.? Isn't that the Russian secret service? Don't tell me the Russians have made it to Grace, Arkansas?"

Towbridge chuckled lightly at his joke.

Lauderdale's pregnant pause and subsequent answer held no symptom of commiserate humor.

"Might be better if it were them, detective. I said *K.G.C.* It stands for The Knights of the Golden Circle. You ever heard of John Wilkes Booth?"

"Who hasn't?"

"Some believe the KGC were behind protecting the promotion of slavery, pushing for the southern states secession, and Lincoln's assassination. You might have heard the organization has new legs."

Towbridge's stomach twisted with unease.

"I've heard of drug running problems up in the area around Bob's Knob," he said. "I've heard hints that an organization of some sort was behind that trafficking."

"Yeah, well, I think Jelinda Gusman took the wrong people's money."

"Are you saying you think it was the KGC who killed her?"

Lauderdale was quiet for a moment.

"If you come up here tomorrow, Detective Towbridge, bring a few more officers, would ya? 'Cause I'm not going to Bob's Knob without back up."

Chapter Twenty-Seven

Missouri Creek
  Northwest Arkansas
  1862

NELLA SAW LEATHERY, CALLOUSED HANDS GRABBING AT THE grey, chalky ground of the ledge she and her family were hiding on. The man pulled himself up onto the flat surface. A face chiseled with dirty lines and two sharp, piggy eyes scoured the ledge for signs of life. They came to rest on the dark corner where Nella sat, holding her pistol pointed right at the new arrival.

In a voice only she, the children, and the new arrival heard, she said, "Don't come any further. Stay on your hands and knees."

Blinking as if he wasn't sure of what his eyes were telling him, he lowered his head and stared. Under the jacket he wore, Nella caught the instinctive quiver of his shoulder muscle.

"I'll shoot you, and if I miss, there's a shotgun pointed at your head," she informed him softly in case that muscle spasm was a physical manifestation of him mentally debating his chances at pulling his Colt pistol from its holster. "Tell me who you are and what you're doing in this valley."

He stared at her, and the shotgun leveled at him, his cold gaze like a mountain lion estimating his quarry's response time. A stray bullet from the guerrilla warfare still in concert below ricocheted off their bluff, making the bearded man instantly crouch.

"Lady," he growled low at her, "I can see you got at least one kid behind you. Who's out there on the ridge shooting? That your man? Your kin?"

Nella shook her head. Her mind was like sludge as it tried to work through the puzzle of how to get her children off the ledge, through a minefield of waring men, and to the safety of her father's farm.

"Answer mine first," she said.

She had the drop on him, and he must have known the deadliest thing on the planet is a woman holding a loaded gun, especially if she's got a child behind her.

The cacophony of fire below made it useless for him to move. With a deep draw of air, he answered her.

"Name's Boscombe, and my men are on their way up from Briar Ridge to Pineville, Missouri."

"You're a bushwhacker," Nella said matter-of-factly.

As he rolled his head to look over the rock ledge, an idea sprang into Nella's mind. If you made a deal with the Devil, you were going to get burned. She knew this truth to be gospel, but she'd run out of choices, and this bearded bushwhacker might be the filthy, devious devil who could get her and her children off this ledge.

"You're on your way to North," she said. "So am I. You get us there safely, and I'll see to it you are paid."

He appeared to study the two separate gun barrels boring down on him, his mouth crumpling tightly into a twisted line.

"What makes you think I'd do that?" he asked.

"Cause I won't let you off this ledge alive any other way," Nella said, the thrust of her threat so quietly guileless, he compressed his eyes and reopened them as if he was swallowing the truth of his fate.

"Okay. Got any ideas what to do about the..."

At that moment, a shot rang out punctuated by a human groan. Her bearded prisoner reacted by slithering close to the edge and looking over its lip. One of his comrades had been hit, and the opposing gunfire was moving closer. A pistol's report was answered by another human cry in the vicinity of the cedar grove below followed almost instantly by a rifle's cracking discharge delivering up to those listening on the bluff ledge the unmistakable groan of a man hit by a bullet at close range.

Compete silence ensued, falling over the valley like a suffocating blanket. No one moved. The bearded man shot a worried look at Nella, almost as if he wanted to have her permission to pull his pistol in defense of his own life.

She shook her head and indicated with her pistol to keep his head down and low to the ground. Men's voices with slightly different accents rose to Nella's ears. Her weary, overly strained mind threw up the frightening notion these men were Jayhawkers or Union soldiers moving back across the line.

They were inspecting the wagon, and it was clear they were trying to understand why rebel guerrillas would bother with moving an entire household complete with farm animals.

"Probably they're Confederate rangers," one said. "They're most likely moving sympathizers, who've gone on ahead, to a safe place. How many dead?"

Nella's heart contracted with fear. She was truly between a true rock and a hard spot. Union guerrillas, like Confederate ones, operating this close to the Mason-Dixon Line in Arkansas, were known to burn the homes, kill the men, and rape the women of families they decided were sympathizers in their enemy's cause. She needed a miracle. The Lord's Prayer whispered from her lips.

"Seven, sir," the soldier below yelled. "We counted eight as they came through the holler, so one has either escaped, or he must be hiding somewhere."

"What's that up there?" the leader asked. "Where that bluff looks like a man's face?"

The sound of boots climbing up the gravel path toward them immediately followed. There was no holding back the bearded man any longer. He reached for his pistol, pulling it from the holster, and rising onto his elbows. Steadying himself, he aimed the gun at the edge of the ledge's lip. Nella's heart beat wildly in her breast as she squeezed her brood even tighter into the cliff's shelter. All seemed lost.

The bearded man's pistol fired three times in rapid succession, wringing a guttural cry from the unlucky underling dispatched to climb the cliff's face. A hellish lead-soaked backlash ensued, making the bearded man's body jerk and jump with each bullet that punctured his frame. Nella, her body, pulled into a tight ball, squeezed her eyes shut at the horror, the Lord's Prayer racing through her brain. With her arms wrapped tightly around her knees, her own body twitched with each explosive blast until all sound echoed to a stop.

"He's dead!" a voice yelled from below.

Nella unclenched her hands all energy having gone from her body. She slowly opened her eyes fearful she would see someone crawling up onto the ledge to inspect the dead man's body.

No one came.

"Hitch up the wagon!" a voice commanded. "Bring the livestock!"

Horses' hooves and the wheels of her wagon crunched along the dry creek bed. In time, the sound receded into the distance as the men headed in the opposite direction of Grace.

It was best to stay put until the men were far, far away. She didn't dare move anyway. Her babies were safe for this precious moment, and she would not risk the slightest, treasonous movement.

Finally, the silence was complete, and as she sat motionless deep within the rocky shelter, Nella became aware of the first floating snowflakes wafting down from the grey, darkening sky. The tiny flakes landed indiscriminately: on the ledge's dusty surface, on the bearded man's useless coat, and on the coagulating blood pooling about his dead body.

In that instant, Nella accepted nature's will. It had an agenda, one completely independent of any human machinations, moral perceptions, or rational insights. For some unaccountable reason, she and her children had been given another chance at life.

Her body stirred into motion.

"Glen, are you all okay?"

"Yes, Mama," came his sweet voice from behind the boulder. "We're all fine, but there's been an accident."

Everything was gone; horse, cow, food, but they'd make it somehow. Shaking her head slightly, she asked, "What happened? You *are* okay, right?"

"Yes, but Coin dropped your bag, and it's wedged down in a hole. We can't reach it."

Nella took a deep, life-affirming breath of the cold air. A tired but tender smile stretched across her mouth as all three of her children's sweet faces peered out at her like owlets hidden in the corner of a barn's hayloft. Nothing but their lives mattered. The heirloom would have to wait in its dark home to be retrieved later.

A renewed sense of life's purpose and a desire to live again welled up in Nella as she sat looking at her children. Somehow, despite the odds and by some incomprehensible grace, they'd survived. For whatever it was worth—this second chance—she'd cut her losses and grab it.

"Honey, it doesn't matter," she said, her words full of relief and even a tinge of joy. "Someday, we will come back for it when things are better, but for now, come out of there. I want something more precious than diamonds, pearls, and sapphires— *hugs*— from each one of you."

Chapter Twenty-Eight

Ned Potter's Cabin
   Grace, Arkansas
   Thursday Morning

UNDER THE DOUBLE LAYER OF TWO HANDMADE QUILTS PULLED tightly up to their chins, Martha and Helen were in a deep sleep when something, a low whining sound, awoke the dreamers at the same time.

"You awake?" Martha whispered.

"Yep, and you're hogging all the blankets," Helen fussed.

Waiting for their eyes to acclimate to the loft's darkness, they stared up at the slanted wooden ceiling not more than four feet above their heads.

"It's kinda like we are Mary and Laura Ingalls living in a cabin out on the prairie," Martha said, her mouth pulled up at the corners into a wistful smile.

"Well, I don't want Tater for *my* Pa," Helen grumbled back, trying to scoot closer to Martha for warmth. "He's a far cry from Michael Landon."

"I always loved that show when I was a kid," Martha went on, oblivious to Helen's squirming attempt to pull the bunched flannel nightdress once belonging to Ned's wife back down from around her knees. "I guess I'd be Laura. She's the cool one—the tomboy. You'd be Mary because she was more prissy. Not that that is bad, Helen, but you do worry a lot about doing everything the right way."

"You mean like getting it right when crawling down a bug and snake-infested hole in the morning?" Helen asked, her tone snippy as she, with sisterly stealth, squeezed her cold feet closer to Martha's warm ones.

"Those things are freezing!"

"I'm freezing. Do you think there are any other blankets up here?" Helen asked, flipping over to her side into a fetal position with her back to Martha and her feet pressing without impunity against her friend's fleece-lined leggings.

"I don't see any. There's a cowhide on the floor. Looks molted, though. You should have bought the fleece underwear at The *Farm and Feed*. I'm not cold at all."

Burrowed completely under the covers, Helen's muffled, sleepy voice came back, "Is molty a word?"

"Probably not," Martha replied, her eyes shutting again, "but it could be."

Silence, the kind experienced in the deep woods in winter, filled the tiny space until it enveloped the loft completely. Not a sound came from the dogs or Ned, who'd gone off into one of the cabin's back bedrooms.

Warm and cozy, a feathery drowsiness settled once again over the Pretend Laura and Sulky (still herself) Helen until they drifted off into a soft-as-cat-paws sleep.

It was the woman screaming that brought them bolt-upright into a sitting position in the bed.

"What was that?" Martha whispered.

Helen grasped the covers and pulled them quickly up under her chin, nearly burying Martha in the up swell of quilts.

"It sounded like a madwoman roaming around outside."

"Oh, no," Martha said, sounding like an eighth-grade girl at a bunking party who's about to tell a particularly gruesome ghost story. "What if...Tater's wife isn't dead...like he said, but roams around the hills because she's insane...killing people...especially women because they are alive and she's dead...because Tater killed her?"

Each successive stanza of the rambling, off-the-cuff tale was delivered in an ever-increasing crescendo of dramatic angst. Martha turned to Helen, her eyes wide with alarm.

"You're wearing her nightgown!" she hissed. "What if she knows you've got it on? She might think you're trying to take her place with Tater."

But as Helen raised a pillow to stuff over Martha's mouth, another wild, long plaintive scream burst forth again, this time much closer than before, sending both women into an all-out, arm-wrapping hug.

Martha's inventive, fervid tale of a crazy, nomadic Mrs. Potter seeking vengeance against rivals for her darling Tater's heart had been like throwing lighter fluid on the smoldering embers of fear already existent in the two overly tired and anxious women. Though she was always the main instigator of excitable, exaggerated storylines, this time, she, too, was snagged by her Marthaesque fabricated fiction. The bed practically rattled with the terror of two middle-aged, scaredy-cats.

Their eyes plumbed the room's shadowy darkness. Layers of mingling translucent grays melted into inky blacks, making it difficult to discern shapes. The moonlight filtering in through the window's white curtains backlit tree branches swaying outside, making witch-finger silhouettes dance across the walls and floor.

A heavy thump directly above them like something (or someone) heavy landing on the roof and a third blood-curdling shriek sent Helen and Martha flying from the bed.

"Get out of that nightdress and get your clothes on!" Martha cried as she balanced precariously on her right foot while trying frantically to push the other through her pant leg.

With the nightgown up over her head, Helen, like one of those inflatable flailing tube creatures seen in front of businesses, waved her arms wildly about as she tried to free herself from the voluminous flannel nightdress.

After some minutes of frantic reassembling of their *Farm* and *Feed* clothes upon their bodies, the two women's harried movements came to an abrupt stop as scratching sounds upon the roof accompanied by guttural moans erupted only two feet above their heads.

Grabbing their purses and their shoes, they hurried down the ladder into the half-lit hallway.

"Get your shoes on," Helen breathed. "I'm gonna go find Ned."

But she'd no sooner rounded the corner into the kitchen than the man himself threw open the cabin's front door. He bustled inside with an armload of cut wood and a wide grin on his face.

"Well, good morning, Mrs. Cousins!" he said with friendly warmth. "I'm just gonna throw some wood on the fire, and we can get going. How about coffee and some breakfast first?"

Helen, with Martha bringing up the rear, stood limp-armed and confused under the kitchen's single burning ceiling light. As Ned leaned over, unloading the wood into the fireplace's mouth, Helen found her voice.

"But there's a woman outside screaming? Didn't you hear her? She's wailing and crying, scratching and moaning..."

Martha pointed to the roof and finished Helen's sentence.

"...on-the-roof! She's crawling around up on the roof!"

Ned straightened his back and settled his free hands on his hips, an expression of befuddlement on his face.

"You girls drank too much of Cooter's Reserve last night. I told you that stuff had the power to unsettle your reason..."

But before Ned finished his chastisement, a bawling howl broke loose across the nighttime air, sending the dogs into fits of whining.

"See!" Martha cried. "There's a woman on the roof!"

Ned's mouth dropped open and immediately spread up into a huge smile. He slapped the side of his leg and chuckled while shaking his head.

138

"Ladies, that's no woman out there. That is a mountain lion. She likes to lie up there now and again. The roof is warm this time of year. Time to get your shoes on. We're leaving right after you eat some rib-sticking food. How does a plate of hot flapjacks, maple syrup, and bacon sound to ya?"

Chapter Twenty-Nine

Briar Ridge Military Park
Thursday Morning

LUCAS HATHAWAY, THE FEDERAL POLICE OFFICER AT BRIAR Ridge Military Park, was scrolling through a social media site. His day had started early that morning. By six o'clock, he'd already made it into the office to clean up some details from the day before.

Civil War enthusiasts and treasure hunters liked to post information and share stories about their searches for hidden caches of gold bullion. It was a competitive circle, and someone might inadvertently or deliberately drop a lead about possible locations of the hoard. Some estimates put the monetary value at around five million dollars.

His phone buzzed. It was Detective Towbridge trying to reach him. Hathaway's mouth turned down in a grimace.

"I'll give him this much; he's tenacious. What the hell? Let's throw him a bone."

He tapped the phone and answered, "Hathaway here. How can I help you, detective?"

It was clear the man on the other end of the line hadn't expected him to pick up.

"Uh, good morning, Officer Hathaway, I know it's early, but I was hoping to talk with you about our teams liaising on these homicide investigations."

Hathaway's expression was pure boredom. The last thing he wanted was to share information with the local county sheriff's department. He'd already had to answer some tough questions from Devon Williams, an FBI agent. It nearly blew his mind when he realized the Special Agent was the same guy as the one who'd found Gusman's body, along with Deb. Best to give this detective an empty promise to appease him, thereby gaining some time.

"Well, we are still in the early stages of our investigation, Detective Towbridge. I'll be happy to work with you, but give me a few more days."

"That would be great. I've been following up on the coins found in Jelinda Gusman's pockets..."

Hathaway leaned forward at Towbridge's statement.

"...and we may have some forthcoming information on where she got them."

"You *know* where she got them?" he asked, his heart beating faster.

"One of the witnesses to her death called me last night and has offered to take me and a few Benson County officers to the place tomorrow."

It was like being slapped with a crowbar. Hathaway's brain lit on fire.

"You had a witness to Jelinda Gusman's murder?" he asked, trying to sound casual. "Who was it?"

"Well, I can't divulge names, of course, but..."

Did he hear real concern for police procedure in Towbridge's tone, or was that an ante being thrown down at the table? He'd take that ante and raise it. Play the man, not the cards, he told himself; and he had the perfect bait to reel in the detective.

"I tell you what, Towbridge, I *have* kinda hit a wall, to be honest on this case regarding Richard Gusman's relationship with the Peace Party, and my superior in DC is breathing down my neck. There is an extremely powerful and old organization in this country. They call themselves the Peace Party and were born out of the Civil War. Basically a bunch of weak, anti-war types who stashed money around the Arkansas hills to support the resistance against the Confederacy. I believe Jelinda Gusman was the heir apparent to the Peace Party, and she may have had her husband murdered. She may have wanted the gold for herself."

There was dead silence on the other end of the line. Was the bait taken?

"Are you saying," came the response, and Hathaway heard the sincerity in Towbridge's tone, "she was in Briar Ridge's Visitor Center at the same time as her husband?"

Perfect. The nudge's desired effect had worked. Towbridge was going down the right road for Hathaway's agenda.

"She didn't show up on our cameras. The salient point, Towbridge, and I want you to keep it under your hat, is Ricardo Gusman was really Richard Gusman; and when he was found, he had a note pinned to his shirt. Not sure, but it may be The Peace Party's calling card."

"A note?"

Towbridge's snap at his bait gave Hathaway a happy tingle in his brain. That stupid note pinned to Gusman's shirt needed to be handled the right way, and this was perfect.

"Yeah, it was cryptic and had this unusual drawing on it."

He let that sink in, but before Towbridge replied, Hathaway went for the real prize. He'd resurrect the long-gone slip of paper, even if he had to draw it himself.

"Hey, I don't mind bringing it to you. I'd like for you to see it. We can share information."

A thin smile pulled at Hathaway's mouth. He hoped Towbridge would offer to bring him along to where this 'witness' was taking them today. He knew Towbridge was considering the pluses and minuses of bringing the federal police officer along.

"I'll be back from Grace, hopefully around two this afternoon. I'll drop by the military park afterward if you have time?"

The last sentence blew up a cloud of black frustration in Hathaway's mind. Towbridge was one of those by-the-book cops, but it didn't matter. There were other ways to skin a cat, and if Towbridge had a witness able to take the detective to the place where Jelinda Gusman found the gold coins, he—Hathaway, had to know where that was. There had to be more coins stashed close by.

Again, he kept his tone modulated and answered, "You bet. Give me a call when you get back, and I'll see where I am in my duties. I'm sure we can work something out."

Ending the phone call, Hathaway pulled up the in-house messaging platform used by the park. A few short sentences later, he'd let the park's superintendent know that for most of the morning, he'd be following up on some investigative issues.

Grabbing his keys, he let himself out of the building into the cold morning.

"Grace, huh? Twenty-minutes, tops."

Chapter Thirty

***

Springdale, Arkansas
Thursday Morning

KARI ROLLER WAS NUMB FROM SHOCK. HER DAUGHTER, JELINDA, was dead. The call no parent ever wants to receive came from a Detective Towbridge of the Benson County Sheriff's Office yesterday. He informed them of their daughter's murder and asked if they would come to identify her body.

This morning, they'd awakened in an economy motel in Springdale. The darkness hung thick and heavy, both inside and out. Kari lay motionless with her head facing the wall. Any willpower to get up, dress, and go to the county morgue was nonexistent in her exhausted mind and body. Her baby was gone, and she was a woman drowning in a surreal, hellish nightmare.

"Honey," Lou said, sitting on the side of the bed opposite of where she lay, "we need to get up. I told them we would be there at eight o'clock this morning when they open."

Great, hot tears welled up in Kari's eyes and rolled down onto the already damp pillowcase. A quiet death was all she wanted—to shut her eyes and never wake up again. Her mind went back to the night before as her tired eyelids slipped shut.

Lou wanted to drive to Springdale immediately, but the morgue wasn't going to be open late, so he'd made Kari get in the truck, drive the two hours, and stay in a motel. Maybe it wasn't real for him until he was able to see Jelinda with his own eyes.

On Kari's mouth, a faint whisper of a smile trembled into life, a memory taking hold in her mind. The images flittered and flashed, rolling like an old movie until Kari was completely removed from her reality and back with Jelinda on her knee as a baby.

A chubby, laughing six-month-old with brown ringlets bounced on a young mother's lap. Covered in carrot goo and gripping a two-handled sippy cup with her dimpled hands, this cherub of adorability gurgled and cooed at each sentence her mother spoke to her. It was a conversation so intimate, so pure, with their souls and gazes intertwining in the perfect, blissful moment together... just her and her daughter.

The hazy film sputtered and died with Lou's shifting as he stood up from the bed. A desire to see Jelinda, even though she was dead, stirred Kari's resolve to get up. Lifting herself, she rolled over to see her husband's back. He was already dressed.

"I'm going out to warm up the truck. We need to hurry."

He didn't look at her but walked out of the room. In a few moments, she heard the truck's engine turn over and rumble into life. Standing up, Kari found her clothes lying over a chair's back and assembled herself, like a ghost going through the motions of life but feeling nothing of its visceral realities.

Minutes later, they were in the truck and traveling down the interstate highway. Husband and wife were mute. Lou reached over and turned off the radio he'd been listening to for any news reports regarding the murders of Ricardo (known to the news as Richard) and Jelinda Gusman.

Once Lou had told her their sweet girl was dead, Kari's mind froze. She remembered him crying, a retired Marine who'd always been so manly, so fearless, holding her hands and kneeling in front of her promising to find their daughter's murderer and see justice done.

She echoed his last words.

"See justice done..."

That was the last verbal exchange of any length between them, and for Kari, it was probably the last one she'd ever have with Lou. He'd been right—it was his fault, but only because she, Kari, had *allowed* him to pull Jelly into the organization. She should have protected her daughter and said no to Lou when he'd first suggested instructing Jelly in the Peace Society's ways—but she didn't.

She was willing to trade on the pleasure it gave her to see her family as a tight, loving unit, even if deep in Kari's heart, she sensed the instability and uncertainty of trusting in an ideal, an organization, a set of beliefs drawn up for the ingestion of men no matter how ideal it all was meant to sound.

In the end, Kari had opted for believing the lie she wanted to believe, for supporting Lou's vanity, and this resulted in Jelinda being the unwitting sacrifice to keep both their delusions afloat. That delusion was over.

Looking out the windshield, Kari saw the early morning traffic swirling bumper to bumper, eight lanes across. Vehicles weaved in and out at top speeds, their headlights floating and dancing the way fireflies will in the twilight of a summer evening. People trying to get somewhere, she thought. Egos trying to tread water.

"We are almost there," Lou said, not taking his eyes off the road in front of them.

Kari laughed. His tone and the statement sounded ludicrous to her. Her laughter was free from bitterness but continued to burble and spew forth as if a dam had broken deep within her. Lou brought the truck to a stop at a traffic light.

"Are you okay?" he asked, his tone edgy.

The laughter trickled away as she turned to him. Looking him squarely in the face, a feeling of utter incredulity welled up within her, followed by perfect calm.

"The buck stops here, Lou," she said, her words reeking with a sinister calm. "*You* are looking at the person who killed Jelinda. I—will—never—be—okay—again. Do you understand?"

His accusing stare sickened her.

Turning away, Kari returned her dead gaze out the windshield.

"Also," she added softly, "*we* are not almost *there*, Lou. That place is gone, forever."

Chapter Thirty-One

Bob's Knob
   Grace, Arkansas
   Thursday Morning

"A MOUNTAIN LION IS OUT THERE, HELEN," MARTHA SAID, HER voice hushed but raspy with fear. "I heard on the news one attacked a guy riding a bike. We will be walking meat sticks for that animal."

Sitting opposite one another, Martha and Helen were enjoying steaming pancakes at Ned's kitchen table. A pile of crispy fried bacon, more than three people could ever eat, occupied another plate. The cook, his apron announcing him to be "Too Hot To Handle," was digging for something in a drawer.

"No need to worry yourself, Mrs. Littleword," he said, pulling out a pistol and holstering it in his heavy duck-canvas coat's front pocket. "I'm taking Waylon and Willie with us. They'll tell us if any mountain lions come sniffin' around. That old cat laying on my roof won't bother us. She's gonna sleep the day away up there where it's warm."

Helen looked down at Ned's menagerie of dogs lying about the kitchen table and tried to discern which two among the scruffy scroungers might be Waylon and Willie.

"Which ones are going with us?" she asked, hopeful at least one of the larger dogs was part of the chosen duo to accompany them on their trek up Bob's Knob.

"Willie is the Beagle cause he's unpredictable and has a way with women. Waylon's the Mastiff 'cause he looks bad and has a big bark, but he's a good-hearted, old dog. They work well as a team."

The pancakes were the best Helen had eaten since her childhood. Delicate crispy edges with a hint of buttermilk made them irresistible. She decided to have another one. As she reached over to snag seconds, her foraging fork was parried by one of Martha's forks.

Helen's gaze snapped up from the pancake plate.

"Why'd you do that?"

Not missing a beat, Martha explained.

"You can't fluff up this morning. I need you to fit down that hole."

Helen sat back in her chair.

"Are you serious? I've got to climb a mountain today on *one* sugared-up carbohydrate and *one* slice of bacon?"

Martha sat, chewing, her eyelids lowered in a cat-like way.

"I'm trying to keep you from getting stuck."

"Well, *I'm* trying to not pass out on the way up there, so *I* can crawl down that hole."

Martha pushed the bacon plate toward her while stealing a quick look in Ned's direction.

"Eat the bacon. Protein is what you'll need to make it up there."

Taking a napkin, Martha wrapped up three pancakes.

"I'll take these in my pocket, and once you're back out of the cave, you can have these to snack on."

Grabbing three more pieces of bacon, Helen chewed on one.

"Thanks," she grumbled.

"Speakin' of," Ned announced, taking his apron off and hanging it on a hook. "Let's roll. Sun's up, and I don't have all day to fiddle around playing nursemaid, cook, and Davy Crockett for two city gals. Put on your coats, boots, and let's go find that cave."

He pulled down his shotgun, stuffed his pockets with shells, and headed out the door with Willie and Waylon bringing up the rear.

An hour later, the drizzly morning had transformed itself. The Ozark hills were full of sounds, the air was cool and clean, and a timelessness, always present in natural places, lifted the hikers' spirits and removed earlier traces of anxieties and fears. The party followed a winding deer trail up through sweet-smelling pine and cedar forests. Gray limestone cliffs and rock formations like wizened old men with jutted chins watched, as the hikers made their way along a ridge at least a hundred feet above the valley below.

"I'd forgotten how blue the sky looks in winter here in Arkansas," Helen said. "The green pine trees up against that vivid blue almost makes me want to cry. It reminds me of being a child and lying under this ancient pine we had in our back yard and looking up through its boughs. At the time, I remember being transfixed and wishing I could drink it in somehow."

"Oh, I know what you mean," Martha replied. "I used to go with my mama when I was little up to this spot overlooking the Bostons. She would always tell me the pines and the oaks were the old grandfather spirits who watched over the forests. There is something noble, aged, and gentle in them."

Their conversation came to a halt as the path narrowed considerably.

"Watch your step, girls," Ned yelled back. "It gets kinda dicey through this part. We've only five minutes or so before we're there."

Below them, a river wound through the long valley.

"What is the name of the river?" Helen called up to Ned.

"That's Missouri Creek! It's swollen from all the rain we've had lately. Normally, I would have brought you through the valley, but we never would have made it up the cliff face with the water being up."

The path reached the top of the hill, bringing Ned to a stop. Below where he stood and out through a few young slender trees, Helen caught a glimpse of a limestone outcropping that created a protruding shelf. Their guide stepped out onto this precarious platform and waved for them to join him.

Helen followed Martha, Willie, and Waylon until she joined the entire party. Hilltops poking up through an early morning mist spread out to the horizon, creating a spectacular vista for their eyes.

"Wow," Martha said, her utterance so soft it was almost lost in the sudden uprush of wind coming down through the valley.

"Yep, she's a beauty," Ned added. "Gawkin' time is done. Now's time to scramble down the side of this here cliff."

He reached into the knapsack he'd been carrying on his back, pulled out a rope, and tied it around a thick girthed pine tree. Pointing to a rut running down along the outcropping they currently stood upon, he said, "All you got to do is lower yourselves down that path, and you'll see the cliff overhang we are standing on now. There'll be a wide-open ledge. Wait on it for me. Once you're there, you'll see the cave opening."

Helen exchanged nervous looks with Martha, but taking the rope in her hand, she lowered herself along the goat path.

"Once you get there," Ned yelled, "let us know you made it. We don't want two holding onto the rope at the same time."

The path was manageable if she held onto the rope. Below her about twenty feet, she saw the creek's muddy water rushing through the narrow valley. Ned's instructions were perfect, and as she rounded the cliff face, the protruding limestone lip was easily achieved. No more than ten minutes had elapsed for her descent to the landing spot.

"I've made it!" she called. "It was pretty easy to..."

But before she finished her sentence, Helen's cell phone vibrated in her pocket as the rope retracted quickly back up the rocky cliff. Taking out her phone, she saw Martha had sent her a text.

"Be quiet!" it read. "Someone or something is coming along the trail. We're hiding. No one should be out here. Stay put and don't move!"

Chapter Thirty-Two

※※※

Thursday Morning

A HEAVY FROST LAY ON THE GROUND AND ROOFTOPS OF GRACE'S three buildings as Detective Towbridge pulled into the uninhabited post office parking lot and parked his vehicle. Two officers, Curt Seymour and Stan Campbell, whom he'd called last night to join him on this investigation up to Bob's Knob, sat in an SUV with the motor running. He gave them a wave, and they raised their coffee mugs in a friendly salute.

The men climbed out of their warm cars. As they came toward him, another utility vehicle pulling a jet boat drove into the parking lot. Towbridge recognized Terry Lauderdale. The new arrival rolled down his window.

"Good morning," he said and gave the other two officers a nod.

"You look ready to go fishing this morning," Towbridge said with a smile.

"No, the rain has brought Missouri Creek up to almost flood level," Terry answered, "so I brought my jet boat. It'll be faster than walking along the valley as I'd planned. Besides, we can't hike through that area anyway; it's too boggy with all this rain."

"That's good of you to bring your boat," Towbridge said with a smile. "Where do we drop in?"

"We'll put the boat in right above the low water bridge at Roller Cemetery. It'll take about fifteen minutes going upriver from there. I hope you brought warm clothes. It can get pretty chilly at fifteen miles an hour."

"Not a problem," Towbridge answered. "We came prepared."

"It may sound like a stupid question," Lauderdale said, "but I gotta ask. You did bring guns, right?"

A soft smile broke across all three of the police officer's faces.

"We don't go anywhere without them when we are on duty."

"Good. Climb in."

Within ten minutes, they were pulling into a public river access along Missouri Creek and backing the jet boat down the cement ramp into the muddy, fast-moving water.

"There's lots of debris coming down with the flooding," Campbell said.

"That's the beauty of a jet boat," Lauderdale replied. "We can go over low-lying logs and maneuver easily in fast water. It's an excellent boat for these conditions."

Soon the men and the boat were skimming across the water's surface, the frigid morning air rushing against their faces making it difficult to catch their breath. The creek nestled among the gentle curves of the tight, tree-laden valley, plunging always forward as if it was in a hurry to see what the next bend would reveal.

Occasionally, the boat would enter and break through low lying mist, inflicting momentary blindness on the men followed instantly by an exhilarating feeling as the sunlight broke through and their vision was restored once more.

As the boat banked sharply around a forty-five-degree turn in the creek's course, Towbridge couldn't help but smile at the thrill of the centrifugal force. Lauderdale nudged him and pointed at one hilltop standing out among the others.

"That's the spot," he yelled. "Bob's Knob. They used to call this Penitentiary Bend a long time ago. Supposedly the Union Army used it to barricade prisoners up along the limestone outcroppings.

It would be a good place to hold people. They sure as hell wouldn't want to jump!"

"That's amazing!" Towbridge yelled back over the engine's roar.

Twenty feet above the creek's water line was a massive face of an old man with a protruding lip sculpted into the limestone rock face.

"Yeah! That's what a few millennia of water and wind erosion can do in the Ozarks. That's why it's called Bob's Knob. Looks like a guy with a head full of hair!"

The two men smiled broadly as they continued to admire the scene, but a glint of reflected light coming from Bob's mouth caught their attention. Terry pulled back on the engine's throttle as he maneuvered the jet boat in the direction of a good landing spot.

"Hey, what's that?" Towbridge asked as the engine died away. "Did you see that?"

"I did."

Terry Lauderdale's body language told Towbridge this was why he'd wanted backup today.

"I'm going to tie the boat onto that tree trunk. You can see the gravel bar is usable. Let's get off there, and we can start the climb up. The place I found the coin and the engraving is not far from the old man's face."

As the four men stepped onto land, a gunshot exploded over the valley. The sound ricocheted off the cliff faces making it difficult for Towbridge to be certain of its origination. Another shot followed. Looking straight up, Towbridge saw a woman's head poke out over a cliff edge and disappear again.

"I think there's a woman up there," he said to the other three men.

Lauderdale shook his head.

"Was it gray, wiry, and standing out like lightning had hit it?" he asked.

"It looked like it was brown."

"That's not Tater Potter standing up there, and this is his land.

Glad you boys are here. There's no telling who or what is up there."

"Did you have time to reach Mr. Potter to ask permission to come on his land?" Towbridge asked.

"No, but Tater's not gonna fuss if it's me."

All of a sudden, a tawny-colored animal the size of a German Shepherd dog came scrambling down the hillside in a straight line toward where the men stood.

"Is that a cougar?" Campbell exclaimed.

"That animal is coming right at us!" Lauderdale yelled. "Have your guns ready!"

"Don't shoot!" came a man's voice high above them. "That's Miss Betty! I loaded her backend with buckshot, and she's mad as a hornet! Get out of her way!"

The four dumbfounded men watched the mountain lion growl, flounder, roll, and finally catch her footing. Coming to a stop thirty feet from where they stood, Miss Betty laid her ears back, crouched, and screamed at them. Turning away, her tail flicking with embarrassed irritation, she stalked off into the underbrush.

Terry Lauderdale let out a hearty chuckle.

"Guess we don't have to worry about getting permission to be out here. I'd recognize that voice anywhere. It's Tater, and he knows we are here."

Terry pointed straight up the cliff face.

"He's somewhere up there. Let's get going."

156

Chapter Thirty-Three

"Oh my God! You shot that animal!" Martha cried out in shock, her ears still ringing with the two successive blasts from Ned's shotgun.

"Well, that *animal* is Miss Betty, and she's been following us for over three miles!" Ned blustered back. He craned his grizzled neck out to see over the hillside. "At first, I thought she was taggin' along for entertainment purposes until I caught sight of that "mealtime" look about her muzzle."

He shook his head back and forth.

"I hope that buckshot stings her back end all the way home. That'll teach her to get spicy with me."

Martha was sitting where Ned had pushed her—up against a pile of boulders with Willie and Waylon, the two lap dogs who were supposed fearless protectors . Shaking her head, she asked, "You named a mountain lion Miss Betty?"

"Yep, after one of my girlfriends," Ned said and whistled. "Both females and both full of spit and vinegar. Can't trust either of 'em, and they'd sooner claw ya than cuddle ya. Dang women! Thank goodness a man can always trust his dogs."

"I don't know, Ned," Martha said, petting the furry canine

heads resting on her lap. "These two aren't much help in a pickle, are they?"

"Well, they're more for moral support and..."

But before he finished validating his reasons for bringing Willie and Waylon along, Martha's brain shot up a burning red memory flare.

"Helen!" she cried and disentangled herself from the two fur-logs lying on her. "Helen! Helen!" she yelled as she hurried to the ledge. "Can you hear me? Are you okay?"

Turning to look at Ned, Martha's brain flashed horrific images of Helen wrestling an angry, hungry cougar on the cliff's edge.

"I'm here!" she heard Helen calling. "Look down below me! Men are coming up the hill!"

This information rallied Ned to join Martha.

"I know who it is!" Ned called out over the ledge. "Looks like Terry Lauderdale has brought some of his friends for a social call!"

He waited until the men were close enough to hear him.

"Whatcha doin' bringing your boat this far upriver, Terry?"

Martha saw a party of four men climbing up the hillside.

"Sorry to not tell you about our visit, Tater," Lauderdale yelled. "Tried to call you all evening. Did you get any of my phone messages?"

Ned, Martha noticed, had brightened up considerably at the men's appearance. Taking hold of the rope once more, he tied it to the same tree trunk and motioned for Martha to descend Bob's Knob to Bob's Lip.

"Come on, Mrs. Littleword. You're next. I know this fella, and he's a good 'un. I'll be right behind you."

While Martha lowered herself down the hillside, the conversation between Ned and Terry continued.

"Yeah, I had me a commotion back at the cabin, Terry. My chicken house burned down, and these city gals showed up wanting to see Bob's Knob. Miss Betty decided to sleep on my roof last night and planned her menu for the next week based on my old hide. Haven't had time, Terry, to check voicemails."

"We came up, Tater, because I found something up here a day

or two ago. I brought these police officers along because you know how unholy these hills can get if The People are skunking around."

"Amen, brother!" Ned returned.

By the time Martha reached Bob's Lip, the four men were finding their footing on the limestone shelf ten feet below where she stood. Seeing Helen there, safe and unharmed, filled her heart with relief. Going over, she wrapped her arms around Helen and gave her a squeeze.

"I'm so glad you're okay."

"I'm fine," Helen said, her words muffled from her mouth being pressed against Martha's shoulder. "I can see the cave, and I think I'll fit. We're gonna get through this situation, and when we find the necklace, I can't wait to finally meet your Aunt Tilda."

Martha let go of her friend, sighed, and chuckled.

"Oh, Aunt Tilda, the original con."

Ned and the four men landed on the limestone lip with handshaking and introductions following.

"So, what are you up here for, Tater?" Terry asked.

"These two ladies from England and Peg helped me put out the chicken house fire last night. These ladies want to see Bob's Knob. Mrs. Littleword has family buried around here."

All four men's faces registered mild surprise mixed with consternation.

"Hello," Martha said. "I'm Martha Littleword, and this is my friend, Helen Ryes-Cousins."

Another round of introductions proceeded as Terry Lauderdale pulled something from his pocket.

"Tater, I found this before the creek came up. It was down below this outcropping near a hand-sized chiseled symbol on the rock face. There was a hole there, as well, about the size of a man's head. I looked in there, but this was all I found. It rightly belongs to you."

In Lauderdale's palm lay a gold coin with a woman's profile wearing a crown stamped upon it.

"Nooooo," Ned said long and slow, pushing the coin in Lauderdale's hand gently back away from him.

Looking up, the old mountain man scanned the ridges until bringing his focus back to the four men.

"That might be found on my land, boys, but I'll not claim it. That is The People's money. The devil's money, and they don't cotton to people messin' with it. Best to put it back wherever you found it."

Lauderdale's mouth screwed up into a tight pucker, and he sighed.

"We got a problem, Tater," he finally said after a long pause. "I watched someone kill a young woman yesterday out in my field when Ashley and I were deer hunting. I found a whole bunch of these in her pocket. We can't put this one back. That's why the police are here with me."

Martha's chest constricted. Everyone standing on Bob's Lip joined in her mute horror at what had happened to the young woman.

"What was her name? The girl who was killed?" she asked, a nameless fear growing in the pit of her stomach.

"Jelinda Roller Gusman," Detective Towbridge said, looking her straight in the eyes.

Martha felt Helen's hand on her arm.

"Jelly," she whispered.

"Ma'am," Towbridge said. "Do you know Mrs. Gusman?"

"I do. She's my cousin," she said, feeling nauseous. "Oh, Helen, what have I gotten us into?"

Chapter Thirty-Four

Tampa, Florida
Thursday

CATCHING HER REFLECTION IN A STORE WINDOW'S GLASS, TILDA saw the boring wig she was currently wearing had gone askew.

For her phone-finding excursion early that morning to call and update Lou, she'd made sure to dress seriously down. A light brown wig, cut in a simple bob, a pair of plain khaki capris, and a short-sleeved sweatshirt was the current ensemble, but not by choice. The only flecks of pizazz she'd allowed herself were the flower encrusted flip-flops and the white cat-eye sunglasses.

With a martyred sigh, Tilda pulled her favorite lipstick, Coral Pink, from her purse and applied it using the window's glass as a mirror.

Watering down her fashion panache was proving exceedingly difficult and downright depressing. In fact, since being on the run with Jackie, they'd both been forced into adopting a fashion approach employed by most typical, middle-class Americans. Sinking into stylish oblivion was becoming a painful thorn in their diva sides.

But it had to be done. It wouldn't do for someone to recognize them while wearing their deliciously gorgeous designer clothes or one of their truthfully famous headdresses. All their brilliant red (blonde, brunette, platinum, etc.) wig beauties would only be flashing, treasonous beacons on their heads, making it easier for the mob to find them.

Tilda shivered at the notion and readjusted the brown wig on her head once more.

"I look like old Uncle Charlie when he'd wear that horrible brown toupee at holiday dinners."

Her pink-enhanced mouth turned down into a frown at the indifferently boring woman looking back at her from the glass.

"My hair is hardly worth adjusting," she thought as she gave the wig another tweak. "Who honestly pays any attention to a woman like this? Even I'm having a hard time seeing myself."

Giving up her bodacious style, exotic ornamentations, and weekly spa treatments was having a serious impact on her happy, joie de vivre personality. Jackie was feeling the bite, too.

Last night at the motel, when she'd returned with food from *El señor de los tacos Grill*, Jackie was preparing for an impromptu poolside party he'd organized for everyone living at *The Sea Shell Motor Court*.

Tilda put a smack down on his plans, sending Jackie into a tantrum worthy of any high-strung, temperamental, and exceedingly bored prima donna. Flicking with contempt the bag of proffered burritos she'd brought for his supper, he retreated to his quiet-time enclave (the bathroom), claiming he couldn't eat what she'd brought because he'd gained five pounds eating junk from the vending machines.

For a while, they both sulked, feeling sorry for themselves but ended up eating the burritos together on the same bed, watching old episodes of *The Bachelor* on Jackie's laptop and criticizing the antics and clothing choices of the reality stars.

Backing up from the glass storefront window, Tilda read the name written across the pink and white striped awning—*Cassandra's Nail & Brow Boutique*. A mad longing gripped Tilda's beauty-deprived soul. Looking down at her pathetically normal, colorless nails (both fingers and toes), all restraint simply melted away.

She soon found herself sitting in a state-of-the-art pedicure massage chair with air conditioning wafting deliciously about her sweaty body and sipping a chilled wine spritzer from a hot pink plastic glass in the shape of a flamingo.

Letting her eyelids drop, Tilda's feet went limp in the swirling, warm, lavender smelling water. The nail techs' chatter with their clients produced a white noise effect on Tilda's ears, making her sleepy. She barely noticed the human commotion following the doorbell's tinkling announcement of a new client's arrival.

Raising one limp eyelid, a blissfully relaxed Tilda languidly scanned the cozy, pink-walled boutique to see what or who had caused all the fuss. If her massage chair had somehow short-circuited and bounced about like a country bar's mechanical bull riding machine, Tilda wouldn't have jerked and trembled less at what her gaze beheld.

Standing with her arms wrapped about another woman's neck and sobbing piteously was Constance Rodriguez, the wife of Ernesto Rodriguez, Miami's Cuban mob boss, the man hunting for Tilda and Jackie.

An 'eerrpp' noise escaped Tilda's frightened, constricted throat. She hastily scanned the room. No one appeared to have heard the croak. Quickly, she gave her brown wig another tweak and reached for the cat-eye sunglasses.

Slipping them on, she said to the nail tech, "My eyes are so sensitive."

To her utter horror, the woman who'd been Constance's shoulder to cry on led the elegant Latino woman to the pedicure chair on Tilda's right.

"Sit here," she said soothingly to the sniffling Constance. "I'll get you a glass of wine and be right back."

Calling over her shoulder to one of the nail techs standing behind her, the woman said, "Go find Rolando! I want him to take care of my sister."

Tilda tried to breathe and curse the Fates at the same time.

"Of all the nail joints, in all the towns, in the entire world, Constance Rodriguez walks into mine?" she asked wordlessly of the Universe.

An internal, seething chastisement was her answer. It unrolled like a scroll of sins listing her vanity, her bad timing, and the hubris-filled moment when she'd chosen to play craps one night instead of poker at the nightclub where Jackie worked as an entertainer, also owned by Rodriguez.

"I've always lost at craps," Tilda thought. "Why in the world would I ever, ever play anything but poker?"

With a quick look at the pretty middle-aged woman sitting composedly beside her and dabbing at the corners of her eyes with a tissue, a feeling of sympathy took hold of Tilda. It was clear some terrific injustice was at the core of Mrs. Rodriguez's troubles.

"Always play your strong hand," the twice Over Sixty-five Poker Champ thought. "Just because my chips are down doesn't mean I can't offer a kindness to my enemy's wife."

Steeling herself, she turned her head and spoke.

"You doin' okay, honey?"

Constance shook her head.

"My husband has lost his mind! A week ago, he was interviewed by a slut of a news anchorwoman, and now he's off in the Caribbean on his yacht. I think she's with him! He's ignoring his business, not keeping up with his managers. It's not like him. He's acting loco."

Tilda's mind whirled. Ernesto was distracted at the moment. As the idea of her and Jackie slipping town while Ernesto was off on some sort of Love Boat excursion filled her heart with glee, Tilda's conscience tapped her on the shoulder. Sometimes you have to reach out to your murderous enemy's wife. That's what decent people did.

"It hurts when someone you love loses all reason," Tilda said. "You're in a powerful position, though, my dear. Don't blow the opportunity."

Constance's expression morphed from hurting wife to quizzical postulant. Taking a drink from her wine glass, she studied Tilda's profile.

"What do you mean about not *blowing* the opportunity?" she asked.

"Well, I'm sure you love him."

Constance shrugged petulantly with one nostril flared, and a corner of her mouth pulled up in an expression of distaste.

"I've given him three brilliant children and twenty-five years of my life. I've been a nursemaid, mother, and cheerleader to him. I've loved him with my whole soul, body, and heart even when he was acting like a spoiled, selfish child—too busy for his family. Do I love him *now*? Not so much!"

"If you've loved him like a good *wife*"—Tilda reached over and laid a comforting hand upon the younger woman's arm—"when he comes back, if he asks for a divorce, handle him like a good *mother*. Don't act bitter. Be regal, positive, and fair. You'll get more, and he'll be much less vindictive. Your children will admire their mother's strength and love you all the more for it."

Constance, her pensive gaze never leaving Tilda's face, sat back in her pedicure chair and said nothing. When she did finally speak, she said, "You are a wise woman. My children will come first, even before my pride. What Ernesto has done, I can't change, but I can be proud of my behavior going forward."

"Darn right!" Tilda said, giving Constance's forearm a few more encouraging pats.

"You have given me the benefit of your wisdom today. Thank you. I will give you *something* in return."

Constance's tone threw up a warning signal in Tilda's brain. Her chest immediately tightened, but she managed to say, "Oh, dear, you don't need to give me anything, please. I am just glad you're feeling better."

"No," the composed Constance said. "I like you, and I am grateful for your kindness. Business is business, and though I can't call off Ernesto's dogs, I can distract them with other meat for a short time."

Tilda rolled her head over, lowered her sunglasses, and locked gazes with a serious Constance.

"You know who I am?"

"I do. My husband's business is my business."

"I'll get the money," Tilda said. "My niece is bringing it to me. I've got to sell a necklace."

Constance Rodriguez shut and raised her eyelids.

"The dogs will be busy hunting elsewhere for one week, but you need to leave town. It's safer for you because—she looked around the room full of women making minimum incomes—"there are those who need money. You understand, of course."

She raised a single index finger on her right hand.

"That's the best I can do."

"Thank you, dear lady," Tilda said, stepping free from her pedicure chair and giving an approving glance down at her own brightly polished, tidy toes. "Yours is a generous gift and one I promise to honor with bringing *you* the money. I'll have it here in one week, at your sister's shop."

Tilda paid the receptionist and exited *Cassandra's Nail and Brow Boutique.* Out on the sidewalk, she blew a kiss to the Fates. Shipwrecking Constance Rodriguez in the same nail joint as Tilda was a gift from Heaven.

"Thank you, girls. Way to keep your hand in the game. Now, if you don't mind, please, please, please help Martha to find that necklace."

Chapter Thirty-Five

Thursday

LOU ROLLER, AFTER DROPPING OFF HIS WIFE AT THE MOTEL, HAD followed one of Arkansas' most scenic highways through the Boston Mountain toward Beaver Lake. An automatic rifle lay on the seat next to him, two full magazines, and another .45 was in his coat's left breast pocket. The retired Marine was going to find the man behind his daughter's death, and he intended to make him pay with nothing less than his life for killing her.

He'd had lots of time in the last twenty-four hours to think through what he wanted to do to Jessie Stacker. They'd known of each other for over twenty years, and though politically opposed to one another, they'd never crossed paths, until now. Though Lou was the leader of The Peace Party, he'd served as a Marine for his country. He wasn't a pacifist by any means. He was a realist.

When Stacker's organization grew, he needed money. He sent men into the hills, especially into Arkansas' mountains, to find the gold and silver coin caches hidden by the Peace Party adherents and the KGC during the Civil War. Lou never guessed Ricardo Gusman, or Richard, as he'd learned, was a plant by Stacker to get close to the Rollers and hopefully learn the caches' locations. Gusman went for Lou's Achilles' heel and wooed his only daughter, and in return Lou treated Richard like family and trusted him with sensitive information.

When he'd realized Stacker's men would probably unearth the lost necklace of the Roller women, he'd trusted Richard to try and find it. It was, if historic family accounts were true, worth a king's ransom. Richard had jumped at what Lou thought was a chance to prove himself to The Peace Party and his father-in-law by going to find the necklace. Instead, he'd found gold. Jelinda's last phone call to him made that clear, but she was certain her husband had not located the necklace.

It was easy enough to find Jessie Stacker's house. Anyone with a boat was forced to witness it. Built on the top of a hill that sat like an island in the middle of Beaver Lake, the gigantic English Tudor-on-steroids looked weirdly ill-proportioned in size to the hill it crouched upon. A thin isthmus of land with a well-guarded road was the only access to the estate other than by water. So Lou rented a boat.

The day was half spent but still sunny. With the windchill below thirty degrees, crossing the lake in the boat should have frozen Lou to the bone, but he felt nothing. Wearing only a regular coat, no hat, and no gloves, he pushed the boat to go faster. The real numbness began with the call that Jelinda was dead. Cold air had nothing on a dead heart.

The mega-mansion came into view. Lou maneuvered the boat to a nearby cove. Slinging a backpack over his shoulder, containing four tear gas grenades, an animal tranquilizer gun, and six prepared darts inside; he harnessed the rifle in a sleeve attached to the pack and stepped off the boat. He'd come prepared for war, with no illusions of Stacker's henchmen rolling out the welcome wagon. With the right timing and some luck, he should take Stacker's compound single-handed, and he'd brought a surprise along.

Dogs barking brought Lou's progress up the hillside to a slower pace. Having trained and handled hunting hounds, he'd become sensitive to bark tones, and these dogs sounded happy, even excited. They weren't onto him yet, so he plunged along, fighting brambles and crawling over fallen debris until he was right below the house's retaining wall facing the lake.

The breeze was picking up. As he followed the fifteen-foot wall, he saw a wrought-iron fence enclosing the compound with a camera mounted to the house's corner. If there were dogs, they would be kept within the gated area, but the men would be responsible for canvassing the entire estate.

Carrying his rifle, Lou walked straight toward the fence and the camera. He'd let them come to him.

It didn't take much time.

A voice spoke to him from the camera.

"You're on private property. Please turn around."

Lou kept walking right at it.

"This property is protected by armed guards and trained security dogs. Turn around."

The tone was commanding.

Lou raised his rifle and shot the camera, exploding it into a hundred pieces. Dogs arrived immediately, barking and snarling at the iron fencing, but Lou came prepared. Being a dog lover, he'd never shoot one. Putting the rifle down, he took the backpack off and reached inside, pulling out the tranquilizer pistol and inserting one of the prepared darts.

He aimed, fired, and one dog went down. This he repeated in rapid succession until three of the Dobermans were out of commission. The men arrived.

"Drop the gun. Put your hands above your head. You've trespassed on private property, and the authorities are on their way," he heard a voice from the corner of the house.

Lou didn't feel like talking. Words were useless. Taking out one of the tear gas grenades, he removed the safety pin and tossed it over the iron railing. Five seconds later, he heard the wailing cries of men and feet running away from the area.

Taking out his gas mask, he put it on and skirted the fence. The circle drive was empty but for the dogs still lying unconscious on the asphalt. Lou headed straight for the door. Kicking it open, he tossed in another tear gas grenade and let it do the difficult work. More cries and men running gave him time to navigate the wide hallway.

Luck was on his side. He saw a movement to his left. Pressing himself against a wall, he waited. A man struggled forward, his eyes shut against the thick cloud of gas. It was like plucking an apple from a barrel. Lou reached over, grabbed the man around the neck, and pulled him into his chest.

"There's a .9mm pressed against the back of your neck. Take me to Stacker."

There was no struggle in the captive. He simply nodded and said, "He's in his safe rooms in the lower section of the house. Even if you had dynamite, you couldn't get to him."

"I've got something better," Lou said. "I've got you. Take me there, get me in, and I promise not to kill you."

Shoving the gun deeper into the man's neck, he finally got another answer.

"Okay, okay. Follow me."

Through the smoke, Lou followed his captive down a flight of stairs.

"Stop," he commanded. "Which way are we going?"

The man pointed to his left.

"It's through that metal door and down a hallway."

"Go ahead of me," Lou said. "Take it slow."

There was only the short hall in front of them, a camera mounted in a corner, and the door.

"He won't let us in," the guard said. "It's useless."

"Don't worry about getting me an invitation. Get me to the door and open it."

The sound of footsteps coming down the stairs stalled their progress. Taking another grenade, Lou pulled the safety pin and tossed it behind him.

"Oh my God!" his prisoner cried. "I won't be able to see!"

"Move!" Lou growled.

Covering the distance at a run, the guard quickly keyed in the code, and the door swung open. Lou pushed him back into the cloud-filled hall, walked into the antechamber to Stacker's hidey-hole, and shut the door.

Another camera, another keypad waited.

"Stacker," he said, certain the man was listening. "Open the door and let me in. Only a coward won't face the father of a child he's killed."

The door's bolts retracted into their steel housings. Lou waited.

"Come inside, Roller," a voice said from the camera.

Lou pushed the door to one side and walked through the thick steel frame. Stacker, a look of bored contempt on his face, sat in a comfortable armchair.

Lou Roller's soul-wrenching grief blinded him to Stacker's indifferent behavior. As Lou reached inside his jacket and wrapped his hand around his .9mm pistol, he watched a smile spread across Stacker's face.

"I didn't kill your daughter, Roller, and I don't live alone here," was all he said.

A stinging bite pierced Lou's arm, causing all his muscles to clench as if the sky had opened up and a lightning bolt had slammed into his body. Hitting the ground, he saw a guard walk into his vision.

"He's down, Mr. Stacker."

Stacker sighed.

"We are collecting a lot of trash around here lately. Toss him in with Williams. I think Roller will be more than happy to tell us where his Peace Party gold is hidden with some incentive. Go get his wife and bring her to me."

Chapter Thirty-Six

Thursday

"Martha, don't worry," Helen said. "We'll get through this."

"Mrs. Littleword, I'm sorry about your cousin," Ned joined in. "If she got sideways with 'em, they'd do exactly what they did."

Martha nodded and returned a weak smile.

"Mr. Potter," Towbridge said, "the place where Mr. Lauderdale found this coin was below this outcropping."

"Actually," Terry added quickly, "it was off to the West about twenty or thirty feet. You know where the creek comes into the bend between this hill and the next."

"I do," the old mountain man said with certainty. "Seen the carvings, but I'd never touch it. The People have watchers in the woods. Best to stay clear of their markings. They run drugs, and they hide them. Not a good thing to run into them."

Helen, taking a quick scan of the surrounding hills, forest, and deep valley, wondered if at this moment they were being spied upon. Her stomach growled, bringing her mind back to the pancakes in Martha's bag.

"I tell ya what," Ned continued, "why don't you boys check out the spot Terry found, and I'll stay here with the ladies and keep 'em safe."

He smiled gallantly through his stubble.

"Yeah, let's go ahead and hike over there. Shouldn't take us fifteen, twenty minutes. Thanks, Tater. You all want a ride back up the river when we're done? I'll drop you off not far from your cabin."

"Sure, sure," Ned agreed, but though Helen couldn't say why something told her he was itching to be rid of the men. "I'd like that fine. I'll have the ladies stay put, right here on Bob's Lip, while I go fetch my dogs and my pack. Should be down off this cliff in about twenty minutes or so."

Martha, Helen, and Ned watched the men disappear below the cliff edge. As soon as their heads were hidden, Ned grabbed the rope he'd brought with him and hurried to the cave's opening.

"Come on," he whispered and waved her and Martha over. "Time is precious, ladies. Don't want the law, or even old Terry, to know about our business. This is rare luck! The People'll be busy paying attention to the police and poor Terry. Let's get a move on."

"Who are these *People*?" Martha asked, looking worriedly around the hills. "Are they weird hillbillies?"

Ned waved his hands in a gesture of excited frustration.

"Come on, Mrs. Littleword and Mrs. Cousins, we don't have time for history lessons. The hillbillies around here drive fifty-thousand dollar cars, worry about their cell service, and live on golf courses run by POA's these days. The People, on the other hand, run drugs. Enough about all that, get this rope around your waist, and let's hurry!"

As he stamped his foot like Rumpelstiltskin, a warm affection for Ned stirred in Helen's heart.

"Okay, okay, put the rope around me and shove me down the rabbit hole," she said.

"Now you're playing ball," he said with another grizzly, bright grin reminiscent of a smiling terrier.

With great dexterity, Ned knotted and secured the rope about her waist as she stuffed all her hair up into the tight stocking cap she was wearing.

"Thank God, it's winter," she said. "Please, please, please, God, don't let there be any spiders or snakes. I think I can handle anything else, but not those."

Turning to Martha, she grabbed her by the forearms.

"If I scream, you pull me out. Understand?"

"Of course. I promise. Oh wait! I've got something for you. It'll help."

Reaching into her bag, Martha pulled out duct tape.

"What's that for?" Helen asked, giving the tape a nervous glance.

"Give me your wrists."

With a shrug, Helen offered up her two hands as Martha ripped two pieces of tape from the roll and wrapped each wrist so that Helen's gloves and jacket sleeve were seamless.

"Nothing can crawl up your sleeve this way. Zip up your jacket all the way, and"—Martha took a deep breath and offered Helen a grateful smile—"I promise to get you out the minute you ask. Here is your flashlight. Good luck!"

Helen nodded and lay down on her stomach. Scooting and pulling herself into the hole, the flashlight's beam moving over crenelated formations, a dry dirt floor, and a few spider webs.

"I hope no one is at home," she muttered.

With a few good twists of her hips, she squeezed through the tight opening and found herself in a compact space. As she moved forward, the tunnel widened, allowing her to finally pull up onto her hands and knees and crawl.

Ten to fifteen feet into the cave, the air was warmer. Dripping water sounds and the occasional air currents made Helen think another entrance probably existed somewhere at the other end. A fork in the tunnel brought her crawling to a stop. Helen saw two paths, the main one heading off to the right and another, downward in its trajectory, heading to the left.

Ahead, the flashlight beam rolled over something lumpy. The lump moved.

"Oh no," she said softly.

Two jelly bean-sized blinking eyes, followed by two more, raised from the furry pile.

"No, no, no, no, no," Helen breathed. "Not a family of skunks. Please, oh God, please, not skunks."

The fur ball broke into three separate fuzzy units, each lifting itself onto paws and scuttling up the tunnel's left-handed route. Bushy brown and ringed tails, not black and white ones, swept the tunnel's floor as the animals moved away.

"Whew!" Helen breathed. "Raccoons."

But as she watched the tails disappear, Helen saw something caught by a root growing through the tunnel's surface.

"Looks like a bag or an old sack. Raccoons probably dragged it in here. Better check it out."

Pushing forward, she quickly realized the once dusty path was becoming increasingly muddy.

"Thank goodness I have a rooope!"

Helen's hands shot forward, smacking her chest into the mud, her legs splaying out behind her. With increasing momentum like a kid on a water slide, she slipped down the tunnel's floor faster and faster.

"Oh—my—God!" she cried, plunging forward, her flashlight's beam wobbling wildly, passing again and again over the root with the bag hanging on it.

Seeing the rapidly approaching drop-off ahead, Helen reached behind her and frantically felt for the rope about her waist. She let her hand inch along its length until she managed to grab hold of it.

"Martha!" she yelled with all her might. "Stop the rope! Stop the rope!"

She zoomed forward, the landslide picking up speed. Ahead, the root with its dangling prize rushed toward her.

Releasing the flashlight, Helen reached out for the dangling bag with her left hand and grabbed it as she passed over a ledge head first into complete darkness.

Chapter Thirty-Seven

Thursday

TILDA'S BUS DROPPED HER OFF IN FRONT OF *THE SEA SHELL Motor Court*. The few guests milling about the place were mainly packed into the swimming pool area, and though she and Jackie had made great friends during their stay at the 1950's-style motel, Tilda wasn't in the mood to chat with any of them. Instead, she made a beeline straight to the room she shared with Jackie. They had much to talk about and a decision to make.

The door to their room was propped open in its typical manner with a chair. Murray, the owner, had offered them a discount if they declined air conditioning and cable.

The lack of the first amenity had been rectified by opening a back window and the front door creating a cross breeze that easily cooled the room during the heat of the day while the loss of cable TV had nearly broken their will to go on living. They were both terribly addicted to reality shows, ESPN's coverage of poker tournaments, and Latin American soap operas all of which they'd not been able to watch for what seemed an eternity, but was really only a few days.

"It'll build character," Tilda had said, trying to bolster Jackie's will to live.

"Yes, it will! All bad! It's going to build nothing but *bad* character, Til," he'd fumed.

But they'd survived, and as Tilda crossed the threshold of their home, she heard Jackie singing with the radio from inside the tiny bathroom.

"Bath time," she murmured with an eye roll.

Laying down her satchel on the unmade bed, Tilda went to the mini-frig, opened it, and pulled out a cold diet Fizz.

"Jackie! It's me!" she called at the door. "You'll never believe what happened. We've got to talk!"

The singing and splashing stopped. Tilda figured he was lying there with a cucumber mask on his face and a bottle of orange soda pretending he was back in Miami.

The lack of response meant he was trying to ignore her. Slumming-it had taken a toll on them both, especially Jackie. Fortunately, Tilda knew his bath time was regenerative, so she sipped on her Fizz Cola until he breezed out of the bathroom wearing a silk kimono and a towel around his head.

"Well?" he asked with a peaceful smile and sitting down beside her on the bed.

Tilda, remembering the new do on her fingers, curled them a bit so he hopefully wouldn't notice the manicure, but she'd forgotten about the flip-flops on her feet. Jackie's well-trained eye caught the shiny color and exfoliated skin the same way a flying hawk can see a mouse move in the grass forty feet below him.

"Oh—my—gosh!" he exclaimed. "You got your feet done! I thought...You said...We agreed..." he stammered and stood up in righteous indignation.

"Traitor!"

Ripping the turban towel from his head, he headed back to his sanctuary.

"Jackie," Tilda wheedled, "it was an accident."

"You *fell* into a pedicure chair? Really? I suppose you also *accidentally* got a manicure, too?"

"Well…" she tried, but he was having nothing of her excuses. "Unbelievable!"

She heard hangers clanging against the door.

"I'm dressing, Tilda, and when I'm done, I will be going over to CiCi's Salon across the street to have my spa day!"

"You can't, honey," she said softly, apologetically, through the cheap hollow-core door. "They know we're here, and I think we need to rent a car and go somewhere safe until I can pay Rodriguez her money."

The door slowly opened, revealing a worried, blinking Jackie dressed in an exquisite short-sleeved, white linen shirt, Zebra-striped Bermuda shorts, and a pair of Italian slip-thru sandals.

"*Her* money?" he asked.

"I ran into Constance Rodriquez."

"At the nail salon?"

"Yes, and she was in the throes of finding out that Ernesto has been unfaithful."

Jackie waved one of his hands in the air dismissively and breezed through the doorway.

"Ernie has been unfaithful for years. Everyone knew it. Does Constance claim she is just *now* finding out? I don't believe it. I once saw her grab a waitress's ponytail who'd delivered Ernie a drink—too much cleavage, mind you—and pull the woman through the bar and shove her out onto the street. Constance was a she-wolf, Tilda. I always played it sweet with her."

Tilda shrugged.

"But she was so upset, Jackie, and we talked. I tried to give her some advice on handling Ernesto for her children's sake."

Jackie raised one brow, pursed his lips, and made a snuffing sound.

"You were playing footsie with a piranha. The fact you have toes left to paint pink is some kinda miracle."

A shiver trickled down Tilda's back.

"She knew who I was, Jackie. To thank me, she said she would give me one week to pay her—not Ernesto."

Jackie's expression, though still skeptical around the pursed mouth, softened.

"Hmmm, Constance playing the generous but wounded wife card—it's a bit unnerving," he said, his eyebrows furrowing, "if not completely unnatural. I don't trust her."

"And that's why you can't go to the spa, honey," Tilda said, patting Jackie on the knee. "Constance *suggested* we leave town —immediately."

Jackie stared off into the ceiling as if trying to mentally process this new evidence of Constance Alvarez's benign behavior towards an octogenarian poker player and a fabulously handsome wigmaker.

"Well, okay, Til," he said, shaking his head. "It'll take me at least two hours to pack. We have Canasta with Murray and the girls. I promised we'd play tonight. Let's leave first thing after lunch tomorrow. I've got water aerobics at ten in the morning. This weight I've put on..."

Tilda held up her index finger to her lips, slowing Jackie's forthcoming diatribe about his slow decline into obesity.

"Honey, we need to be out of here in the next thirty minutes, sooner if possible."

Jackie looked thunderstruck.

"Why?" he croaked.

"Spas have ears, Jackie," she said, her voice low as she turned to look out the still open motel door. "For all we know, some money-desperate nail tech is selling us out this very minute. If we don't hustle, we will be the most glamorous fish bait ever fed to sharks."

"Oh, Tilda," Jackie said, chewing on his thumbnail, "they'd toss us overboard, and our bodies would wash ashore on Miami Beach. All my friends would cry and say things like 'he was so beautiful, so young, such a talented entertainer and wig artist."

"Yes, but they'd probably take our clothes and our wigs and go on to win all sorts of contests."

Jackie bolted upright from the bed, flinging his arms and hands about like a frazzled, soon-to-be-cooked exotic fowl.

"Get your bags together, woman!" he commanded. "No one,

not one single dancer, entertainer, or balding poker maven will get their filthy, greedy cat claws on even one of our wigs! Not one!"

Chapter Thirty-Eight

Like a free-falling yoyo, Helen's plunging momentum was forcefully arrested as she was yanked right-ways up and in the opposite direction. The rope once around her waist, now slid up her abdomen and caught under her armpits.

"Helen!"

She heard Martha's voice coming through the tunnel, echoing down through the cavern below her.

"I'm here! Pull me up!"

Looking up, she saw the faintest whisper of light coming through the tunnel from the outside. Clutching the bag, Helen could feel the rope lifting her.

"Better stuff this somewhere safe. I'm gonna need both hands," she mumbled to herself.

An idea sprang into her mind. Once both hands were free, she reached up, took hold of the rope, and helped her upward movement by pushing with her feet against the pit's wall.

Reaching eye level, she saw the flashlight wedged between two rocks, its beam pointing at the root wad she'd slid past only moments earlier. Where the bag had once hung, a tiny blue light flickered deep within the roots' fibrous mass, catching her eye.

"What is that?"

"Helen? Are you okay?" Martha was yelling.

"I am! I am! Keep pulling, but…"

She looked once more at the roots hanging right above the approaching ledge.

"Go slow! I've got to try and reach for something!"

Like a rock climber, Helen continued pressing her feet against the wall producing an upward momentum. With this action, she found enough leverage to lift herself closer to the root wad. Once she'd almost crossed over the ledge, reaching up and out, Helen pushed her arm deep into the matted root's debris toward the tiny blue beacon and wrapped her gloved hand around something globular and hard. With a gentle tug, she pulled the object free and lifted a dirty, fur-entwined blob to her light-deprived eyes.

"Holy smoke," she breathed, shoving the clump into her pocket and zipping it shut. "Martha, get me the heck out of here!"

Five minutes later, a mud-covered Helen squeezed free from the cave's mouth. Ned and Martha lifted her to her feet.

"Are you okay?" Martha asked, clasping Helen by the shoulders. "The rope flew through our hands. What happened?"

"It doesn't matter," Helen said. "Reach into my pants."

Martha's expression registered serious confusion mixed with distaste.

"Did you hit your head in there?"

"No, no, no," she said, patting her tummy with mud-encrusted gloved hands. "It's okay. I don't want to reach in there with these dirty gloves. I found something in the cave. Go ahead, pull it out."

Martha's face brightened with excitement. Ned, wide-eyed but mute, waited patiently in their three-person huddle as Helen allowed Martha to pull the tatty bag from where she'd stuffed it down in the front of her tight leggings and under her coat.

"Oh my gosh, Helen," Martha whispered as they gathered closer. "It looks kinda…nasty."

"For God's sake, open it before the police officers come back and we gotta explain," Ned demanded.

The bag showed signs of being chewed upon by an animal with

tiny teeth. Martha gently stretched the puckered mouth apart. Reaching inside, she pulled out a black case with a brass latch.

"I think it's an old photo," Helen said.

Indeed, upon pushing back the latch, a daguerreotype in a gold frame lay open in Martha's hand. Using her glove, she rubbed the dirt from the glass. A man and woman with their children around them and a baby girl sitting on her mother's lap stared out at the group on Bob's Lip.

Tater cleared his throat like a parson about to give a sermon.

"I think what you're looking at, Mrs. Littleword, is Nella Roller and her family. They say she and three of her children survived being nearly killed by bushwhackers. I think we've found the lost treasure of the Roller clan."

Martha, her eyes warm with tears, smiled at Helen and Ned.

"She must have been very brave. What do you think happened to her husband?"

"He was said to have died, along with the baby girl sitting on her lap, from influenza during the Briar Ridge Battle. Nella Roller took her children and fled to Grace. She hid up here with her two sons and one daughter on Bob's Knob trying to evade bushwhackers."

Martha rubbed the glass tenderly over the faces so long since departed.

"I'm going to keep this," she said. "They deserve to be remembered."

Taking a deep breath, she let it out and wiped the tears off her cheeks. Reaching over, she wrapped Helen in a strong hug.

"Thank you so much. You risked your life, Helen. I don't know how to ever repay you."

"Ahh, I'm sure we can think of something."

Martha released her.

"I'm still in the same mess, and so is poor Tilda. How are we going to save her and Jackie's bacon now?"

"I'm sure it's going to work out fine. Now, would you help me get this duct tape off my wrists?"

"Sure, sure," Martha said, unwrapping the sticky stuff.

Pulling her hands out of the dirty gloves, she tossed them on the ground and unzipped her pocket.

"Oh, I forgot. I found something in there," she said in a disappointed tone as the other two were walking away toward the path. "I think some raccoons had been using it for...dress-up."

Martha and Ned slowed their progress.

"Dress up?" they said, turning around.

"Yeah, and who would have thought raccoons have such good taste, too."

Dangling from Helen's hand, held high so that the sun reflected its dazzling beauty, was Nella Roller's, Serepta Guyon's, and Lady Anne Warwick's long-lost, wildly valuable, pearl, diamond, and sapphire necklace.

Chapter Thirty-Nine

"Tater? You and your friends still want a ride?"

The sound of Terry Lauderdale's voice calling up to them made the three on the ledge nearly jump out of their skins.

"Yeah, yeah, that would be great, Terry!" Ned called over the ledge. "We're comin'! Let me get my dogs! I tied 'em up so they wouldn't go chasin' squirrels and get lost."

He scanned the hillsides. Turning back to Martha and Helen, he said, "Put those things somewhere no one's gonna look for 'em. Understand? The boys down there will wanna know why you look like a pig fresh from a good roll in her mud bath, Mrs. Cousins. Let me spin the tale. I'm going up to get Willie and Waylon."

The two women nodded, and Helen handed Martha the necklace.

"Helen," Martha said softly as Ned whistled for Willie and Waylon. "Where should I put it?"

They each replayed Ned's furtive scan of the area.

"Come over here. I've got an idea."

Following Helen, Martha was forced to stoop over as they pressed deeper into the bluff's overhang.

"Stuff the necklace in your stocking hat," Helen whispered.

"Ya think?"

"I don't think anyone's going to mess with us, especially with three police officers on the boat, but to be on the safe side, put the necklace in your stocking hat and wear it. If we are stopped, tell them we pulled the bag out of the cave and show them the daguerreotype. Go ahead, I'll stand in front of you and hold up my coat."

The idea had its merits. Martha nodded and let Helen do the coat-blind. Taking the necklace from her pocket, she stuffed it down into the stocking hat and pulled it over her head.

"I'm ready."

"Good. Let's go."

The girls came free of the overhang and went to the edge of the cliff. Below, Martha saw the boat waiting for them with the three men.

"Isn't Ned back yet?" Helen asked.

"Ned!" Martha called. "Everything okay?"

The hills echoed her last word, but nothing more.

The two women exchanged uncertain glances. Martha watched Helen go over to the path that scaled the hillside back to the top of the bluff. The quiet was pierced by a sharp bark.

"It's Willie," Martha said. "Do you think Ned's hurt?"

"The rope's still hanging down from the tree. I could climb up and see," Helen said.

But Martha's instincts told her something was amiss.

"Wait. Don't go."

Leaning once more over the cliff, she saw the men waiting in the boat below.

"Hey!" she called. "Would one of you please come back up here? We think Ned may be hurt. He's not returned with the dogs."

She watched as the men talked among themselves, and two of the police officers left the boat.

"Stay put, Helen," she said. "Let them go up. It feels wrong."

Another bark followed by a whimper sent a chill of fear over Martha's skin. Helen backed away from the path.

"Something is wrong. I'm going up. He may be hurt..."

"Not hurt, not Ned."

Detective Towbridge and Officer Campbell arrived.

"He should be at the top of this hill," Helen said, pointing up to the place they'd stopped before climbing down to Bob's Lip.

The two men nodded and continued up the path disappearing from view. Martha and Helen waited with only the sounds of birds talking to each other, wind blowing through the valley making the pine trees whisper, and the occasional crunchy leaf sounds from tiny animals scurrying about for their supper. Ten minutes passed and another five.

"This is so weird," Martha said. "Should we yell up there and see what's happening?"

Helen shrugged, her eyebrows knitted together.

"Um, I don't know. Let's stay quiet."

"I'm getting a creepy feeling about this, Helen. Let's climb down to the boat. The two men are still there. I'd feel safer."

"Okay."

They walked over to the cliff's edge and peered over. The men were gone.

"Oh, stink!" Helen squeaked, her eyes the size of silver dollars. "They're gone, too!"

"I think we're surrounded," Martha said, backing closer to the bluff's overhang. "They're here."

"You mean The People Ned kept going on about?" Helen whispered as she followed Martha. "What are we going to do?"

Huddled once more under the overhang, the two women didn't speak. Martha tried to think.

"I got it," she said.

"What?"

"Let's go back into the cave."

"No way," Helen replied. "They might seal us in there. There's a huge pit."

"Our only other option is to get down to the boat."

"Nooo," Helen argued, drawing the word out and shaking her head. "We don't know how to drive a boat."

"I grew up fishing with my uncle on Greer's Ferry Lake. Running an outboard motor is easy."

Helen, her lips compressed, blinked her eyes twice.

"How do we get down there and not be nabbed like the others?"

"Helen, I can't think of all the answers! You think of one."

"Okay, okay, give me a minute."

They were quiet for a few moments while Helen chewed on her lip.

"I bet the boat needs a key."

"It has a trolling motor, too," Martha replied. "It doesn't need a key."

"I got it! Both ideas are good and probably the only ones available to us. We will do them both."

"Thanks," Martha said, feeling pride at Helen's compliment.

"Rocks and boulders are lying all over this ledge," Helen began. "I put my mace in my backpack when I emptied my purse. Did you bring yours?"

"They've got guns, Helen. Pepper spray is useless," Martha said.

"We might need it in the cave. Some things are living in there, trust me. Let's throw rocks over the ledge, make them think we're coming down, and we will squeeze into the cave to wait."

"Wait? For what? And how will I get my amazing booty through that hole?"

"Suck it in. Come on. We don't have much time. You go first, and I'll shove you through."

"If anyone comes near that cave opening, blast them with the mace, Helen."

With a tentative approach to the edge, they grabbed the rocks, threw twenty or so over the precipice, rolled a few larger ones over for good measure, and talked loudly about climbing down the hillside. Men's voices came from above them as Martha headed straight for the cave with Helen right behind her.

"I think I can make it through," Martha said, half of her body already through the cave's aperture.

"Yep, I do, too. You're gonna need a shove."

Taking her two feet, Helen placed them firmly on Martha's bottom and pushed. The tushy disappeared as Martha exclaimed, "God! I'm getting so skinny on this trip!"

"Yeah, now move your butt, so I can get in there, too."

Martha moved forward in the darkness.

"Do you still have the flashlight?" she asked, hoping Helen hadn't lost it during the first trip inside.

"Yes. Move. I hear something coming down the hill."

Hurrying deeper into the tunnel, Martha felt Helen's hands occasionally landing on her shoes.

"Are you in?" she asked.

"Yes, and I've turned around, and I'm trying to smooth away our footprints. I'll put a few rocks near the opening. They might think we didn't go inside if these are near the cave's mouth."

"I hope there aren't rats in here."

"Shhh! Martha," Helen whispered. "They're not in *here*, but three have arrived out *there*."

Chapter Forty

"What do you see?" Helen heard Martha asking behind her.

"It's three men dressed in camouflage clothing, black stocking masks covering their entire faces, and carrying rifles," she whispered back. "They're looking over the ledge at the river. Crud, they're pointing at the cave. Hang on. One is coming over here. Get back further."

Feeling for her pepper spray, Helen pulled it from her pocket and flipped the safety latch. She scooted backward until she was hidden by a curve in the tunnel.

"I don't think they could have crawled into that cave," the one said to the other two. "Only a kid could fit in there."

"Oh my gosh," Helen heard Martha say behind her. "You did hear him say only a child could fit in here. God, I hope we don't die. I may be having my best body year ever."

"Shhhh! You're a freaking pubescent if that'll get you to be quiet."

Helen pressed herself against the earthen wall as a light beam flittered over the cave's dusty, muddy interior.

"There are footprints over here," one said to the others and pointed at the cave.

Helen wondered if the man doing the pointing was possibly their leader.

"Tater said they'd tried to get inside but couldn't fit," another man said. "Lauderdale offered up the coin after I hit him. He said the stash was down on Bob's Adam's apple near a chiseled mark on the bluff wall."

"No mark on this wall," one man said. "We're wasting time up here. If they found anything, you can bet they'll be high tailing it like the other woman did—back to town."

"What are we going to do with Tater, Lauderdale, and those cops? I'm not going to kill a cop," one said to the others. "If they don't go into work tomorrow, these hills will be swarming with police trying to find them."

"We're gonna march them back to the park's entrance, leave them there, and let someone come along to set them free."

"We should take the boat."

"No," the leader answered. "Someone might see us transporting them. I'm going to climb down to the river and see if the women are down there. I'm kicking myself for not leaving someone with the boat."

The flashlight's beam was gone. Helen heard the man move away from the cave's opening. She didn't dare crawl forward to see what they were doing.

"Martha?" Helen asked her voice barely audible.

"Yes?" came the hushed reply.

"You doing okay? The floor is slippery, and we don't have a rope."

"I'm fine. I won't go near the slope."

They sat in silence until the men's voices faded entirely.

"How long should we wait?" Martha asked.

Helen shook her head.

"I think we should give it at least an hour. They're going to leave the boat. Interestingly enough, they may be psychopaths, but they're not thieves."

The two friends, quiet for the first time since Helen's

emergence from the cave, sat still for a while until Helen's stomach growled.

"Whoa," she said. "I'm starving. Do you have any of the pancakes left?"

"I do," Martha said. "They're in my bag. Do you want me to get them out? My hands are dirty."

Helen thought about it. The idea of eating a pancake with raccoon or bat droppings quelled her appetite.

"I'll wait."

"I was thinking," Martha said. "Even if we get to the boat and manage to find where Lauderdale left his vehicle, we still don't have a way to town. I've never hot-wired anything in my life. These men will be looking for us. How will we avoid them?"

"Good point."

She thought for a few moments.

"What if we call Peg?"

"What if she's one of them?"

"No, not Peg, she has integrity."

"True. Okay, let's go see if they've left."

Helen took the lead. Once at the opening, she saw no one and heard nothing. The sun was lower in the sky, and she guessed it had to be close to one o'clock in the afternoon. If they waited much longer, they risked being either on the river or walking in the dark along some dirt road alone at night. Not a good idea for anyone worried about aggressive dogs or people hunting for them.

"I think we're going to have to take a risk and go for it," she said back to Martha.

"Right after you."

Sticking her head out much the same way a turtle might assess the safety of its surroundings, Helen was able to see the cliff ledge. It was completely free of masked men. They'd gone.

"I'm going all the way. Wait here."

Squeezing once more through the cave's opening, she popped free.

"If I never crawl into another cave again in my lifetime, it'll be too soon," she muttered as she peeked over the ledge and up the pathway.

"Seems all clear."

Going to the cave, she helped Martha, and they quickly scrambled down the path to where the boat sat in the water. Here, too, no one waited for them.

"You undo the rope tied to the tree and jump in, but go to the back. I think I can push it away from the bank," Martha said. "I'll get in and start the trolling motor."

Helen did as she was told, but as she passed the boat's center console and sensed Martha pushing the boat away from the creek's edge, she saw the keys were still in the ignition.

"Hey, the keys are here. That's a lucky break," she said, looking up.

Far down the creek's embankment, she saw two of the masked men hurrying towards them.

"Martha! Get in the boat! It's the men!"

Turning the ignition switch, Helen heard the outboard jet motor roar into life. Martha quickly joined her at the console, and with amazingly deft handling, she turned the steering wheel, pushed the throttle forward, and maneuvered the boat out into the rushing water.

"They're pulling out their guns!" Helen yelled.

"Get down in the bottom of the boat!" Martha yelled back.

"They'll shoot you!"

"Do what I said!"

Helen bent down and watched. One man, with a handgun, was aiming at the boat while the others struggled through the underbrush.

"Go! Go! Go!" she yelled at Martha.

The boat shot forward, almost sending Helen out over the aft deck. Two shots rang out, but the boat zagged and zigged at tremendous speed across the water's surface. Helen watched the men recede, finally disappearing as the boat cornered a bend in the river. Turning around, she saw Martha's red hair blowing in the freezing wind out from under her stocking cap.

"You okay?" she yelled.

Martha nodded.

"Dang straight, I am. Stand up here by me. You can see better."

Helen pulled herself up on her feet and stood next to Martha at the console, the wind beating them but also assuring them they were both still alive.

"Let's have some fun. Zip up your coat, pull down your hat, and hold on tight!" Martha yelled, a mischievous twinkle in her eye. "Let's see what this baby can do!"

Chapter Forty-One

Thursday

A STRANGE PRICKLING AT THE EDGES OF HER CONSCIOUSNESS needled Kari Roller the minute Lou left the motel. It was as if the animal in her, a survival instinct, had sniffed the air and smelled the danger coming toward her. Let it come, she thought and positioned herself at the laminate table in a chair near the room's wide window. Pulling the curtains back, she waited and watched for the dogs to arrive.

It took four hours for them to do so. She recognized them without even an increase in her pulse rate. Getting up, Kari went over to her purse and took out the cell phone and her wallet. She'd leave those for the authorities to find later. The only thing she removed from the plastic photo sleeve was a picture of a four-year-old Jelinda sitting on the Easter Bunny's lap. It was her favorite, and she kept it with her always.

A knock came at the door. Kari tenderly tucked the precious photo into the left side of her bra, down next to her heart, and went to the door.

"You must be here for me," she said without emotion to the two men standing there. "I'm ready."

Dressed casually, they stepped inside the room and shut the door, expressions wary. She watched as they moved about, checking the bathroom, looking through her purse, and going through her suitcase.

"We need to pat you down," one man said.

Kari raised her arms and let them look for the gun that wasn't there.

"Okay," he said. "We're taking you to your husband. Come with us."

Snow spit at them as they left the room—Kari flanked on both sides by her angels of death. Nobody stopped or thought to retrieve her coat. She'd never need it again anyway, and it didn't matter because the SUV was warm inside as the door shut behind her.

Strapping the safety belt about her lap, Kari couldn't help a soft, mirthless smile at the irony. An hour later, the vehicle pulled through the ten-foot-tall retracting gates. It climbed a road curving through forests of pines with fleeting glimpses of a blue lake down below. Jesse Stacker's manor home finally revealed itself like a putrid boil sitting on one unlucky hill's back.

She waited for the man to open her door. He hadn't bothered to flash a gun or use rough handling. Kari posed no physical threat to a man twice her size, and she'd willingly let herself be led to whatever fate awaited her.

The wind swirled the snow in eddies about her feet as they waited at the front door. Dogs barking far away made Kari think for the first time about her little dog, Winks. She'd left him at home with her neighbor, and now he'd be waiting for her; my poor boy, she thought. A wave of anger flared at the ridiculous, horrible situation Lou had put them in and how she'd give anything to bury her nose in Winks' furry neck.

As they ushered her into the great room, Kari Roller never made a sound but simply wiped away the hot tears from her face as the man she'd been brought to meet walked into the room.

"Mrs. Roller," he said, "thank you for coming."

She didn't bother answering but stared at him without contempt.

"I want to offer my condolences for the loss of your daughter."

Again, she felt nothing, so she said nothing.

He sighed.

"Your husband is downstairs. I respect him and his passion for his family, however misguided his actions were earlier and the organization he represents."

Kari waited. Stacker sat down in a chair by the roaring fire in his massive fireplace.

"If you will sit down," he said, motioning to a seat opposite him, "I think we can straighten some things out. Afterward, you and your husband can go home and bury your dead."

His last three words were like a fist punch. Kari hadn't yet thought about her daughter being slipped into a box and lowered into a grave. The yawning hole she saw before her mind's eye sucked her daughter down into its cold emptiness, Jelinda's face retreating into blackness.

Kari swayed, her legs buckling, and as she collapsed, a moan like only mothers who've lost their children know welled up, poured forth, and seared her soul for eternity with its virulence. The two men caught her as Stacker stood up.

"Sit her down in the chair and bring me some brandy."

With an odd tenderness, the two men put Kari into the wingback. She sunk into the down cushion and laid her head into one of its wings. The fire crackled, and in its flames, she drifted like an ember between one reality and another.

A glass snifter was thrust into her line of vision, its brown liquid, almost amber from the fire's backlight. Kari accepted the glass taking a sip from its contents and letting the brandy burn its way down her throat.

"I apologize for the shock and what you've been through, Mrs. Roller. I am not your enemy."

Kari, as if being woken from a dream, looked at Stacker. His last five words swam around her mind.

"Not my enemy," she repeated, trying to decipher his language as if he'd spoken to her in Russian.

With complete clarity of her situation, Stacker's insanity, and the world's utter perverseness, she laughed.

He stared at her, and she laughed even harder. Taking her brandy, she drank it and threw the glass in the fire.

"What do you want, so I can get out of here?" she asked, her tone cold and direct.

"Your organization has a complete list and maps of all the locations of Civil War gold caches."

"Not *my* organization," she corrected, "Lou's."

Stacker didn't miss a beat.

"You get it for me, and you can leave with your husband."

In her mind, Kari tried to work out if she wanted to take Lou home. Wherever the master list might be, she hadn't a clue, nor did she care. The KGC, the KGB, the IRA, Peace Party, or the IRS could have it if they wanted it. Give it to the GOP, the Liberal Left, the Conservative Right, Yankee Unionists, or Rebel Confederates for all she cared. Not a damn one of them had ever done one thing that didn't serve themselves over the individuals they supposedly represented. Jesse Stacker, like Lou, was one more person, one more group selling an idea to people desperate to believe in something and willing to pay for it, even with their lives and their children's lives. It was simply a game of craps. Kari was done rolling dice and praying for a winner.

She stood up.

"I don't have whatever it is you're looking for."

She walked over to the armed flunky standing by the door and turned around to Stacker.

"Tell your man, here, to take me out and put a bullet through my head, if you'll be so obliging. I'll be forever grateful to you. If you want something from Lou, though, better talk to him yourself. He's never told me a damn thing about any of it. I live at 12 Roller Lane outside of Paris, Arkansas. Go there yourself and take whatever you want."

"You're not a very faithful woman," Stacker said with arrogant self-righteousness.

"You're a power whore," Kari responded with boredom. "I guess we both have our faults."

"Mrs. Roller, I have the perfect hell for you," he said with a grotesque smile. "Take her down to her husband and lock them up together."

Chapter Forty-Two

"I think we've more than lost them. Would you please see if there is cell service?" Martha asked as she slowed the boat down.

They'd traveled at least five miles upriver without seeing anyone. With each bend in the river, they half expected to be bushwhacked by the thugs who'd chased them. Helen reached for her knapsack and found her cell phone.

"I have two bars. If you will quiet the engine, I'll call Peg."

Martha pulled down on the throttle gear until the motor was only idling. The boat slowed and came to rest in the creek's middle. Nothing stirred but a few crows fussing overhead.

"I hope she answers," Helen said, pressing the speaker option on her phone so Martha could hear everything, too. "Fingers crossed."

Grey clouds were bumping up against one another in the sky as if the atmosphere was having a traffic jam overhead. The warmth of the sun was gone, and the smell of snow tinged the air as the phone rang four, five, six times.

"This is Peg," came the no-nonsense voice through the cell phone, causing both women's heart rate to jump.

"Peg?"

"Sure am and have been all day. What can I do for you?"

"I'm so glad you answered," Helen almost gushed with relief. "This is Helen Cousins."

"Hey!" Peg said, sounding pleased to hear from them. "You girls find your cave?"

"We did find it, but we've got one doozy of a problem."

"Okay, spit it out. I had to come to work late, and my sister just told me one of my maintenance men hit a pipe with his backhoe. I could kill that idiot."

"Oh goodness, well..." Helen hesitated.

Martha took the phone.

"There were some men wearing masks. They came and took Ned, Terry Lauderdale, and three policemen away. I think they might be the people Ned was always so worried about."

The other end of the line went quiet.

"Peg? Can you hear me?" Martha asked.

"Girls," Peg's voice came through once more, but her tone was different; kinder, but serious, "You're in a heckuva mess. Ned's a good old cuss, and they better not mistreat him, or they're gonna have some angry people on their backs. They've been pushing their weight around here for years, and we're all about sick of putting up with their hate talk, stirrin' up people against each other, and bullying those who can't fight back."

Martha heard the heat in the water department manager's words, not to mention it was the first time she'd heard Peg call Ned by his given name.

"We are sorry to ask this," Helen pressed on, "but we took Terry Lauderdale's boat because they left it, and Martha drove it up Missouri Creek. Would you tell us where to take this boat and give us a ride back to our car? We are calling the Benson County Sheriff's Office when we hang up."

"Girls," Peg said, sounding oddly like a friendly drill sergeant, "I'll call Terry's wife, Ashley. She'll help you get the boat back on the trailer. Be ready, though. When I tell her what's happened to Terry, she's gonna be chewin' nails and spittin' barbed wire. Do what she tells you, and don't get worked up if she's packin' heat. If she offers you a gun, for God's sake, don't shoot a hole in her truck. She *will* kill you."

There was a pause. As Peg drew breath, Martha couldn't help a chuckle at Helen's horrified expression.

"Now," Peg resumed her interrogation, "did you hear anything about where they might have been taking Ned, Terry, and the officers?"

"Yes," Helen said, remembering one of the leader's comments. "They are taking them back to a park's entrance."

"Did he mention a name?"

"No, I'm sorry. The man who I think was in charge didn't say which one."

"Let me chew on that for a bit. First things first. At some point along the creek, you're going to see a gravel bank on your right-hand side with a cement ramp. That's your spot, but don't beach the boat until you see a red dually pull into the lot. That'll be Ash. Anyone else could be the wrong person looking for you."

"Got it!" Martha said.

"Call the police and tell them what you know. Get ready, girls. Once the boys in blue are in this game, plus a few people I intend to round up, it's going to be a wingding."

Peg almost sounded excited, even happy.

"Should we meet you at the water department?" Martha asked.

"No. My sister is here cleaning right now, and she's leaving to take her new boyfriend out for his birthday. No one will be here. Stay with Ashley and have her bring you to My Mama's Kitchen."

The girls exchanged confused expressions.

"Ashley does know where your mother lives, right?" Martha asked.

A great guffaw of hearty laughter erupted through the phone, infecting the girls with its cackling merriment. Their smiles weak but hopeful.

"Not my mama! That woman's as crazy as a March hare. I wouldn't send my worst enemy to her house. I'm talking about the cafe in town...that's its name— *My Mama's Kitchen*. They do a wonderful breakfast any time of the day. Best bacon you'll ever eat."

Martha's mouth watered with the thought of bacon.

"Food," Helen breathed. "Please tell me they're open this late in the day."

"You girls need to get out more. Our restaurant stays open until eight pm Wednesday thru Saturday. Sunday, it's open after church until two o'clock."

Helen and Martha grinned at the marketing plug.

"Thank you so much, Peg. You're a real gem," Helen said.

"Girls, don't thank me, yet. I've done nothin'; but if I save your bacon, you can buy me breakfast at Mama's. It won't be cheap. I'm a good eater."

"It's a deal," Martha said. "See you in Grace."

Chapter Forty-Three

"I've bought us plane tickets," Jackie said with a regal closing of his laptop.

"You did what?" Tilda asked with a sharp intake of breath.

"I'm not going to be mashed into an economy car for twenty hours, eating lousy salads from drive-thru restaurants, and forced to frequent restrooms a prison inmate wouldn't be caught dead using."

Tilda turned to make sure it was Jackie she was talking to. Granted, he didn't look like any of the regular people on the bus at that moment. For safety's sake, they'd decided to dress in disguises. He was currently styled as a bobbed redhead in a retro aquamarine jumpsuit while Tilda was sporting a pink beehive, white cat-eye sunglasses, and a tie-dyed sixties shift dress in bright purples, pinks, and greens. Had their harsh circumstances caused Jackie to forget their poverty? She shook her head.

"Where did you get the money?"

"I called in a favor."

Her jaw slackened with surprise, but she rallied.

"A *favor*? From *whom*?"

Jackie drew himself up in the seat, his gaze straight ahead with one eyebrow slightly lowered, and his mouth pulled into a soft bow. It was his favorite, spirited impression of Joan Crawford at her enigmatic best.

"You're not the only one with loving family members you can turn to in a pinch," he said, patting her arm. "I've got an uncle in Wichita who follows my career. He thinks the money is for a trip to LA and an industry convention I go to every year."

Neither spoke for half a minute. Tilda was completely overwhelmed by this sweet act of friendship. Granted, he'd been a terror to live with for the last week, but in her darkest hours, he'd borrowed money twice because he wanted to help her.

"Thank you, Jack," she said, tears burning her eyes. "You are such a dear, dear person. If I'd had a child, a son, I would have wanted him to be like you. I know we are in a mess, but I promise to get your money back, every penny, Jackie."

Tilda pulled her tissues from her purse as Jackie reached over and took hold of her hand.

"We will be in Arkansas in three hours this way, Til dear, and I'll finally get to meet this wonderful niece of yours. You haven't been home in two years since you broke up with what's his name."

Tilda knew Jackie still had hard feelings for her ex-boyfriend, Harvey, whom he'd never called by his name since they'd gotten into a fight over a rhinestone bedecked wig.

"That's true," Tilda said, her tone reflecting her worries about the obvious downturns in her fortune and style. Her family would certainly know all about the first and see the frumpy ramifications of the second.

Jackie squeezed her hand.

"Now, don't you worry. I'll brush out your best wig; the platinum one with the sixties' flip would be perfect for a homecoming. And wear that gorgeous tangerine pantsuit and turquoise scarf. You've got to fake it 'til you make it, girl."

The image he'd painted in her mind made Tilda catch her breath, bringing an uplift in her spirit. She smiled brightly.

"Oh, Jackie, that would be so perfect. They will die from visual overload when they see me. I love an audience, even an uptight one."

"I know, dear. Me, too. Your people back home will be both shocked and awed. They'll love talking about it long after we've left. I always say, leave 'em with something stuck in their craw. They remember you forever that way."

"That is, if they don't choke."

They broke out in laughter.

"*And*," Tilda said, drawing out the word for effect, "what will you be wearing?"

"When we get off this bus," Jackie said, his nostrils slightly flaring with restrained contempt, "we will go into one of those private bathrooms at the airport and change. Mine's a surprise, but not to worry, I promise to be the perfect understated, elegant companion."

"Italian designer?"

"Perhaps for the return flight to Miami," Jackie said with a tender, benign smile.

"French?"

"It's true. I adore them, but I left those clothes behind. When it comes to the French fashions, I tend toward the Baroque. Frankly, the heat in Tampa doesn't allow for the heavy brocades, silks, and embroidered loafers."

"Okay, tell me," Tilda gently pleaded. "I'm dying to know."

"We are going to the heartland of America, Til, so it has to be in keeping with that theme. Something manly, something that says gentleman hobby farmer or rugged, handsome ranch owner."

Tilda considered his proposal.

"Well, honey, everyone I know back home dresses in khaki's, t-shirts, yoga pants, lots of workout shorts, and jerseys with numbers. Once in a while, you'll see a few blue jeans and the occasional button-down Oxford."

Jackie put his right hand over his heart in mock horror.

"Noooo, and God willing never, but I will give you a one-word hint," he said with a coy smile. "Tweed."

"You've thought this through, Jack? We won't clash too much?"

"Trust me. Have I ever been wrong before?"

Tilda considered that statement. When it came to fashion, he'd never failed.

"You're the guru, Jackie."

"It'll be divine, darling. Simply Jackie Boy Divine!"

Ten minutes later, they arrived at the airport. As Tilda stepped from the bus, her cell phone rang. It could only be Martha. Handing her suitcase off to Jackie, she pulled the phone from her pocket.

"It's Martha calling."

She put the phone to her ear.

"Hello, honey! How are you doin'? You'll never guess what dear Jackie has done so I can get there..."

Martha's words came through loud and clear halting Tilda's usual longwinded greeting.

"Aunt Til, we've found the necklace."

Tilda gripped the phone tighter, her heart beating hard.

"Martha, did you really?"

"Helen found it."

"I could kiss you both!"

Elation filled Tilda's body only to be arrested by Martha's next words.

"Til, you probably need to get here ASAP. Things are heating up here. Some rough stuff. I think you better call Jelly's parents."

Tilda's stomach constricted.

"What's happened, Martha?"

"Are you sitting down?"

Finding a bench, Tilda breathed in and said, "I am now."

"I'm so sorry, Aunt Til, but Jelly's been murdered."

"Oh, dear God in heaven! Martha, get to the police, and please, please don't let anything happen to you. I'm calling Kari and Lou. I'll see you in three hours. Meet me in Grace. You name the place."

The answer came back.

"Ever heard of a place called My Mama's Kitchen?"

Chapter Forty-Four

Detective Towbridge was sitting on the side of the road blindfolded and restrained, along with the other three men: Ned, Officer Campbell, and Officer Seymour. Falling snowflakes landed on his face, and the cold seeped into his bones. They'd been there for over two hours when in the distance, the unmistakable rumbling of a diesel truck approaching made him get to his feet. Jumping up and down as a way to attract the driver's attention, he prayed they'd stop.

Tires crunching over gravel and the diesel's engine coming closer told him he'd been successful.

"Terry?" a woman's voice cried as a car door slammed shut. "Honey! It's me, Ash!"

"Ashley!" Terry's voice called back. "Oh, baby, I've never been so glad to hear your voice!"

"Peg called me. I came straight here."

"Get these ties off me, Ash," Terry said.

After a few moments, Detective Towbridge's blindfold was removed from his face by a young woman he guessed to be Terry's wife.

"Better?" she asked.

"Thank you so much," he answered as she cut the zip ties off his aching wrists.

Towbridge looked around to see Terry and his wife removing the other men's blindfolds and ties.

"Do you have a phone?" he asked Ashley Lauderdale. "Would you take us to our vehicles?"

They needed to hurry. His sheriff, Paul Carmichael, needed to be informed. Looking around, he tried to guess where they'd been dumped.

"One more request," he said, addressing the married couple. "Where in the hell are we?"

"It's a parking lot not far from Tater's house. Horse trails, bike trails, and hikers use it, too."

Terry turned to his wife.

"How did you guess we were here?"

"I've been to three since Peg Sanderson called me. I was supposed to go find the two women, but I couldn't, honey."

Terry's wife, standing by her husband, did a face dive into her husband's chest, letting him wrap two strong, safe arms around her.

"It's gonna be okay, Ash," he said soothingly. "Right now, we've got to get these officers to their cars and let one of them use your phone."

The buried head nodded but didn't come up immediately. Towbridge and his fellow officers walked to Lauderdale's truck.

"The women: Mrs. Littleword and Mrs. Cousins," Ned asked, "where are they?"

"They supposedly drove Terry's jet boat up Missouri Creek. Peg called me back. She's going to go get them. We still need to get the boat."

"Let's drop these men off first," Terry said.

Ned jumped into the conversation.

"I promised to watch over those ladies. Those men will be after them. They're in real danger. They have something valuable in their care. It'll get 'em killed if we don't find them before those men do."

Towbridge nodded. Ned was right.

"Forget taking us back to our cars, Mrs. Lauderdale. Get us to this boat takeout on Missouri Creek."

Chapter Forty-Five

The sun was below the tree line and slipping fast. Snowflakes the size of quarters fell through the air; lacy, filigreed bodies landing on the water, the boat, and the two huddled women hiding behind a fallen tree trunk. They'd decided hiding in the forest near the boat ramp was better than sitting like two ducks in the jet boat.

With their backs to the oak tree's carcass, its girth similar in circumference to a tractor's tire, Helen and Martha were effectively screened from anyone seeing them who might be looking.

Helen put her hands deeper into her coat's pockets.

"Those pancakes stopped the gnawing hunger, but I could still eat a horse."

Martha nodded and pulled her hat down tighter over her ears, making sure the necklace was still in its safe spot.

"Wouldn't it be nice, though, if the horse were made entirely from buttermilk pancakes, with a bucket of hot syrup strapped to a saddle made from bacon? He'd be dragging a cart full of hot hash browns, too."

A happy sigh from Martha followed.

"That necklace still in your hat?" Helen asked.

"Yes, Killjoy, it is."

Headlights flashed across the trees. Quickly turning around, the two friends peeked over the old trunk to see a vehicle approaching.

"Hope that's our girl, Ashley," Martha murmured. "Remember, it's supposed to be a red truck."

A hoot owl's plaintiff call, followed by the rush of wings directly above where Helen and Martha were hiding, made them crouch once more behind the log. Looking up, they watched the beautiful creature land on a thick oak branch off to the left from where they sat. It cocked its head and considered them with a regal stare.

"My granny used to say," Martha whispered, "if you hear or see an owl at night, he's telling you to act with caution and not make hasty decisions. Owls don't particularly like people, so if you see one, he's come for a reason."

Helen stole a glance at Martha.

"Let's go with that advice and not stand up yet."

"Good idea."

The vehicle was anything but red or a truck. It drove straight for the parking lot and came to a stop. The driver's door swung open, and Peg stepped down. She was wearing a fuzzy stocking cap pulled down over her ears against the cold, heavy muck boots, and a long, down-filled black coat.

"Hello! You girls out there?" she yelled into the twilight.

"It's Peg."

Helen grabbed Martha's arm, holding her down.

"Nope, don't do it. She was supposed to send Ashley."

"Maybe Ashley couldn't come, so Peg came instead."

"She never called us to tell us," Helen argued. "It's not Peg's truck."

"We shot a hole through the roof and it's snowing. Maybe she's driving another vehicle."

Peg walked over to the cement ramp. Putting her hands to her mouth like a megaphone, she yelled out, "Heelloooo! Ashley's not coming. She had to pick up Terry first! Got a cafe full of people waiting on us!"

Helen's stomach groaned.

"Oh, come on. It's Peg," Martha said, her words in a hushed tone. "I heard your stomach. You know how you get if your blood sugar drops and there's nothing out here to eat but bark."

"Okay, but we need to leave the necklace here. I have this feeling, Martha; we can't take it with us. You're always the one who has all the gut instincts, but this time you need to go with mine."

Martha shrugged and took the necklace from its secured place.

"Let's stuff it in this tree trunk."

"No, an animal might drag it off."

Helen dug a hole in soft dirt under the fallen tree's body where a nubby limb pointed down.

"Give it to me. If anything happens to one of us, the other needs to remember the necklace is under this nub."

Covering up the pile and sprinkling leaf debris, Helen stood up. Martha followed, and they walked in a wide arc away from their old hiding spot until they emerged from the brushy forest.

"Peg! We're over here!" Helen called and waved to attract her attention.

The tall blonde turned around, smiled, and put her hands on her hips.

"Hey! Man, I'm glad you two are all right. Let's get over to the cafe. Everyone is waiting."

"Thank you so much for coming to get us. We can't wait to eat. What do we do about the boat? We tied it to a tree, but I feel weird going off and leaving it."

Peg's brow furrowed.

"We could wait until Terry and Ashley show up if you want. They should be here soon. No one is going to be out in this weather, so I do think it'll be safe to leave the boat."

She rubbed her hands together and scanned the parking lot.

"Let's climb inside. It's freezing out here."

Peg headed to her SUV, and so did the girls. It was a good compromise, and as Helen climbed into the passenger seat, she breathed a sigh of happiness. The vehicle's interior heat was good medicine for her cold-weary appendages. Martha's back door shut, and Peg cranked the heat higher.

"You two have been through it. When you found the cave, did you find any of the old Civil War gold in it? I'm on the county historical board. We've been trying to plot those caves for years."

With the sunlight gone from the sky and darkness filling in between the trees, Helen saw the owl take flight once more. Huge wings stretching out in a five-foot spread lifted the spectacular bird as it flew through the parking lot's open space. Martha's granny's words echoed in the back of Helen's mind.

"No, we didn't find anything," Helen hastily answered with a lie. "It was much too small to get into."

"Yeah," Martha chimed in, scooting up and inserting herself between the front's bucket seats. "By the way, would you have Ned's telephone number? I want to check on him."

Helen turned to see a twitch, barely visible in the lowering light, pass across Peg's face. It was confusion, and it hinted of something not right, something odd.

"Ned?"

"Yeah, Ned," Martha said.

Helen lowered her right hand casually until it lay on her door's armrest. She turned her attention back out to the gloom-filled forest that lay far beyond the SUV's windshield. As she wrapped her hand around the door latch, she heard the locking mechanism slide into place.

Peg shook her head.

"They've figured it out," she said into the air, her tone resigned. "What do you want me to do?"

"Hey," Martha asked, "are you all right, Peg?"

Peg put the vehicle into gear. Helen couldn't find the button to unlock the door in the evening's complete darkness. Feeling frantic, Helen turned back to look at the driver.

"I'll bring them to you," Peg said, a hopeful smile on her face. "I'll bring them to you, darling."

Chapter Forty-Six

Thursday Evening

"I WENT OUT THERE. THE BOAT WAS FLOATING IN THE DARKNESS tethered to a tree. No one was about. Do you think they might have tried to walk?"

Terry Lauderdale stood in the middle of My Mama's Kitchen among a group of at least twenty people listening to every word passing between Detective Towbridge, his sheriff, Paul Carmichael, and Ned Potter.

"Those ladies are in a heap of trouble," Ned said forcefully over the cafe's constant chatter. "We've got to find them."

Carmichael, still with snow covering his shoulders and his wide-brimmed hat, addressed Ned's concern.

"I've got the state police and half the sheriff's department combing those hills, Mr. Potter. There's even a chopper in the air. We'll find them soon. It's a pity we don't have their cell phone numbers, but we should have them soon. My information officer is getting an investigative subpoena."

The cafe's door swung open, making a cowbell tied to its handle clang, announcing new arrivals. Initially, no one turned to see who might have walked in, but with a strange hush descending upon the once loud space, the three men turned around.

An amazing, colorful duo stood in the door's entryway looking pleased by the silent reverence being paid to them by the crowd. In Grace, rarer birds had never been seen.

The woman was wearing a platinum wig with a one-piece pantsuit and a cosmic blue faux fur cape reaching to her knees. The younger man was dressed like a fashion-forward English gentlemen in a slim-fitting tweed suit, plaid vest, hunter green tie, and matching bowler hat upon his bald head.

"*I* know my niece's number, and I have it right here on my cell phone," Tilda said with authority, her head held high.

"Ma'am," Sheriff Carmichael said with a respectful nod, "thank you. That would sure speed things up. As soon as we have the judge's approval, we'd like that number."

With Tilda and Jackie's spectacular appearance, no one had noticed another arrival, nor had there been time for her to speak.. A woman in her late forties dressed in a gray overcoat stepped around Tilda and Jackie.

"I'm Leigh Alexander, Special Agent in Charge of the FBI Little Rock Division. You must be the sheriff. Your dispatch officer told me your location and the situation unfolding here."

A renewed silence took hold of the cafe patrons once more.

Sheriff Carmichael offered his hand to her.

"With your involvement, we should have much more traction in managing this situation," he said.

"I'm expecting another agent from our Miami division in the next hour. One of her team has gone missing. His name is Devon Williams, and his last known location was approximately fifteen miles from here. If you have a moment to talk privately, sheriff, I'd like to brief you on what we know."

"I have a mobile command unit outside; they're getting into place."

As they left the cafe, Sheriff Carmichael turned to Tilda and Jackie. "If you'll come with us, please, we should be able to access your niece's cell number to triangulate her location soon. It will help immensely to have her number."

"May I come along?" Ned asked.

"Not at the moment, Mr. Potter," Carmichael said, "but I promise to keep everyone informed at intervals. This has become more than a local murder investigation or abduction situation. The involvement of the FBI puts this in the realm of national security."

A nervous silence descended over the entire cafe.

The door swung open once more. Ashley Lauderdale burst in, her face white with shock.

"I just found Peg Sanderson on the Water Department's floor. I'd gone to look for her because she wasn't responding to my texts about the two women. I think Peg is dead!"

Chapter Forty-Seven

Thursday Evening

Martha heard her rubber-soled shoes squeaking on the floor's linoleum as someone with their hand under her elbow continued to guide her through a series of rooms. She knew Helen was still with her because, occasionally, Helen's heeled boots would clatter softly when they tread across different flooring surfaces. It was impossible to talk. The man Peg had stopped to pick up had taken Helen's phone, blindfolded them both, and gagged them with duct tape.

"Put them in here with the others," she heard him say. "Tomorrow, we will throw out the trash. Tonight we need to get back up to that cave."

A door shut behind her. Martha stood unmoving. Cold hands gingerly removed the blindfold. Standing immediately in front of her was a petite older woman with hazel eyes. A long-forgotten memory nudged Martha's mind.

Reaching up and tenderly removing the duct tape from Martha's face, the woman stepped back.

"Thank you," Martha said once her mouth was able. "Do I know you?"

"*You* are the spitting image of my Jelly," the woman breathed, tears welling in her eyes. "Who *are* you?"

The name nailed it. Martha's stomach knotted. This was her Aunt Kari, Jelinda's mother; but Martha couldn't imagine what the woman was doing here.

"I'm so sorry...about Jelinda. I...I haven't seen you in probably thirty years," Martha said, her words barely audible. "I believe I'm your niece, Aunt Kari. My mother was your husband's sister."

Another man came forward, an expression of dismay mixed with exhaustion written across his face.

"Martha," he said like it was a spell to open up a shadowed past. "Carolyn's daughter?"

The two stood staring at her and hesitantly moved in to wrap her in a timid hug. As they put their arms around Martha, Kari sobbed. No one spoke. The room was like a tomb for the grieving. After a few moments, Lou stepped back and gave Martha a sad smile.

"Our Jelly is dead," he said, his voice breaking at the last word.

Martha wrapped her arms tighter around Kari, putting one hand gently on the back of her aunt's head.

"She's okay, Kari," Martha whispered.

"She's where no one can ever hurt her, and you'll be together forever someday. God's angel is in the safest hands of all."

Across the room, Martha saw Helen wiping tears away from her eyes. A handsome man stood silently beside her, looking awkward.

Kari stepped free of Martha's embrace, a fragile smile on her lips.

"You look just like Jelinda. We weren't close with your mother and father. When they died, we didn't see you again. I'm sorry."

Martha nodded.

"That's why I'm here. Tilda's in a mess, and she asked me to help."

Lou cleared his throat.

"I know. She told me about you and that she'd called in some experts to help, but..."

His words died away. The handsome man stepped forward.

"I'll introduce myself. I'm Special Agent Devon Williams with the FBI's Miami Division. The people we are dealing with are a dangerous organization. Meeting Mr. and Mrs. Roller, even under these circumstances, has helped me understand clearly the situation and the KGC's agenda. Mr. Roller is going to help us in our investigation when we get free."

"What can we do?" Helen asked. "They tossed my knapsack out the window. Martha left her backpack at the top of Bob's Knob. We can't communicate with anyone."

Williams took a deep breath.

"My last communication with my division supervisor would have given my team an exact location. They will come when I don't check-in or respond to their communication attempts."

"So we wait?" Helen asked. "They could kill us before anyone finds us."

Agent Williams shrugged.

"We have no choice unless someone has a way to contact the outside world."

Martha signaled for Helen to come over.

"Would you help me with a little personal privacy, please? We may have an ace in the hole, so to speak."

Looking befuddled at Martha's request, Helen joined her.

"What is it?"

Martha took her coat off.

"Hey, would you boys please turn around? This is gonna be tricky."

The men did as they were told, and with Helen's and Kari's help, Martha lifted her shirt, her thick undergarments, and revealed a cell phone tied in red embroidery thread around her lower waist.

Helen burst out in a surprised giggle, infecting Kari, who also had to laugh.

"What in the world?" Helen cried. "How did you ever get this thing tied to you?"

"Just help me with my pants," Martha said, trying to scrunch the tight leggings down around her knees. "It was tricky, but I saw a bag of embroidery in the back seat, and it made me think of Emily Dickinson."

Helen looked up at Martha with amused confusion.

"So," Helen said, drawing the word out, "you tied the phone to you."

"Yep, do you remember how Dickinson hid her knots? She wanted to be discrete. I saw the red thread and I needed to hide my phone. I knew they'd pat us down wherever Deb was taking us, and I was right; they did. So while she was driving, I reached down into her knitting bag, and I took the embroidery thread. There was a thick needle in there as well and made holes as Emily did on her fascicles, but I put them at each corner of the phone's case. While we were driving, I slipped my pants down and wrapped the thread around the waist and through my legs until I had the phone up against my lower belly. Figured that was the safest spot. No man goes there unless invited."

A chuckle-like snort from Kari, who was trying to unlace Martha's handiwork, grew into a full belly laugh.

"You did a bang-up job of securing it," she said.

Helen, finally freeing Martha's phone from her body, handed it to her and nodded.

"You are extremely resourceful, Martha, and I think Emily Dickinson would have been proud."

Pulling up her pants and reassembling her clothing, Martha walked over to Agent Williams, who still had his back turned.

"You can turn around. I'm decent," she said.

"That's always debatable," Helen teased.

Williams faced Martha and accepted the phone. Turning it on, he studied it for a moment and glanced back at Martha.

"Something you said about the embroidery thread made me think about Deb Sanderson."

"That is Peg's sister," Martha said.

"Is that the woman who brought you here?" he asked.

"Do you mean Deb or Peg?" Helen asked.

Williams was quiet for a moment.

"Deb Sanderson was the person along with me who found Richard Gusman's body at Briar Ridge. The next day, she was doing embroidery at the Visitor's Reception desk when I went to talk with Officer Hathaway. What did *Peg* Sanderson look like?"

Martha turned around. Helen was staring at her. She wondered if they were both having the same thought.

"Peg didn't seem like the type to do needlework," Helen said with slow deliberation. "That wasn't Peg who brought us here. I thought something was weird about her in the car."

"You're right," Martha agreed. "I'd bet that necklace we found that it was Deb, her sister, not Peg who handed us over to the man dressed like an ex-soldier."

"Holy smoke!" Helen cried. "They are..."

"Twins!" Martha finished. "I remember now. Peg once mentioned something about her twin sister working at some park or military place."

Turning back to Williams, she pointed to the phone in his hands.

"Better give your FBI friends a call and tell them to hurry. It's time to call in the cavalry."

Chapter Forty-Eight

Special Agent Leigh Alexander's phone rang.

"Hello? Yes. He has? You do? Fantastic! I have the Benson County Sheriff with me. His SWAT team is set to go. Send the coordinates. I'll be in touch."

She ended the call and turned to Sheriff Carmichael.

"That was my colleague from the Miami Division. Devon Williams, her agent, has contacted her using Martha Littleword's phone. He, along with four other hostages, are being held at a location near Beaver Lake. A Jesse Stacker's home. We will have the coordinates in a few moments."

"My men are ready..."

A knock on the mobile command unit's door and an officer poking his head in interrupted Carmichael's sentence.

"Sir."

"Yes, Stephens?"

"We have information on the victim Ashley Lauderdale found at the Water Department. The woman, Peg Sanderson, is still alive and in route via ambulance to the hospital. Took a bash across the back of the head."

"I want an officer there and her statement when she's able to talk." Turning back to Alexander, he asked, "Do you have the location?"

Alexander stayed focused on her laptop, not answering immediately. No one spoke while she continued to work.

"We have it!" she announced.

Thirty minutes later, a highly trained tactical team moved into positions around Jesse Stacker's compound. Agent Alexander and Sheriff Carmichael waited in a mobile armored surveillance unit with two communications officers watching and listening to the intelligence data being gathered and disseminated among the initiative's key players.

"Ma'am, we have the Counterterrorism Division Director being patched through."

A woman in her early fifties appeared on the monitor in front of them.

"Alexander, you have full clearance to initiate the action. Jesse Stacker is wanted on three counts of inciting domestic terrorism, collecting, generating, and disseminating propaganda, drug trafficking, and conspiracy to finance terrorism. The Miami Division has closed the link between Stacker and a Cuban money-laundering organization. There are hostages involved, so I don't need to tell you this is high risk, and we need Stacker alive."

"Yes, ma'am, I'll be in contact with you when we have it wrapped. I'll start the negotiations."

The monitor's screen shifted back to multiple viewpoints from a night drone relaying video, cameras attached to SWAT officers, and enhanced satellite imaging of the area above Stacker's house.

Alexander nodded at Carmichael.

"It's go time, SWAT Commander," he said into his own headset's microphone. "Agent Alexander is coming out. She'll initiate negotiations."

Chapter Forty-Nine

There was no mistaking the situation unfolding above them. The occasional muffled voices, irregular movements, and thumping sounds sifted through the floor to where they waited below. Devon took command. He directed his flock of nervous humans into the safest corner of the room.

"It's going to be fine," he said. "Negotiations come first. Most times, this can take some time. Jesse Stacker is most likely on his phone with his attorneys."

Agent Williams' interpretation of the situation was positive.

"Make yourselves comfortable on the floor. If they should come in and remove one of us, I'll volunteer to go."

"No," Lou Roller said. "I will go."

Devon shook his head. His tone was firm and unyielding.

"Sir, you will stay here. I am trained for this situation, and my team out there is trying to bring us out safely. Stacker knows I'm his best bargaining chip, so please sit down."

Martha leaned over to Helen and whispered in her ear.

"If we get through this, I want to do something happy."

Helen couldn't help a smile. Martha's tone was so sincere.

"What would that happy thing be?"

Martha pushed closer to her.

"Well, how about a fun get-together with all our friends? Polly's barn would be perfect. Everyone should bring food. Polly might want to share her beer."

"Sure she would," Helen added, but making a mental note to secretly pay Polly for 'watering' the thirsty Marsden-Lacey herd.

"We need dancing, and the Irish fiddle band should do the music. I thought they were amazing last year at The Traveller's."

Multiple gunshots exploding somewhere above their room constricted the group's tight huddle.

"Where do you live, Martha?" Kari asked.

"I live in Yorkshire, in England. It's an adorable village called Marsden-Lacey."

Helen, sitting between Kari and Martha, pulled her arm free and wrapped it around Kari's shoulder.

"Martha has a boyfriend," Helen added, trying to sound like a tattletale. "She won't let him move in with her. Says she doesn't want him underfoot unless they are married."

Martha jabbed Helen gently in the ribs.

"Well, I think that's always a wise approach," Kari said with a tiny twinkle in her eye. "Better to take your time finding out if he's worth all the trouble."

A loud bang made the room shudder. The three women trembled, holding on tighter to each other. Lou wrapped his arms around his wife while Williams placed himself in front of his charges.

"Kari, would you and Uncle Lou come and visit?" Martha asked, her words sounding more like a plea. "I don't have much family. My daughter, Kate, would love to meet you."

"You have a daughter?"

Martha smiled tenderly at Kari's softly asked question.

"I do. She's such an amazing person. What if you came for the holidays? I promise to make it cozy, jolly, and we will have the best food. You would fall in love with Helen's house. It's straight out of an Agatha Christie mystery."

Kari turned and flashed Helen a quick smile. In her eyes, Helen saw the tiniest flame of hope kindling there. Martha was good medicine for this grieving mother, and it didn't hurt that she probably reminded Kari of Jelinda.

"I promise to think about it, Martha," she said. "I've got a lot to come to terms with, but I will definitely think about it."

Martha wrapped Kari in a tight hug.

"You do what's best for you, Aunt Kari. When you're ready, I'd love to have you and Uncle Lou for as long as you want to stay."

All the chaotic sounds coming from above suddenly ceased, causing everyone to look up at the ceiling. Collectively, it seemed they held their breath waiting for something to happen, an oppressive, fearful silence hanging in the expectant air around them.

Like a jolt from a cattle prod, the entire huddled group jumped as Martha's cell phone erupted into an insanely loud honking ringtone.

"That's my phone!" she cried.

Devon took it from his pocket and studied the screen.

"It says..."

He hesitated, an expression of befuddlement upon his face. "Tampa Til?"

"Give me that phone," Martha demanded. "It's Tilda!"

Williams handed it over with one last request.

"The police may try to reach us..."

But he was ignored as Martha answered.

"Tilda? It's me! Yes, yes, we are fine, well, I say that, but who the heck knows."

Everyone groaned at the last comment but maintained their focus on Martha. She was quiet for a few moments.

"She and Uncle Lou are here. Yes, I know. Did you and Jackie make it? Uh-huh... Okay... Let's meet in the morning. That is, of course, if we make it out of here alive."

Helen punched Martha in the shoulder.

"What is wrong with you?"

Martha ignored her.

"Oh, my gosh, that sounds so good. I'm jealous, Til. Yes, it's hidden. I'll text you the location," Martha said, lowering her voice to a whisper, "in case we don't make it out alive."

A man's voice from right outside the room's door squelched any further phone time with Tilda.

"Are you in there?" the voice boomed. "This is Lieutenant Collins with the Benson County Police!"

"Yes! This is Agent Devon Williams! Your entry is clear!"

"Stand back from the door!"

"They'll use a battering ram," Williams quickly explained. "Let's get up and stand over there."

The group moved to the place he designated. A massive boom exploded at the door, causing everyone but Williams to jump. The door flew open, and a powerful light beam at the height of a man's head broke into the room. Four men, dressed in black body armor, helmets, and gloves, walked through a dust cloud carrying assault rifles.

In her ear, Helen heard Martha whisper, "Hot, huh?"

The comment was pure Martha. Helen looked at her friend, who offered her a wicked smile and an eyebrow wiggle.

"Seriously hot."

"I'm going to hurt you," Helen replied.

Martha drew back slightly.

"Why? They *are* hot."

A feeling like a tiny fire was taking light inside her head made Helen reach over and pinch Martha's arm.

"What," Martha squeaked, "did you do that for?"

"It made me feel better, and what about Johns?"

"Am I not supposed to appreciate beauty now, Helen?" Martha declared righteously. "We are finally out of this mess—saved by gorgeous, strong men, and you're being bad-tempered."

"No," Helen said, drawing out the word, "I've been shoved down a filthy, raccoon infested hole, covered with mud, sat out in the freezing cold, been chased by psychotics, held in a Neo-Nazi's basement, involved in a hostage situation, and wasn't allowed to eat enough this morning."

"Oh, *that's* it," Martha said, giving Helen a smug look.

"What's *it?*"

"You are hungry. You always get like this when you don't eat."

"YOU wouldn't let me eat!"

"Oh my God! I'm sorry I ate most of the pancakes. I'll get you some food!" Martha cried and turned, walking over to one of the SWAT officers. Offering him an admiring smile, she looked up at him. "You wouldn't have a little something like a granola bar tucked into one of those fabulous pockets?"

The man's eyes crinkled at the corners as he smiled down at the pretty, demure Martha.

"Come with me," he said with warmth in his voice and offered her his arm. "Let's see what we can find you."

Martha blushed but took his arm, letting him lead her out of the room. As they exited through the bashed-in door, she turned around and shot Helen a wink.

As they moved away down the hall, Martha murmured, "Thank you so much for saving us. That gun of yours is huge! Did you have to shoot it? No? Wow! What a frightening job you have! My boyfriend..." Helen sighed, smiled, and hoped My Mama's Kitchen was still serving breakfast.

Chapter Fifty

Two days later, My Mama's Kitchen was packed with busily chatting people. All the chairs were taken, and the waitresses were weaving between and around tables like rubber shuttles through a human loom. The lack of seating meant nothing to new arrivals. Instead of turning away to leave, they simply pushed inside and found places to stand or sit along the sills of the cafe's frosty front windows. All small towns have a place to congregate in good times and bad. Fortunately for Grace, it had Mama's, and she served the best breakfast within a forty-mile radius, and no one left feeling sticker shock, once they got the tab.

The air was alive inside the cafe with disbelief, shock, and gossip. People were talking across the backs of booths and milling from table to table, rehashing fresh news about the infamous goings-on regarding Jesse Stacker, his twisted KGC organization, and how poor Deb Sanderson was so infatuated with her lover, Lucas Hathaway, she was willing to do anything for him, even commit two murders and attempt a third.

The general consensus was Deb had been too desperate. Most people knew about her loneliness and desperation to get away from her mother. Heads shook at the unfairness and the eventuality of a situation like hers to lead to a bad end. In low tones, they discussed Peg and how Deb's messed up situation would affect her. There wasn't a man, woman, or child in a tiny town like Grace that hadn't benefited from Peg's friendship. Best to close ranks around her and the widow, her mother, to ease the horror they'd both be feeling.

Blame for Deb's actions was laid at many feet: her own, the nature of women, the pressure of society, lust, her family, and even her neighbors' indifference. Generally, though, deep in their hearts, they knew Deb had had a choice, and she had chosen to gain something from hurting others. It was the age-old problem all humans face daily. People living close to the land, the Bible, and each other wrestled with the same moral struggles as people everywhere. Do you follow the Golden Rule or stuff it somewhere so you can get what you want, no matter the cost?

It was a tragedy, but it had also finally galvanized the community together. Grace's townsfolk and farmers had been scared and uncertain each time they ventured into the hills, rivers, and pastures for work, to hunt, or even for pleasure. They'd only heard whispers regarding Jesse Stacker's possible involvement in the drug trade corrupting the area, but they'd long since come to fear The People who made the drugs and ran them. Fear had held them hostage, it had separated them, and it had become its own drug. Deb Sanderson had crumpled under the weight of her fears into a hard rock of self-centeredness.

This wasn't the time, though, to kick someone when they were down. It was time to forgive and offer a helping hand. Peg would need that hand, one she'd so often in the past offered to others down on their luck.

Stepping first into this busy communal haven came Martha. She pushed through the door and scanned the heads, her gaze finally landing on a powder blue beehive in the center of the cafe.

"Tilda's over at the middle table," she said to Helen, who followed close on her heels. "Jackie isn't with her. That is odd."

Threading her way through the crowd, Martha bumped up against a man. His head swiveled around, the face and eyes lighting up as his gaze met hers.

"Mrs. Littleword!" he exclaimed.

"Ned! I'm so glad you are okay."

The grizzled head bobbed up and down.

"I'm doing fine. The men took us, me and the policemen, down to a parking lot. Had to go find my dogs late last night, but Willie and Waylon are back home, too. Glad to see you girls are safe."

He lifted his head like a meerkat to see past her shoulder.

"I see you have Mrs. Cousins in tow. Come sit down at my table. I just met your aunt. She's a real looker!"

Martha nodded and smiled.

"Thank you. We'll follow you, Ned. Lead the way."

Luckily the middle table had two benches leaving plenty of space for Helen and Martha across from Ned and Tilda.

"You two took your time getting here this morning," Tilda said after she poured them both a cup of coffee.

Helen grabbed the menu wedged in between the napkin holder and the sugar shaker.

"Yes, we had an errand to run before we got here."

Martha, looking around for the waitress, asked, "How are the waffles in this place? I'm starving."

"The waffles are the best you'll ever eat," Ned bragged. "But it's Mama's griddlecakes she's famous for. They're a perfect golden brown."

Tilda leaned in over the table, her mouth pulled into a tight, business-minded Coral Pink bow.

"That brings something to mind," she said in a low, hushed voice, furtively scanning Mama's other patrons. "You never texted me the location the other night. Is *it* okay?"

Helen's voice came from behind the menu she held in front of her face.

"Martha got sidetracked by a muscular man carrying a gun."

"He was *saving us*, Helen," Martha said, rolling her eyes.

"Sounds yummy," Tilda said, leaning closer with a mischievous smile.

Martha winked at her aunt.

232

"I think I will have the waffle," she said without going into any detail about the officer who escorted her out of Stacker's mansion.

"Did you girls learn anything from your meeting with Detective Towbridge yesterday?" Tilda said, turning the conversation around. "There is so much scuttlebutt going on in this place; who knows what the real story is."

Helen nodded and took a sip from her coffee.

"Martha and I had to give our statements, but Towbridge called us back in yesterday to talk with Agent Williams. It took some time to piece it together, but they had a confession from Deb Sanderson. She admits to killing both Richard and Jelinda Gusman."

"Oh dear," Ned said. "Poor Peg and Widow Sanderson. What a heartbreak for them to carry!"

Tilda reached over and put a plump, pink-nailed hand on the old mountain man's forearm. Martha caught the blush on Ned's cheeks.

"You need to shore up support for that family, Mr. Potter. People can't be allowed to turn their backs," Tilda said softly.

He nodded and shot a shy smile back at the blue-bouffanted Tilda.

"I certainly will, Miss Tilda," he said, leaving his hand under hers.

The waitress came over and refilled their coffee thermos.

"What'll ya'll have?" she asked.

Martha jumped in with enthusiasm.

"I want the waffles, a side of crispy bacon, and an order of grits, please."

"Tammy, do you have those scuttle browns still?" Ned asked.

"We do; you want sausage in 'em?"

"Sausage, two eggs on top, and tell Mama to leave the yolks a bit runny, please. You got that?"

"I do." Tammy pointed her pen at Helen. "And you?"

"Blueberry pancakes, please, a side of crispy bacon, hash browns, and two eggs over hard."

Helen put her menu down, revealing a huge smile.

"My goodness!" Tilda said with a chuckle. "You sure about all that? Where are you gonna put it all?"

A tinge of pink rose in Helen's cheeks as she reached for the cream.

"Don't worry about me, Miss Tilda," she said, shooting the older woman a grin. "I know how to put away a good southern breakfast."

"Honey, please bring me some oatmeal with brown sugar," Tilda said to the waitress. "I've got to watch my cholesterol and my figure."

She shot Ned a wicked, flirty smile and turned back to Helen and Martha.

"Tell me, Helen," she said, "what made Deb Sanderson do what she did? Was this a story of tragic love, or was she coerced by a manipulating brute?"

"Deb was in love with Lucas Hathaway, who was the park police officer at Briar Ridge Military Park. Richard and Hathaway both worked for Jesse Stacker, but Hathaway was his right-hand thug. Stacker was trying to raise money for a stab at a political career, according to Agent Williams. He was waist-deep in drug trafficking and other sordid things, but his real passion was finding the caches of gold stashed during the Civil War era by secret societies like the original KGC and Lou Roller's organization, The Peace Party. According to Detective Towbridge, there's a lot of money in those hills, probably millions."

"Well," Tilda said in a hushed tone, "they can dig up all the gold they want, but thank goodness no one ever found that necklace."

"Yes, and you were lucky, Tilda, because Richard Gusman did find a gold stash on Bob's Knob not far from where we found the Roller's necklace. A triangle symbol marked the spot. Richard took his booty and went to the park to tell Hathaway he had it. The men argued because Richard wanted to be the one to take the gold to Stacker—a chance to rise above his rival for Stacker's admiration, but Hathaway refused to let him meet the great KGC leader and tried to stop Gusman from leaving. Deb Sanderson overheard the ruckus and, thinking the man she loved was in danger, grabbed the closest thing available—a knife called an Arkansas Toothpick she'd brought in as a present to her lover, and plunged it into Richard's back."

Tilda and Ned sat dumbstruck across from Helen and Martha.

"Not a woman to mess with," Ned mumbled.

Martha nodded and picked up where Helen left off.

"Not when it comes to the man she loves anyway. She and Hathaway stuffed Richard behind a display, trying to hide him until they could move the body elsewhere. What they didn't know was Jelinda brought Richard to the park. The Benson County Sheriff's Office has placed Jelinda's cell phone at Briar Ridge on the same day and at the same time as when Richard was killed."

"Poor little Jelly," Tilda said. "She must have been so frightened."

Martha nodded and put her hand on top of Tilda's.

"Uncle Lou admitted that Jelinda found out her husband was working for the KGC. She'd come up to Grace to find him, and she obviously did. Richard surely admitted finding the gold to Jelinda, but probably spun a story about having to go to the military park and confront Hathaway. Jelinda and Richard were certainly together at Briar Ridge, and she most likely waited in the car while he went inside to talk with Hathaway. When he didn't come out, she went inside to find him. Jelinda may have even seen Deb and Hathaway hiding Richard. Detective Towbridge says the handwriting on the note found on Richard Gusman matches Jelinda's. She must have hurriedly pinned the note on her husband to point at who she thought killed him."

"That poor child must have been terrified," Tilda said.

"Without a doubt," Helen agreed, "and she had Deb Sanderson and Hathaway looking for her. When a child pointed out the body and the note was found, Hathaway went back to the security camera tapes and saw Jelinda come into the Visitor Center. Hathaway must have believed Jelinda had the gold, and she was a witness to a murder who needed to be silenced. The parking lot's cameras made it easy for them to find Jelinda's car and a quick look through Richard's coat revealed a plastic door card for the only motel in Briar Ridge."

"So, it was Hathaway who killed Jelly," Tilda asked.

"No," Helen said, picking up as Martha took a sip of her coffee. "Detective Towbridge says it most certainly was Deb Sanderson. Hathaway wanted to keep his hands clean. He sent Deb to find Jelinda at the motel immediately after they watched the tapes. Deb admitted to finding the gold hidden in the trunk of Richard's car. She kept Jelinda at gunpoint in the motel, waiting until it was two o'clock in the morning, and then made her get in the trunk. Deb drove out to what she thought was a secluded place and made Jelinda start walking into the forest. It would have been a good place to kill someone because it could have looked like a deer hunting accident. I think Jelinda managed to get away from Deb, but unfortunately, the rest we know from the statements of Terry and Ashley Lauderdale."

"It's like poor Deb was out of her mind," Ned said, shaking his head and staring down into his cup. "I've known that girl since she was born. Breaks your heart."

The three women sitting with him either offered Ned a gentle pat on his shoulder or his two outstretched hands.

"I'm sorry, Ned," Helen said softly. "It's going to be hard for her family and those who knew her."

"Lou told me they found coins in Jelly's pockets," Tilda asked, "why were they there?"

"No one knows," Martha said. "After she knew Richard was dead, she may have found the gold in the car's trunk and simply slipped a few in her pockets, but if she hadn't done so, Detective Towbridge might never have connected her murder with the FBI's investigation of Stacker."

"Why do you think Deb tried to kill Peg, her own sister?" Ned asked, looking back up at Martha.

"Because *I* realized she'd killed that man at Briar Ridge with one of my father's knives made by James Black back in the 19th century."

Helen, Tilda, Ned, and Martha froze. They had been so

embroiled in their conversation; they hadn't noticed the hush that had fallen over the cafe. Right beside their table stood Peg Sanderson with Jackie Boy by her side. She offered them a weak smile as they each, in turn, looked up at her.

"Mind if I sit down?"

"Please do," Helen said. "We've got plenty of room."

Martha added, "Would you both like a cup of coffee?"

Ned jumped up and came around to Peg and pulled out a chair for her to sit down. Jackie found his place next to Tilda.

"So glad to see you're doing okay Peg," Ned said. "Are you both hungry?"

Peg shrugged and took the offered cup of hot coffee, but instead of sitting down, she stayed standing. The floor was hers, no one in the cafe moved, and the steady drip from the coffee machine was the only noise. Softly clearing her throat, she said, "I thought about taking my family and leaving Grace, but the thought of it..."

She shook her head.

"I'm sorry for the terrible things Deb has done, but I can't lay all the blame on her. She's my sister, and I always knew she was fragile, but I ignored it. This is what comes from ignoring problems—they only get bigger. I won't abandon her, so don't expect me to."

Ned stood up and went over to Peg. He gently encouraged her to take her seat. Once she was sitting, he turned to the silent crowd.

"I'm gonna say this, and I believe you all will understand. We've been touched by a cold, cruel wind that's reached deep into this town's soul and has taken one of our own. It's time for forgiveness and trying to heal the damage done."

The previous chatter resumed in the cafe as people nodded and went back to their private conversations. Tilda leaned over and gave Ned a nudge.

"You think you might flag that Tammy down so she'll hot-foot it over here? This lady and my dear Jackie need something to eat." Turning to her adoptive son, she said, "This is the man who saved my life, Mr. Jackson Divine. God love him; he went to find you, Peg. He understands how it can be when you feel on the outside, so to speak."

Peg smiled at Tilda and Jackie.

"I feel so much gratitude to this man who showed up at my door. I didn't know who he was, but he walked right in and explained what I needed to do."

"Jackie's a peach," Tilda said. "I hope he didn't insult your home decor."

Peg chuckled.

"How'd you guess?"

"Not to worry, yourself," Jackie chimed in. "I'm gifted when it comes to redos."

Everyone laughed, and as they sipped coffee, each in their way fussed over Peg. Ned managed to catch Tammy's eye, who, in her good time, sashayed over to the table.

"Somebody want something?" she asked.

"We owe this lady a breakfast," Helen said, indicating Peg who sat beside her. "She *claims* to be a good eater."

Peg chuckled.

"You remember that, huh?"

"Never one to squelch on a deal," Helen said. "Thank you, Peg."

Once the breakfast was served, they found things to laugh about, complained about eating too much, and finally, got up to leave.

Tilda grabbed Martha's arm as they got out into the chilly air.

"I hate to beat a dead dog, honey, but where is the necklace?"

Martha reached into her purse and handed a dirty drawstring bag to Tilda.

"Here you go, Til. Here is your infamous Roller necklace. It's seen bushwhackers, caves, raccoon nests, and probably passed through many hands down through history. A rare jewelry dealer in New York who we sent pictures of the necklace to says the setting is from the seventeenth century. The sapphire and the pearl pendant alone are worth a few million. The dealer said it would have belonged to either royalty or at the least a woman of noble

238

birth. I guess we'll never know the necklace's entire history, but wouldn't it be fun to know where all it's been?"

Tilda nodded as she looked down at the worn, muddy bag.

"Yes, Martha, it would. It really, really would, but there is one thing I know for sure."

"Oh yeah, what's that?"

Tilda gave the bag a kiss.

"It's laid around in that dirty old cave long enough. Might as well get it back around some rich lady's neck and give our family and friends a second lease on living." Tilda slipped her arm through her niece's and they began to walk toward the car where Helen and Jackie were waiting. "Tell Helen to get on the horn with New York, Martha, and find us a sugar daddy. It's pay day, honey!"

Chapter Fifty-One

"Where is Tilda?"

Martha craned her neck up, trying to see over the passengers streaming up the gangway behind her.

"She's saying goodbye to Jackie."

"Geez, those two are practically joined at the hip. He was still giving her fashion advice at the hotel. You'd think she was going to visit the Queen."

Helen kept moving forward despite Martha's attempt at staying the human current.

"It wouldn't surprise me if she did get an invite. Whether it was Grace, Arkansas, or New York City, those two knew how to draw a crowd."

"Tilda and Jackie have that effect on people. Did you see how Peg loved them? They cackled and hooted like a bunch of gossipy old women during our breakfast at Mama's. I think Peg was touched by their idea to go with her to visit her brother in Dallas. They've got big hearts, Helen, big hearts."

"I'm glad Peg and Ned were okay. That little town has been through so much. It was good of your Uncle Lou and Aunt Kari to offer some of their share from the sale of the necklace towards a community foundation for Grace."

"It'll be in Jelinda's name," Martha said. "I hope they will come to visit us at home."

"It *is* home, Marsden-Lacey. Isn't it? When we flew out over Little Rock, I was thinking how nice it would be to get home. I'd held on to the idea that Arkansas was home for so many years, but it isn't anymore. Home is where Piers is and where my friends are."

"Same for me," Martha agreed. "Stick with me, buddy. My friendship is like underwear—I've got your backend covered, no matter what."

Helen snort-laughed.

"That goes ditto for me."

The two friends made the deck and waited for Martha's aunt to arrive. Soon, a bobbed redhead with fringe bangs wearing a lime green silk suit and white cat-eye sunglasses came up the gangway.

Helen sighed, and Martha echoed her.

"Marsden-Lacey won't know what hit it," the latter said.

"She's going to have all the old ladies' tongues wagging and the old men's eyes roving."

"God help me, I'm bringing Hurricane Tilda to Yorkshire."

Helen's laughter caused Martha to look over at her.

"You know I'm right."

"Absolutely, you're right. Within two days of arriving, she'll have them in a poker game."

Martha groaned.

"Of course she will, and then she'll clean them out. I'll tell her no poker, no dice games, no betting of any kind."

Helen made a scoffing laugh-grunt.

"Good luck with that."

Tilda arrived, her smile brilliant in its favorite Coral Pink shade.

"I'm here!" she trilled. "Jackie was such a dear. He's going to fly over when the necklace goes to auction next month. London! I'm so excited! Shopping until we drop!"

Martha put her hand up.

"First, did you get the money to that woman in Tampa? We don't want a visit from her henchmen in Marsden-Lacey."

"All done. Thank you for loaning me the money, honey, and for bringing Jackie to New York. He had so much fun."

"One more thing, Til. Did you work out with the family how the money would be divided up among them?"

"I did. Everyone in the family gets a cut from the sale, including Jackie. That was hard for the rest of the family to accept, but he deserves his share. After all, if it hadn't been for Jackie, we'd never have gone looking for the necklace in the first place. Plus, he bankrolled our getaway."

She gave a nod and a flirty smile to an attractive older gentleman who tipped his hat at her.

Helen waited for the man to get out of earshot and slipped her arm through Tilda's right one.

"Technically, what he did is called stealing from the criminal underworld."

"Potatoes, potat*hoes*," Tilda replied with a wave of her hand. "The point *is*, Jackie saved me, and he will have a cut of that money. I owe him."

The three women strolled along the deck, taking in the views of Manhattan and New York Harbor. Martha tucked her arm through her aunt's left one.

"Of course, he should have his share. By the way, Helen, what is the necklace's sale estimate?"

"Well over six million."

"Thank you, Jesus!" Tilda exclaimed. "Talk about your potatoes! And not those boring, bland kind people eat, no! I'm talkin' about southern fried potatoes with pepper and onions! Big, spicy *money* potatoes!"

Tilda squealed and pulled the two women closer making them laugh.

Soon the talking slowed, and they were quiet as they stood at the ship's rail. Manhattan's skyline, backdropped by a smattering of white evening stars playing peek-a-boo through crimson and orange clouds, made the perfect picture-postcard memory for Helen and Martha to remember America by.

Helen sighed.

"Going home by boat, isn't it romantic? I can't wait to relax, go to the spa, eat freshly prepared healthy food, catch up on my reading..."

Feeling a slight nudge in her side, Martha turned to Tilda, who led her away from where Helen stood talking to herself.

"Hey," her aunt whispered a mischievous twinkle in her eyes, "how about we hit the buffet and the casino. I'm feeling lucky."

It was Martha's turn to sigh.

"Okay, fine, but on *one* condition."

"What?"

"No dice games. That's what got you into the last mess."

Tilda reached up, pushed her sunglasses to the tip of her nose, and put a hand over her heart in a gesture of reverent honesty.

"I swear—no dice."

As they walked away, leaving Helen to murmur on about massages, catching up on her reading, and daily workouts, Tilda uncrossed her fingers on the hand hidden behind her back and patted Martha on the shoulder.

"You're a good kid, honey."

"And you, Aunt Til, are truly one of a kind."